HELL ON EARTH

SIN DEMONS

MILA YOUNG

HARPER A. BROOKS

DEDICATION

CONTENTS

HELL ON EARTH

The journey's been Hell... but it's time to give the devil his due.

This is it. This is where it all ends.

It's me, my shadow, and my demons against Lucifer.

With the relics stolen, the only way to get them is to go back into the hellfire--back to Hell where Lucifer awaits. Defeating him may mean making the ultimate sacrifice, but even with so much at stake, I don't know if I can.

Things heated up fast with Cain, Elias, and Dorian, and now Maverick, but I'd sell my soul a hundred times to keep them as mine. Forever.

What if that's impossible?

There's so much danger ahead of us, but I'll bring Hell on earth to save the ones I love. I just wonder that when all's said and done, who will be the one wearing the unholy crown?

"Speak of the devil and he appears." —Anonymous
CAIN

The absolute fury that's clashing inside me is unlike anything I've ever felt before.

Every inch of me is trembling with it. I can barely see straight. The monster inside me rips at my core, wanting out. Wanting more blood. Wanting death for those who wronged me.

I tear past everyone and throw open the balcony doors. Aria tries to move toward me, but Dorian quickly snatches her and pulls her back. He knows me too well to know that when I get like this, I'm like a tornado, taking down anyone in my path. I'm uncontrollable, and it's not safe for anyone to be by me right now. Aria included.

Once the frigid air of the night hits me, my wings explode from my back, the transformation into my demon too fast for even my human side to process, and pain ricochets through me. It's easy to ignore it, though. Especially with so much adrenaline and hellfire pumping through my veins.

The roar I unleash booms across the quiet landscape. Animals flee from their resting places and birds take off for the skies. Not only did I lose my club tonight, I lost six of the seven pieces of Azrael's harp, and any chance of us returning to Hell along with them.

Why? All because of my fuckwit of a brother.

He conned me. He convinced us all that he was on our side and wanted to help, only to swipe the relics once our backs were turned and make a run for it.

I should have known better. I should have never allowed him into our home. I should've slaughtered him the moment he showed up. But he knew I was distracted—between what was happening with Aria, the vampires, and the hellhounds—he took full advantage of my overwhelmed mind.

He fucked us all over.

The big question is, what do we do now?

It's more than likely Maverick took the relics back to Hell, and that's the one place we can't go. Retrieving them is impossible.

We may have won with the Nightwalkers and getting our city back, but we've lost so much more.

As my fury boils me alive, another roar raises up my throat. Maverick's lucky I can't go to Hell. I'd rip him from the underworld and peel off his skin with my bare hands. Death is too quick and easy for him. I'd prolong the suffering; he deserves nothing less. Lucifer may be the king of torture, but I'm going to temporarily take the title from him, just for Maverick's sake.

He's going to wish I'd let Father kill him that day. I'll make sure of it.

Stopping abruptly, I sense the change in the air before I see it. That strange skitter in the atmosphere, like time is holding its breath, and what follows is never good.

Whipping around, I notice the ripple of the air in the center of my bedroom. Then the big exhale and pop through the very fabric of time and space as the archangel Gabriel appears in its place.

Dorian yanks Aria farther back, while Elias

protectively steps in front of them both. Gritting my teeth, I quickly hurry inside, only to have the hulk of an angel whirl on me first, eyes blazing with an ancient hatred I'll never understand. He looks over my leather wings and black-lined skin, and his lip curls in disgust.

When he spins again and finds Aria, his body stiffens and the grip on his sword tightens.

He wants to kill her—and the Leviathan inside her—more than anything. I can see it in his stance. She represents God's mistake, and he's dying to eradicate her because of it. Me, Elias, and Dorian are the only things standing in his way.

Well, besides the need to stop Lucifer. But I have no doubt that if one of us blinks, all sense will go out the window and he'll kill her in an instant. And that's something I'll never let happen.

"Gabriel!" I shout, gaining his attention once again. I recall my demon for the moment but keep it close, to appear less threatening. "No one summoned you here."

"You can't just pop in here whenever you feel like it," Dorian adds. "You may be wearing a dress, but you're no fairy godmother."

Gabriel glances down at his tunic and sneers.

"Get out of our home," I tack on, in case it wasn't clear enough. "Or we'll make you."

The cold bastard ignores the threat and lifts his nose at us instead. Unbothered. As if he's staring down three cockroaches instead of three powerful demons. If he wasn't carrying an angel blade—or sword in his case—I would have made good on my word right away. But God-made and blessed weapons are the only ones that can kill any creature. Maybe even God himself, if anyone ever got mad enough at him. It's why they're rare and only archangels have them. How Lucifer got ahold of a dagger before he fell is unknown to me.

"Son of Lucifer. Sin Demon. I would not have come to your..." his lip curls up in obvious disgust, "*home*...if it were without purpose."

"Well, spill it then, Gabe. We got shit to do, places to be," Dorian snaps.

Gabriel waves his sword Dorian's way, and Aria stiffens nervously. "Do not call me that."

"What? Gabe?" Dorian laughs. "It's just a nickname, man. Relax."

The archangel clenches his teeth. "I am not a Gabe. Nor am I a man. So I will not *relax,* as you say. One purpose has brought me to Earth and one purpose only. And that is to find out if you Hell-vermin have obtained the rest of Azrael's harp." He turns to me again. "So, tell me, Son of Lucifer, what news do you bring me?"

Elias's breathing picks up and his nostrils flare as his anger builds. The skin across his face and arms ripple as the power of the shift crawls through him. It's not such a smart move to call a hellhound a rodent. I'm surprised he's kept it together this far.

I have to defuse the situation before it gets out of hand and we have another issue that we don't need.

"We found the foot and the intestine," I interject and step closer, which isn't a lie. We had hunted down and collected the two pieces of the harp. I just don't think he needs to know that they, along with the other four parts, were taken from us.

Gabriel's head tilts and disbelief washes over his face. Did he honestly not think we could do it? Must have.

Bastard.

"And the skull?" he asks.

I clench my teeth. Even though I know it's in Mexico, that doesn't mean it'll be an easy piece to retrieve. "We're working on it."

"You have all the locations," he says. "There is

no excuse."

"I don't know if you saw while you were sitting on your golden pedestal on cloud nine, but we had a little vampire problem to deal with here. And all Lucifer's hellhounds," Dorian says.

"Hellhounds will be the least of your worries," Gabriel replies, which wins him a guttural growl from Elias. "That's not a threat from me, you wretched creature," he spits. "Lucifer will be sending other legions next to retrieve the Dark One. Demons. Shades. Whatever will do his bidding."

Aria glances at each of us, the worry clear on her face, and I know Gabriel's right. Now that he has the relics, there will be no way for us to get to Aria if he does steal her from us.

"Retrieve the skull," he says, gaze sweeping over the room. "Hell is coming." And with that, Gabriel pops out of existence right before our eyes.

The room falls into a thick silence, one heavy with all the doubts and fears we don't want to utter out loud. After battling vampires and losing the relics to Maverick, we're finally coming down from the high of the fight, and rock bottom isn't looking very welcoming.

"Who pissed in his Cheerios this morning?"

Dorian says to break the stillness. "I swear, he needs to get laid. Can angels even have sex?"

"Dorian…" Aria whispers and touches his arm. "Not the time."

He holds up his hands in surrender. "All I'm saying is that it's no wonder Lucifer fell from Heaven. They all have giant sticks up their asses."

Aria looks at me with her mouth tugged down into a hard frown. "Cain, why did you lie to him? Why didn't you tell him about Maverick? Maybe he could've helped us—"

"It would've only worsened things," Elias answers for me. "We don't need Gabriel's wrath on us now."

"But what he said…about Hell coming. What are we going to do?" Aria asks.

Every eye turns to me for guidance, but this time I have nothing to offer them. Nothing that can ease our situation, fix what's been broken, or save what was lost. For once, I have no ideas. No answers to give them all or reassuring words. None.

My chest clenches as the weight of what's happened grips me fully.

We are in deeper shit than ever before.

And we're running out of time.

CHAPTER TWO

ARIA

The mattress bows slightly beneath me as if someone is climbing into bed with me. Fear spikes inside me, until I realize it's probably Elias. It's been too long since he made his way into my bed during the night, and I've missed waking up to find him beside me.

The blanket tugs and pulls behind me as he slides under, and he's doing a terrible job at not causing the whole bed to creak. I smile to myself.

A strong arm loops around my stomach and roughly pulls me back against his solid body, followed by a growl that rumbles in his chest. I squirm in his arms, loving how I'm already feeling wet from such an aggressive gesture.

"Hey sexy," I whisper and arch my body,

pushing my ass back against him to tease him. Seeing he just woke me up, he owes me to help me go back to sleep.

"Felt like some company?" I purr when he doesn't respond.

His cock twitches and hardens as his voice caresses my ear. "Right there, that feels so good!"

I stiffen. Wait! It's not Elias. And I don't move at first, instinctually knowing the danger I'm in.

A squeak leaves my throat. "Maverick! What the fuck!"

I shove my hands against his arm to dislodge myself, but his grip tightens, forcing me to be caged in against his hard body. And not to mention his erection is pressing right up between my ass cheeks, and I'm wearing my thin pajamas. I feel every inch of him pressed to me, even though I can feel he's wearing clothes too.

My earlier boldness dissolves in moments, replaced with a rising anger.

"But we were having fun," he says, his voice carrying a dangerous edge. "Or were you imagining me as one of your demon lovers? Who was it? Can't be Cain since he doesn't seem the type to practically hump you. Maybe Dorian, but no, this has Elias written all over it."

"Let me go before I scream and wake the whole damn house."

"First, I want you to listen to me."

I clench my teeth. "Why? So you can spin a lie about how you vanished with our relics? How you played me like a fool while you pretended you cared." My pulse is racing now, and it has nothing to do with his body glued to mine.

"Aria, I would never—"

"You really hurt me, Maverick. And I feel like an idiot now thanks to you." I hate that tears sting my eyes as the weight of what he really took from me feels like someone is crushing my heart. I realize how much I had let Maverick into my life, how much I truly started to like him. And to have him return is like a blade to my chest, reminding me of his betrayal.

But with those emotions tearing through me, a familiar sensation rises within me, one that comes so fast. In seconds, Sayah pulls out of me. She's darker than the night, her eyes blinking.

Maverick's breath catches, and his grip around my middle loosens. I take the chance and roll away from him, then scramble clumsily out of my bed and right over Cassiel, who doesn't move a muscle and keeps on snoring.

I roll my eyes at the lynx.

Hopping out of bed, I quickly cross the room and hit the light, turning around to face him. Sayah is hovering over him, and with a single thought of, *Sayah come back to me,* she zips into me. There's something rewarding about gaining that sense of control over her once more, to have her listen and not be terrified of my own shadow.

But my attention now falls on Maverick again.

I don't want any surprises, plus I feel safer being near the open door and with Sayah at my fingertips.

"Clever trick. And you've proved your point." Maverick pushes out from under the blankets and stands. I grin when I realize I've startled him.

He's dressed in all black…tight jeans that do nothing to conceal his boner, a V-neck tee that's tight across his strong chest, and combat boots. This guy is powerful and gorgeous, and he's going to destroy me if I'm not careful. Everything about him screams dangerous. There's wildness behind his gaze when he studies me.

"You couldn't help yourself, could you?" I insist. "Just be honest with me for a change and admit you're working with Lucifer."

He runs a hand through his light hair, his eyes

lowering momentarily as a painful expression sweeps over his face. "My whole life I was told to make a call on whose side I'd be on. My father's or my own, which meant going directly against Lucifer, so there really wasn't a choice after all." He lifts his head. "Everything was an illusion. My brothers and I have always been captives in Hell, except we've got more privileges, but a prison is still a prison."

"Why are you telling me this?"

He's shaking his head. "Because, for the first time in my life, I made a call on whose side I'm on. I want to escape Lucifer's oppression. On your side, on Cain's side." He takes a step closer, and I recoil, my heels hitting the wall. "No more second guessing, and I'm not willing to sacrifice myself anymore for him. Believe me when I say, I didn't take Azrael's relics."

"So, what? They just vanished at the same time you did?" I roll my eyes, not sure why he thinks I'm an idiot.

"I know who took them, which is where I've been." He's closed the distance between us completely and he stands in front of me, a hand poised against the wall over my shoulder. He looks down at me, his heavy breath washes over my face, and I can't stop myself from looking at those lips, remembering how they felt against me. His mouth presses into a tight smile, and I kick myself how even in this circumstance I'm admiring him, how my chest pushes toward him instinctually. *Down girl. He could be the enemy.*

It's really impossible to tell if he's lying and about to eat me like the big bad wolf in Little Red Riding Hood, or if he's being genuine.

My gaze moves from those tempting lips to his sharp eyes as I consider my next move. Run and call the others, or give him the benefit of the doubt.

"I've never said I was the good guy, Aria, or that sometimes my heart doesn't feel as black as the darkest pits of Hell, but around you, I'm different. I crave the high of making you smile, to touch you so you'll moan. The sounds you make drive me wild, and I don't think you have a clue what you've done to me."

"Is that supposed to convince me you're inno-cent?" I don't know what's still holding me back from shoving him off me, and the thing is, Maverick knows exactly how he affects me, which is why he's come to me first, why he's flirting this way.

Sure, everything about this demon sends my pulse into a frenzy, but that doesn't make him safe now, does it?

"They're just words," I answer. "Demons lie all the time. It's one of your specialties."

"And how would you know that?"

"It's a known fact."

He leans in closer, and I press my back to the wall. "Maybe people change. Cain's my brother, and you've given him a chance after he bought your soul."

"Good for you in doing your research, but it's not that straightforward. And I've had enough of this game." I shove my hands against his chest, pushing him off me. "The fact is, you took the relics, and you're an asshole for everything you did to me."

He stands several feet away, and I've decided I'm no longer going to fall for his tricks. I can't stand his persistent lies. I want more than anything to believe him, but everything points to him taking the relics, lying to us. Cain hasn't trusted him from the beginning, but it was me who fell prey to his charm. Now I'm burdened with my mistakes and the awful ache that I let myself fall for someone like him.

I should have known better. Dammit. Taking in quick breaths, in and out, my pulse is on fire with anger.

I turn fast and head out of my room and down the hallway, cloaked in the night's embrace.

Footsteps strike the floorboards behind me. "Aria, please, you need to believe me. I am on your side. After everything, do you really think I'd betray you?"

He snatches my wrist and roughly forces me to face him, but as I stumble around I lash out and slap him across the face.

"You don't get another chance to hurt me," I croak, surprised I can even speak straight with how much I'm trembling with anger.

He stiffens from my strike but doesn't release my hand. He instead lifts my palm and places it on his chest. "You broke me from the first moment we met, but I hadn't known it at the time. You've become my obsession and I can't get you out of my head. When I close my eyes, I only see you, I hear your voice, I can't stop smelling that gorgeous scent you have. It's unbearable being away from you. Aria, do you think I'd risk losing someone as special as you for some fucking relics?"

"I...I don't know what to think." I yank my

hand free and stumble back a few steps, my pulse jackhammering in my chest. His words wreak havoc with my head, with my heart.

He lets out a frustrated sound as he stares at me sharply. "I returned to Hell to chase my brother, Lorcan. He took the relics. I'll die trying to help you. Anything you want, I'll give you, because in my heart, I claimed you as mine from the first time we met."

Before I can respond, a terrifying growl floods the hallway from behind me. The hairs on my arms raise when a sudden whoosh of air rushes right past me.

One second, Maverick stands in front of me, and the next, someone slams into him, sending him sideways. The bangs and growls sound like an earthquake is tearing down the mansion.

I know instantly that it's Cain tearing into Maverick. Brother against brother.

My stomach shouldn't ache at seeing them battle, but it does. I'm trying to make sense of what Maverick told me. Why would he return if he got what he wanted, to rub it in my face? It sure seems like something he'd do, except something just doesn't feel right.

I rush down the hallway after them. The pair

are tossing each other into walls, leaving gaping holes. Paintings drop from the walls. It's chaos.

Cain is fighting as his full demon with his wings out. So is Maverick, and there's something almost beautiful about watching these powerful, dark beings battle. Only the light from my room behind me illuminates the fight, their shadows like monstrous puppets twisted in their own battle along the walls.

Maverick is suddenly thrown into the air where he slams into the ceiling. His silver feathered wings sweep against the chandelier, sending the entire thing to the ground. It falls to the floor with a tremendous crash, and the crystals break off and fling like projectiles.

I duck and cover my head, when a large hand sweeps over me, and someone covers me with their body. Dorian, I smell his cologne instantly.

"Stay behind me," he says.

I lift my head to Dorian and Elias, who are now by my side, watching. Neither of them interrupt.

The look in Elias's gaze is filled with blood lust, with hatred.

But my mind swirls with Maverick's excuses about Lorcan taking the relics. With Gabriel's insistence, the knowledge that Lucifer and his demons would do anything to get the relics.

My head hurts and my gut churns while working out who to believe.

Cain's clawed wings slice through the air before slashing Maverick across the chest, his other fist colliding into his face. Maverick stumbles backward, his blood splashing the wall, and he glances my way for a brief moment as he catches his footing. It's enough for me to see a harrowing look in his eyes, of him pleading for me to believe him.

"You couldn't pay enough for ring-side viewing of such a fight," Elias brags, grinning wildly.

Dorian isn't any better with how enchanted he is by the battle. And sure, I won't deny that seeing Cain fight is spectacular. He moves like the dark, barely noticeable until he's savagely mauled you.

But the longer I watch, the more I know this isn't the solution. It's not going to help us.

"Stop," I call out suddenly, and I'm pushing forward when Dorian snatches my arm.

"That's not going to happen," he tells me. "This is long overdue."

"And then what? He kills Maverick! We need to grill him, and he told me Lorcan stole the relics."

Elias barks a laugh. "He'll say anything to not be blamed."

"Then why did he return?" I ask hurriedly, as another thunderous bang comes from Maverick slamming Cain to the ground in what I can only describe as a wrestling flip over his shoulder.

"Gorgeous," Dorian says, still holding onto my arm. "He came to take you back to Lucifer."

His words just add to my tangled thoughts, though I can't help but wonder if that were the case, why did he waste time trying to tell me otherwise? Why not snatch me while I sleep and kidnap me?

My throat tightens like someone has punched me, and all I can think is what if he is telling the truth?

I yank my arm free from Dorian and scream, "Cain, you need to stop, please!"

In the exact same moment that Cain looks up at me, two things happen simultaneously. Maverick drives a fist right into his face, sending Cain falling backward, and Dorian snatches me off my feet and swings me away from the fight.

"Put me the hell down," I yell, slapping his arms.

"Calm down. You don't get it, do you?" he

growls in my ear, then finally puts me down.

The sounds and grunts of the battle escalate.

I look up at Dorian. "What do you mean?"

"This fight has been long overdue. They won't kill each other; in Hell, this is how shit is settled."

I'm breathing heavily. "So, they're not going to kill each other?"

"Not if Maverick accepts his defeat."

I flinch in response as I doubt Maverick is the kind to ever give in. "And if he doesn't, Cain will take him out?"

He shrugs, which doesn't put me at ease.

"This is just crazy. It would be easier if we just talked."

Dorian half chuckles like that's the most ludicrous idea in the world. "You see, Maverick bowing to Cain is also an admission that he's on his side and not Lucifer's. And that's done with battle and drawing blood. Without it, how can we believe him?"

"And what if he's lying?" I huff as frustration pinches along my shoulder blades. Of course, demons only settle things barbarically. It doesn't help that my heart is trying to leap out of my chest, leaving me feeling dark and trembling.

Dorian's fingers skim under my chin, tilting my

head back. I stare into his darkening eyes as he grins. Something about him is different…it's not like before, where he'd never stop me. Maybe I need to let my demons do what they have to do. Even if I don't agree with it.

It isn't Cain I'm worried about. It's finding out that perhaps Maverick has been lying this entire time and I'm about to find out the truth.

I don't know how long Cain and Maverick have been fighting, but it feels like eternity.

The sounds of war rattling the house abruptly ends.

Without warning, Maverick comes sliding out of the haze of dust, on his back, and pauses feet away from us, bleeding and bruised. He winces as he starts to push up.

Cain leaps toward Maverick, his black wings like shadows curling in on either side of him. He lands with a thud by his brother's side. Then he moves lightning fast, and his hand strikes out gripping a blade, and presses it to Maverick's throat. Blood starts to trickle out.

My heart seizes. "Cain, no!" I choke out the desperate words.

His head snaps up, and my eyes connect with his black stare, dark veins standing out beneath his skin, his horns ominous.

"Please, Cain," I say.

He pauses for a long moment, holding my gaze, then abruptly draws back, a heavy growl rolling past his throat. He cracks his neck and, in a heartbeat, his demons slides back into him. Clothes torn, bleeding, and his lip ripped open, but there's no pain on his face. He'll quickly heal the wounds he's gained—it's what demons do, after all—but what I find in his gaze is something else. Something that brings a flare of worry through me.

He looks down to Maverick. "Do you yield and vow allegiance to me?"

Maverick groans and pushes himself to a sitting position and wipes blood dripping from the cut under his eye. He heaves for breath, his chest rising and falling with the strain. The silence drags, and Cain's nostrils flare with what I imagine is impatience.

"I won't ask again, Brother," he growls.

Maverick gets to his feet, and glances at me momentarily, a tiny grin at the corner of his mouth. "Yes," he finally says, looking at me, then swings his attention back to Cain. "I give my allegiance equally to you and Aria."

Confusion washes over me. To me? "What does that mean?" I murmur.

Cain huffs, his hands curling into fists.

"It's my right," Maverick states, lifting his chin.

Cain doesn't look at me but anger crosses his face.

"Fine, have it your way," Cain finally says and brushes past Maverick. He pauses in front of me, pushing a stray strand of hair from my face. "Aria, if anyone ever hurt you, including my brothers, I'd make them regret it."

I blink at him, confusion heavy in my chest. "W-what does that allegiance really mean?"

"It means I don't trust Maverick's intentions. To put it in simple terms, it also means that he considers you his superior as much as he does me."

My thoughts are spiraling out of control and too many things are happening at once. I glance over to Maverick, who watches me with a strange expression.

"Aria, I would give you the world, but when it comes to demons, every deal ends up twisted to somehow benefit them."

"Maverick, can we talk?" I ask, to which he nods.

"Elias, stay close to Aria," Cain orders, glancing over his shoulder at him, then he swings his attention back to me. His brow furrows and annoyance dances across his features. "Come down to the parlor with Maverick once you're ready."

Him and Dorian head downstairs, leaving behind an air of tension. I'm partly surprised that Cain isn't locking Maverick up, but I guess if allegiance has been given, technically Maverick is free.

Elias gives me a lopsided grin as he approaches me. His hands clasp around my waist and he leans in close, whispering in my ear, "Aria, I hold you in my heart and love every inch of your body. No matter what happens around us, you can always trust in knowing I will be there for you, to catch you, to lift you, anything you need."

It is strange that his words make me want to cry...happy tears of course, but who would have thought demons experienced such deep emotions.

I hug him and bury my face into his chest, loving the way he smells so masculine and woodsy. "Love you too, Elias."

Maverick is clapping, which has Elias tensing. "Give me a moment, Elias."

He takes a few steps deeper into the hallway to where I can still see him.

Maverick lifts his head at my approach, and there's a glint to his eyes. If I thought Cain had been badly battered, Maverick is devastatingly so. Blood drips from the cuts across his arms and chest, from the gash over an eye, but he's not wincing or moaning from pain.

I step over the debris, noting the broken paintings and statues, and pass the chandelier that has somehow ended up half sticking out of a wall, like someone used it as a weapon.

A dark look flashes across Maverick's face, and he wipes the blood dripping down his chin.

"Why did you give me allegiance? I don't get it," I say.

He's staring at Elias over my shoulder, and I look back to find my gorgeous hellhound leaning a shoulder into the wall, arms folded over his chest and one leg crossed over the other at ankles. His gaze never leaves us.

He gives me a sexy wink, which makes my heart flutter.

"You can trust me," Maverick says, and I turn back around to where he's running a hand through his white hair, the intensity in his eyes softening my knees. This man…this demon, is stunning. Even bleeding and beaten, he takes my breath away. Strong jawline stained by blood, scruffy and delicious, despite his frown—he's the level of handsome that would stop any girl in their tracks. "And I trust *you* to do the right thing."

"Sure, whatever that means," I murmur.

"Cain and I have never seen eye to eye, and despite me vowing my allegiance to him he'll never completely lend credence to what I have to offer. And when things go bad, I will be the first to be blamed until I can show him I am a man of my word. So, I've given you power over me to stop him ever taking me out, should he decide to do so."

His confession surprises me. It's not what I expect from him, but it reveals how deep the distrust between these sin brothers are. And it's incredibly difficult to ignore that his true intentions no longer side with Lucifer.

"So, you're saying I have control over you now, right?" I tilt my head to the side, wanting to take control of the situation. After what he told me, the deal he made with Cain, I want to give him the benefit of the doubt and believe him.

The corners of his lips curl upward. "Does that turn you on?"

Elias clears his throat from behind me. "Are you ready to head downstairs?"

There is an edge to Maverick that has always intrigued me, aroused me. It also scares me a bit, but then again, my demons aren't exactly safe either.

Maverick lifts his head, his lips curving into a grin. "Let's go."

I find myself giving him a smile back in response. "Are you sure you don't need to be patched up or something?"

His gaze meets mine. "You want to play doctor?"

Elias is suddenly strolling alongside me, and his arm goes around my waist in a possessive gesture. My cheeks flush with warmth.

"The only playing you will do is with me," he growls, and I can't help but snicker a laugh.

Maverick mock-coughs, "Jealous-ass."

When we reach the parlor, Maverick wastes no time and strides across the room like he owns the place. He carries himself very similarly to Cain... full of bravado and arrogant confidence. Must be a sin demon thing.

"To put it simply," he begins, while the rest of us gravitate to the couch in front of the fire, "Lorcan broke into your bedroom, Brother, and took the relics. I spotted him when it was too late, rushing out of your room and mansion. I chased the bastard because you know Lorcan. He's a fucking slippery ass and fucking fast too, but he's always up to something bad."

"Lorcan is a two-faced prick," Dorian adds, then falls quiet. Seems someone's had an encounter with this demon.

"That he is," Maverick continues. "So, I chased him down to a mountain entrance that led to Hell, and like a serpent, he vanished inside."

I swallow hard at the thought that Lucifer may now have the relics. Well, not all of them as one is still outstanding, but still… We are so fucked right now.

Maverick's mouth presses into a thin line. "There is one way to find the relics quickly, but it's risky." He glances over to me, as do the others.

My stomach hardens as the realization hits me too. He's implying that I will be the one to track down the relics in Hell.

Cain roars and is on his feet. "Over my dead body. There is no fucking way Aria is going back into Hell!"

3

CAIN

I've been thinking long and hard about my brother's proposition and what it means for us all.

Do I trust him fully?

Absolutely not.

But I have to trust in Aria. I have to believe she's capable of protecting herself and making the right decisions.

On the other hand, Hell isn't like Earth, and during her last visit, she only got a glimpse of the insanity that lays beyond the veil. If she goes—I won't sugarcoat it—I'm terrified for her. She'll be easy pickings for Lucifer without me, Dorian, or Elias there. Even with Maverick there, he can only do so much.

And that's why I won't let her go. I can't.

But the relics…

I pace across my room, past the closed balcony doors, and glance at the two drained corpses at the foot of my bed. Ramos will be up soon to dispose of them, and although I feel more powerful after devouring their souls, I'm just as anxious and riled up as before. Nothing's changed.

I want another way to fix this. At the same time, I want to keep Aria safe, but the three of us can't pass through Hell's gate without Azrael's harp. How else are we going to get the pieces back?

My head pounds. How long have I been up here, going over the same questions and winding up with the same answers? Must be hours now. There doesn't seem to be any other way.

I'm going to have to let Aria go.

It kills me. Truly. But if Maverick is right, and it is Lorcan who snuck into our home and took the relics, well…the demon of Envy isn't an easy one to catch. While Maverick's slippery, Lorcan's fast, and he'd be the next one on the list of demons pining for Father's attention and favor.

Rubbing the worry lines across my forehead, I sigh heavily. When will my brother learn? Lucifer doesn't care about any of them. Not a single soul in the underworld. I'm not even sure he cares for his own. He's using whatever and whoever he can to get what he wants. That's all we are to him. Pawns in his game.

Then there's Maverick. He may have pledged his allegiance to not only me, but Aria as well, but again… They could be just words. It's near impossible to know for sure.

He cares about her—I can see it whenever he's near her—but he doesn't know how to explore those feelings yet, and that's what troubles me. Any hesitance or weakness will be used by Lucifer. I need to be certain he'll protect Aria at all costs while in Hell. Whatever that takes.

I think back to the dream I had while teetering on the edge of death before Aria, the necromancer, and the others brought me back to life. Aria covered in blood, eyes black as my demons', with Lucifer's crown upon her head. What else could it mean other than her becoming queen and ruling Lucifer's kingdom? But, was it a premonition or just a fever dream? I have no idea.

And then there was the vision we all shared after I touched the foot. Us in Lucifer's throne room while I ran an angel blade through Maverick and then myself. Again—was it a flash into the future or something else? Hard to say, but it did get me thinking about how this war would end for me. Maybe for all of the sin demons.

Shaking my head, I stop and peer out the glass doors. The gray sky is darkening again outside, signaling the end to another day.

I'd been right; I've been confined to my room and my thoughts for too long.

It's about time I go and find my Aria to tell her I've thought things over and changed my mind. We need the relics, and we need her to get them.

Twisting my father's ring around my finger, I wonder if there's a way we'll all come out of this infernal war alive.

Because, if I'm being honest with myself—truly honest—I'd have to say I doubt it very much.

ARIA

That discussion didn't go over too well.

Cain is absolutely against me returning to Hell.

To make matters worse, Dorian and Elias were soon to follow.

"You go," Dorian snaps at Maverick, crossing his arms over his broad chest. *"I think it'll be an excellent way to prove your loyalty to us. Go and bring the relics back."*

"If it was that easy, I would've done it already, don't you think?" Maverick scoffs. *"I can't believe I'm saying this, but I need Aria's magic pinky toe to sniff them out."*

"No." One word, but the way Cain says it makes it slice through the room like the swing of a sword. A final blow.

"Do you have any other ideas? How else are we supposed—"

"NO." This time, Cain's demon emerges to really drive it home, voice deepening and black veins crawling from his eyes and all. Maverick clamps his mouth shut, and that was the end of the conversation.

But as we dispersed and went on with our day, I couldn't help but think about what Maverick was proposing.

Go back to Hell. Me? Right into the lion's den where the lion was waiting to eat me, or in this metaphor, Lucifer? Just thinking about it scares the shit out of me, but I also think he's right. Since Cain, Dorian, and Elias are still banned and unable to use the gate, that only leaves Maverick and me to get the relics. There's no other way to get the demons into Hell to take down Lucifer. They are stuck on Earth without them.

How am I going to tell Cain that, though? He's made up his mind, and there seems to be no changing it.

Maybe I just need to let him stew for a bit. Let it rest and then revisit it later, once he's calmed down. But privately, with just me and him. That way his malice towards Maverick won't leak into his decision.

In the meantime, I want to know more. More about me and Sayah and what lies ahead for the both of us.

What is a Leviathan exactly, and what does it mean for me, since I'm living with one inside me? Now that it seems I'm learning how to control Sayah and use her power to my advantage, I want to make sure it won't be short-lived. I can't have her taking over again and wreaking havoc. I have to stay in control.

And that means I have to do some research.

I head to the library.

Yes, I know Cain already devoured every possible book in this place looking for an answer to the mystery of what I am, but that was back when Sayah didn't have an identity. Now she does.

But, as I spend hours combing the shelves, I quickly discover that Cain was also right about another thing—Leviathans are ancient creatures without many records. The only thing I can manage to find is, ironically, in a Bible Cain keeps on a shelf in his office.

A demon with a Bible? The irony is just too much. Shouldn't it burst into flames or something? Should *I* for touching it? I don't know how this works.

Sitting at Cain's desk, I plop the thick book down and sit at his chair. The last time I was here, I'd snuck in to search for information about the hospital where I was born, only to be found by Cain and *taught a lesson* in the best kind of way. That felt like years ago, not weeks. It's crazy to believe how different we both were then. And how different we are now…

All I wanted to do was leave and have my shitty life back with Joseline. And now, I couldn't imagine a day without my three demons.

Opening the thick cover, I start to comb through the pages blindly. I'm lucky it's in English and not Latin, but the words are so small and I really don't feel like reading through all of this that I'm just skimming rather than concentrating like I should. I do this for a while, turning a page, glancing over the small print, then going to the next. Until I spot the word I'm looking for in the center of the page.

Leviathan.

Bingo.

Stopping, I lean forward and lick my lips. Here we go.

I read—really read this time—the sentence.

In that day the Lord will punish Leviathan the fleeing serpent,

With His fierce and great and mighty sword,

Even Leviathan the twisted serpent;

And He will kill the dragon who lives in the sea.

Well, fuck. That's not what I want to see.

Fierce and great and mighty sword?

I think of the angel blade Gabriel wants to run through my gut and swallow hard. That part may be a little true, but fleeing serpent? Sea dragon? I don't think so. Whoever wrote this thought a Leviathan was a big fish or something. Living with Sayah my entire life, I can tell them firsthand that's not even close. A powerful shadowy ghost thingy, yeah, but no Loch Ness Monster here.

I already met one of those and he's in Scotland. Where he should be.

I flip through a few more pages, seeing no more references to the word I need, and sigh. As I shut the book, I look up to see Cain standing in the doorway, leaning his shoulder against the frame in the most casual way—for him, at least—a smirk playing across his lips.

"At it again, I see," he says, and I can tell by the lustful gleam in his eye that he's thinking back to our sexcapade in this office, on his desk, and against the window. Just like I was.

"Just trying to cover all my bases." I pick up the Bible to show him. "Why do you even have this in here? You're a demon."

"I am aware," he replies and walks over to the desk. "But it's also a part of our history, too."

I'm not sure I'm buying that one. It must show on my face because he follows up with, "You ever hear the saying, 'know thy enemy'?"

"Come on."

He chuckles. "Would you believe that I read it for entertainment, then?"

"Now that I believe," I say.

He picks up the massive book with one hand and holds it up to examine it. "I'll never understand why so many people worship a book written by a few dirty old men who knew nothing about God or Heaven or Hell. Just stories."

"Like fanfiction."

He glances at me, confused. "Fanfiction?"

"You don't know what fanfiction is?" I ask.

He shakes his head.

"Of course you don't." A centuries old demon knowing what character shipping or slash fiction is? I should've known better. "Maybe I'll explain it another day."

But he's unsatisfied with that answer. "Is it when people make up stories for their own amusement?"

Okay… Maybe he did understand. "And those stories become more popular than the original. Yep."

"Ah, then yes. You're right. This is like fanfiction." He tosses the book back onto the desk. "Useless really."

"I was just hoping I could find something else about…about me."

He holds out his hand, and I find myself reaching for it without a second thought. He guides me around the desk and brings my hand to his lips for a sweet kiss.

"Aria, my love, what else do you want to know?" His voice is as tender as his lips.

I blink, a bit struck dumb by his sudden shift in demeanor. Especially when the last time I'd seen him, he was fuming just at the idea of me returning to Hell with Maverick.

"I…uh… Well, you know. Just what being a Leviathan really means? What can I expect?"

"You've lived with Sayah inside you for your entire life. I don't think anyone knows more about what you are than you do," he replies and stares deeply into my eyes.

Heat crawls across my face. How can this demon still make me blush like a schoolgirl from a single look? I don't understand it.

"You know she has a mind of her own. And if I'm not careful—"

He runs his hands along my arms and draws me in closer. "I don't want you to think like that, Aria. You showed that you're fully capable of controlling Sayah during our fights with the hellhounds and the Nightwalkers. It's as if you both aren't two entities, but one. Someone just needs to take the lead, and when you do, you're stronger than any of us combined. Stronger than Gabriel. Even Lucifer."

"Let's not get ahead of ourselves," I tsk.

His serious facade cracks as another smile peeks through. "I saw it for myself."

As I peer up at his handsome face, I see nothing but his admiration and love reflecting back at me, and my chest warms. God, I love this man—this demon. There's no other way for me to describe it other than love.

"You know, you're starting to sound a lot like your brother," I tease but immediately regret it because the change in his posture is sudden and drastic. His muscles stiffen, his eyes flash a shade darker, and his hands fall away from me.

Ah, shit. Why did I have to mention Maverick?

I want to kick myself for being so stupid.

Read the room, Aria. Geez.

When I try to step toward him, he shifts back, his lips pressing into a hard line.

Then he does something else unexpected. He slides off his ring, the one with the dark red— practically black—stone from his father, and holds it out for me to take. I only stare at it in confusion.

"What do you want me to do with this?" I ask.

He holds it up high, pinched between his two fingers. "It's for you to wear."

Instinctively, my hand shoots to the necklace

he'd given me at the beginning of this hell-of-a-relationship with his signature emblem. A single wing. I still wear it everyday.

"You already gave me this," I tell him.

Cain grabs my wrist, presses the ring into my palm, and closes my fingers around it

"But I can't take that from you. It's… It's…" I stammer.

His gaze bores into mine. "You're going to need it."

"I don't under—" But then it clicks, and I look up at him in disbelief. "Wait."

He nods. "As much as it kills me to say this, Maverick was right. You have to go back to Hell with him and retrieve the relics. And I…" He sighs heavily. "I have to let you go."

I don't know why, but those few words make my heart clench. Why? Because I know Cain, and I know this wasn't an easy decision for him. I wouldn't be surprised to find out that he'd agonized over it, obsessed over it, all night and day. From the moment Maverick had returned.

A part of me wonders if what he's saying has another meaning, too. About giving me more freedom and letting go.

"Like Maverick's, it'll help you cross over," he

goes on, and I can't help but notice the hint of sadness in his tone. "It should keep your soul safe while you are there, but that means keeping it on always. No matter what anyone tells you, you must keep it on. If you remove it, even for a second, you will be lost to us forever."

I remember from last time, but it still makes me shiver. He wants the warning to sink in. "Don't worry. It'll stay on me the entire time I'm there. It'll be like you're with me."

"Good." The small smile is back. The one that makes my heart flutter. "If it were up to me, I'd always be with you."

Hell, I love when he says stuff like that. It gives me goosebumps; I don't know why. Maybe because he rarely expresses himself like this.

I slip the ring onto my finger. It's heavier than Maverick's and takes up more space, but it's Cain's and I love it for that reason alone. When I hold it up, the dark stone catches the light and gives me a peek at his blood red center.

"It's no engagement ring, but it'll do." I chuckle.

His brow arches. "Engagement ring?"

Ah, shit. Probably shouldn't have said that.

"It was a joke," I say, swatting away his question.

"Would you...want an engagement ring?" he asks, which throws me for a loop.

"What? No! Well, I don't know. Maybe some-day." I'm babbling, of course. "The binding ritual was hard enough for me to agree to. I never really thought about marriage or anything like that before. Not with my shitty life growing up. I rarely had a steady boyfriend, let alone..." I pause, my words trailing off as I look up at him. He's watching me intently again, taking in my every word.

"Three demons."

"Uh...yeah. That."

"I see," he says.

"Not saying that's a bad thing," I quickly recover, "because it's not. Not at all. I'm all for being with whoever makes a person the happiest. No judgment here."

"I'll have to remember that."

Rubbing my lips together, I glance away, a bit embarrassed I even confessed such a thing.

Silence stretches between us as we're both lost in our own thoughts but, after a while, Cain slides his hand in mine, his finger finding the ring right away. He rubs the stone.

"A ring here does look good on you," he muses,

and I blush. "I can always respect ritual and tradition, and if I remember correctly, a human marriage is supposed to end in a very specific way."

Oh, I think I know where this is going, but I ask the question anyway. "And what's that?"

His eyes darken a shade. "Consummation."

4

MAVERICK

I have no idea what I'm doing here, or why Cain insisted I come to Dorian's bedroom.

As expected, the place reeks of sex, sweat, and who knows what else. It makes me gag just thinking about what vile things happened on this very couch I'm sitting on—why is it so sticky?

Fuck, the demon's disgusting.

Across from the large party-size bed, there's a rack of *toys*, if you know what I mean. Whips, ropes, chains, handcuffs, straps, paddles, feathers, *appendages.*

My eyes widen. I know we all have our kinks, and Dorian's power thrives off pleasure, but damn. The guy needs a hobby.

I really shouldn't talk though. My sexual needs are…a bit on the dark side. But at least I clean up after myself.

But what I still don't understand is why I'm here. What game are my brother, Dorian, and Elias playing at? Especially after the incident with Lorcan and the relics, I doubt they trust me fully. No matter how many times I swear allegiance to Cain or promise my commitment to their cause, it doesn't seem to be enough, so whatever this foolishness is, I hope it's the last thing I have to do.

The door opens and the three demons plus Aria walk in. Her large dark eyes find me immediately, and I can't help the smirk curling the corner of my lips. She quickly glances away, back to Cain, who is guiding her to Dorian's bed with their linked hands.

His claims about loving Aria float back to me, and I clench my teeth. I don't know why it annoys me so much that the idiot thinks he's been struck by Cupid's arrow, but it does.

"So?" I start, that annoyance leaking into my tone. "What's this all about?"

Dorian smiles wickedly, like he's holding some secret he can't wait for me to figure out, because he knows I'll hate the answer. He and Elias stand on opposite sides of the massive bed and start taking off their clothes.

What the fuck?

Aria seems just as confused. "Uh, Cain. What's going on?"

"Do you remember us talking about humans and their wedding rituals?" he explains.

She nods. "The wedding night."

"Consummation. Yes."

She glances at the bed, at Dorian and Elias, who are both now naked, and then me. "Wait, now?" Her voice rises with nervousness. "But Maverick—"

Cain pulls her into him and crushes his mouth against hers in a possessive kiss. My insides twist into a tight knot as Aria melts against him, instantly lost to his hunger for her, his desire.

He breaks away for only a second to whisper against her lips, "If my brother wants to be a part of this cause, then he is going to have to know his place."

He's challenging me. I see it now.

That's what this is. A power move.

The three of them plan to fuck Aria and make me watch so it's clear who she belongs to and to make sure I know that she's off limits.

The fucking bastard.

Anger spikes. I already promised my loyalty to him. I don't need to be here for this and be humiliated.

I push to my feet. "This is fucking stupid," I bite out. "There's no way I'm sitting here while you… while you…"

"Ah, but you don't have a choice," Dorian interjects.

"You leave, you're deemed the enemy," Elias adds, and his hard gaze lights with murderous intentions. "Which means, all bets are off."

Meaning, they plan to kill me.

A quick look at Aria proves that she's unsure about this, too, but I'm not one to fold from a threat. If my brother wants to play his stupid games, fine. I'll play. I'm tired of being seen as a lesser demon because of my age or rank.

It's just sex.

If they want to fuck her, go for it. Fuck her. I don't give a shit.

Unlike them, she means nothing to me. I'm a demon—not some love-drunk fool. Never will be.

I drop back on the couch and make sure to look as bored as possible. "Let's make this quick, then. We got shit to do."

Cain touches Aria's chin, turning her head so that he can resume kissing her. His tongue sweeps into her mouth, and when his hands start to peel away her clothes, she lets him without hesitation.

It's like she's hypnotized by him. Entranced. And it isn't long before she's standing there in just thin black-lace panties with her creamy breasts on full display. His fingers tangle in her hair and wrench her head back, and she groans from the pleasure and pain.

I know all too well how much she loves pain. I got to see a taste of it myself a few times, especially during our little knife fight in the basement. The cuts, the taste of her blood on my tongue... Like me, pain turns her on.

As she slowly gets to her knees, Cain's fingers stay locked in her hair, holding her in place. Face to the stiff bulge in his pants, she licks her lips and my own body tenses, knowing exactly what's going to happen next. My own cock twitches, and I curse myself for feeling anything but disgust or indifference.

She undoes his belt and tugs his pants down. When his dick springs free, she grabs it eagerly and presses her lips to its hardened tip. Her tongue swirls around it, her eyes lifted the entire time to

Cain's, who watches her with a mixture of admiration and starvation. Using his hold in her hair, he pushes her down more so that his cock disappears past her lips.

She takes it all without hesitation, squeezing his balls at the same time. And when he yanks her off, salvia drips from the side of her mouth.

Holy fuck, that's hot.

He does it again, pushing her mouth down, all the way to the base. This time, he tilts his hips, and I can see a bulge growing at the center of her throat. That makes her gag, and Cain jerks her off him just as fast but she pouts, wanting more.

My pulse speeds up, and to my own surprise, my demon stirs. It wants out. More importantly, it wants to be in Cain's place, fucking her throat, making her plead for me to do it harder.

Without waiting for permission, Aria leans forward and takes him back into her mouth, devouring him. Her head bobs, her tongue lapping at him, the sound of her sucking and slurping filling the room. Cain's head rolls back, his ecstasy clear, while Elias and Dorian both watch everything unfold from the sidelines, palming their own dicks and patiently waiting their turns.

Itching to touch myself, too, I clench my fists against my thighs.

Again, Cain yanks Aria off him, but then he forces her head in my direction. Our eyes lock, and sweat starts to slide down my back. She's so incredibly sexy on her knees, lips parted and breasts out, her eyes hooded with lust.

"How do I taste, my love?" Cain asks, his voice husky with need.

Eyes still glued to mine, she whimpers and the sound sends shockwaves straight to my cock. I'm so hard now, sitting is uncomfortable. But I do my best to keep how much this is affecting me off my expression.

"Tell my brother how much you love it when I fuck your throat, Aria," he says.

"I do," she pants. Her breasts swing with every movement. "I love it."

I can see that.

"Do you want more?" he presses and glances at me, gauging my reaction. He's testing me. He's trying to rile me up and see if I walk out, but I won't let that happen.

She nods her answer.

"Beg for it," he commands.

Still looking at me, she says, "Please... Cain." She swallows roughly. "Fuck my throat."

He answers her by grabbing her under her arms, lifting her off her feet, and throwing her onto the bed. Like wild animals, Elias and Dorian take that as their cue and descend on her. Dorian flops onto his back, upside down, and pulls her body over his.

A quick snap and her panties are torn off and tossed away. Like a ravenous beast, he starts to devour her pussy, making her cry out. Elias moves toward her rear, spitting on his hand like a savage, and lubing himself up with it. He then presses his two fingers into her ass crack, and she gasps.

Lifting his shirt over his head, Cain takes his place in front of her, his cock at full attention and positioned right in front of her mouth.

She peers up at him through long, dark lashes, and he runs a finger up her throat to her chin. A smirk lifts his lips. "My sweet, sweet Aria," he whispers. "I don't think he heard you. Say it again. Louder."

She's panting now, her back arching as Dorian grips her legs and sucks on her clit. The hellhound continues to finger her while stroking himself.

She's close to coming. I can tell. And my jealousy and arousal are starting to outweigh my need to win this challenge of Cain's. Even more, I hate that it's even affecting me at all. It shouldn't be, but no matter how many times I tell myself that, I can't ignore the raw desire spinning inside me.

My hand slides to the erection straining against my jeans. I begin to rub myself, imagining myself getting ready to fuck her tight little pussy. Or that delectable mouth of hers. I want to hear *my* name on her lips. Hear her beg for *me* to give her what she craves.

"I… I…" She can barely get the words out. When Elias removes his fingers and rubs the tip of his length along her crack instead, she moans, "Oh fuck."

"Come on, Aria," Cain coaxes. "Say it. Look at Maverick and say it."

Her dreamy gaze flicks my way again. In that moment, so lost and free of any fear or worry, she's the most beautiful woman I've ever seen. My heart thunders, and I stroke myself even faster through the tight fabric, loving the way the friction burns.

"Fuck me…" she says in a weak voice. Since she's looking at me on Cain's orders, it's almost as if I'm the one she's speaking to, and just the thought has me holding my breath. "Fuck me, please."

Fucking shit. I don't think I can do this.

It takes all my strength not to leap to my feet, shove one of them out of the way, and take their place.

As if working in perfect sync with each other, Cain, Dorian, and Elias readjust themselves and do exactly what she asked for. Elias stands in his tiptoes and pushes into her tight ass, groaning, while Dorian continues to eat her out. Slurping. Sucking. Until she's screaming.

Every time Elias rams into her from behind, she's thrown forward. Cain takes the opportunity to hold her head with two hands and thrust himself deeper into her mouth. They all fuck her mercilessly, and she takes it all, moaning loudly.

I feel my own body tensing, getting closer to release. It's not the real thing, but my imagination is doing a hell of a job by itself.

Cain pulls back for a moment, and without missing a beat, her head drops to Dorian's erection, taking him into her mouth and tasting him from base to tip.

"Ssssshit," he hisses, clearly not expecting it.

Cain steps away, letting his friends have their

moment—Elias speeding up so that her ass slaps against him with every thrust. Aria uses both her hands and her mouth on Dorian beneath her, pumping, licking, teasing.

Suddenly, Aria cries out, her entire body tensing as the orgasm explodes through her. Dorian reaches down and keeps her head in place, thrusting his hips up to fuck her mouth through it, and she lets his cock mute her screams. He lets out one last thrust and grunt with his own release, before sagging into the mattress, and simultane-ously Elias slams into her two more times to flood her with his seed.

This time, when Cain steps forward, his demon is released. Huge leathery wings tucked into his back, marble-like skin lined with dark veins, and inky black eyes. A figure of power and darkness, he steps closer to the bed. Dorian and Elias move away to give him space.

Another power move. By bringing forth his demon and taking her like this, he's saying he's the strongest. The one in charge. In hellhound terms, the alpha.

He might not want to hear it, but it's a very Lucifer thing to do.

With a confidant strut, he walks around the

bed, grabs Aria by the ankles, and rolls her onto her back. Then he crawls over her, his wings and her legs spreading wide.

Without warning or mercy, he thrusts into her. Hard. The entire bed shakes and the headboard slams against the wall.

Boom.

My demon rears up again, and jealousy replaces all the earlier desire, followed by fury. My spine prickles as my own wings push against my skin, wanting to tear through.

I don't know why, but seeing him fuck her to oblivion as his demon hits me harder than watching it in his human form.

Maybe because, like he's said before, there's something more to this than sex. He *loves* her, and she loves him for what he truly is.

And he wants me to see that.

He rams into her again.

Boom goes the headboard against the wall.

She cries out.

I can't stand it. I can't even look. My gaze drops to the floor, but I can hear it—the crash of the headboard every time he thrusts.

Boom. Boom. Boom.

Faster. Faster.

Plaster falls from the new hole quickly forming in the wall.

I'm getting flashbacks of hearing similar sounds from above the rafters and the dust raining down on me when I was in the basement, which only fuels my anger.

Boom. Boom.

"Fuck, Cain! Fuck!"

I jump to my feet. Every inch of me is shaking with rage, and if I don't leave now I may do something even worse. Something I'd regret that could ruin everything.

Fuck this. I really don't care if Elias hunts me down and kills me, at this point. I'm out.

Heading straight for the door, I refuse to look back. I'm sure Cain, Dorian, and Elias are loving my weakness.

Even when I slam the door shut behind me, I can hear the thudding of the bed against the wall. Mocking me. Calling me out.

As I trudge down the hall, I'm surprised neither Elias or Dorian come after me to drag me back.

I guess there's no need. Cain has gotten what he wants in the end… For me to obey and learn my place among their demon trio.

Which is at the bottom.

The same ranking I was in Hell.

Problem is, it's not where I fucking want to be.

ARIA

This is it. The moment I've dreaded since I escaped Hell's fiery clutches last time.

I swore I'd never go back, yet here I am, standing at the base of the mountain that is supposed to be a hidden gate to Hell, holding a flashlight in the dark.

Cain, Dorian, and Elias stand behind me, the collective tension between them pulsing through our invisible link. It only heightens my anxiety, too. It also reminds me that while Maverick and I are in Hell, I'll lose contact with my demons, even with the bond between us. The magic is too weak to reach across the planes, and that's worrisome in itself.

Not like they would be able to come down and rescue me if I was in trouble anyway. But still...

I guess I am just going to rely on Maverick.

Speak of the devil—or one of his sons, I should say—Maverick steps up to my side and rolls his shoulders and neck like he's about to head into a fight. And maybe we are. I don't know.

"Have the ring on?" he asks, glancing at my crossed arms that I have wrapped across my chest to keep out the cold. It has to be below thirty degrees and there's snow on the ground, but I'm only in leggings and a sweater, and he's in jeans and a button-down. Definitely not dressed for this weather.

I pull out my hand to show him Cain's ring on my finger. "Got it."

"I don't have to tell you to never take it off, right."

I narrow my eyes at him, feeling so tense I might burst. "I know the deal."

"Good. Because I won't have Cain skinning me alive because you decided to be stupid and got your soul lost forever."

I clench my teeth. Maverick has a knack for getting under your skin, and it seems I am no exception. It's no wonder Elias wants to punch him in the face ninety-nine percent of the time.

"Maverick." Cain's voice rumbles across the darkness, but the warning rings clear in his tone.

"Yeah, yeah. I know."

I don't understand where all this attitude

came from. He seemed to be enjoying himself quite a bit during Cain, Dorian, Elias, and my group session last night. Well, in the beginning. The next time I was able to glance over, he looked miffed. And then when we had… you know, finished, he'd stormed out. I guess he wasn't happy watching me with the three demons.

"You are to go to Hell, retrieve the relics from Lorcan, and come back. Nothing more. But Aria is always—"

"My first priority," he sing-songs as if Cain's repeated this very phrase to him a million times. "Don't worry your pretty little head about it, Big Brother. She'll be safe with me."

Dorian and Elias exchange looks that say they still aren't so sure about this arrangement. I'm not so sure about it either.

Without warning, Maverick snatches my left hand and tugs me toward the mountain's rocky face. My pulse races, and I glance over my shoulder at my three demons standing in front of Dorian's Ferrari, the bright headlights casting them in shadows. Despite that, I can still see the worry and fear etched on each of their faces. Especially Cain's. He's wound so tight, he looks like he might just leap forward, seize me, and wrench me back to them after changing his mind.

Part of me wishes he would, but he doesn't. He only stares at me, lips pressed into a thin line, the internal war he's fighting clear in his eyes.

I don't want to leave them.

I hope to god I'm coming back.

At that moment, Maverick and I pass through the rock, the mountain swallowing us whole and engulfing us in blackness. I lose sight of every-thing, and the air becomes so thick, I can barely take another breath.

I lose sense of Maverick's touch, even though I can vaguely feel him tugging me along, but it's like we're moving through sludge. Slowly. Agonizingly so. And I wonder if we'll ever get to the other side.

It feels like forever but eventually the immense pressure eases and I can feel Maverick's firm grip on my hand again. The darkness gives way to a blaze of colors, making me squint.

Then comes the heat.

5

ARIA

An oppressive heat bears down on me like someone's smothering me in a woolly blanket. How can it be so hot in a place with no sun, where there is permanent cloud cover?

But with the way my feet overheat with each step, I have my answer. It's coming from underground, like we're walking on a blazing fire that roars beneath us.

Maverick and I are moving quickly down a dingy alleyway between two buildings made of black stone. Something drips sluggishly down their surface, and because of the sulfur stench in the air it reeks. I don't want to know what the gooey stuff collecting in puddles on the sidewalk is.

"Where are we exactly in Hell?" I ask, feeling I have to keep my voice down to not attract attention.

"Outskirts of the city," he replies, not giving me more. Someone's still in a pissy mood. I glance behind us to where we'd been spat out after entering Hell from the gates. At the end of the alley lies an adjacent road peppered with trees, though I'm not sure if they can be called that. They have no leaves, the branches are gnarly, and even the ground looks like it's been scorched by flames.

We pause at the corner as Maverick peeks out on either side. I turn Cain's ring on my finger over and over, partially terrified that it's not going to mask my human side from the demonic beasts living here. The metal feels cool against my fingers despite me perspiring.

"All clear," Maverick mutters and turns around. "We're heading to Lorcan's place, and I'm hoping you can detect if the relics are anywhere near without us having to go inside."

He takes my wrist and hauls me alongside him roughly, then we're moving out from the alleyway.

"Hey." I tug my arm back. "Not so rough."

His hand loops around my waist and pulls me against him instead.

I cut him a glare.

"Relax," he whispers, which only makes me elbow him in the ribs. But his grip is like iron, and he turns on me swiftly, towering over me, and I can swear his eyes are darkening. "Listen, Aria. My brother's ring can only protect you so much. But you don't exactly look like you belong here with your deer-in-the-headlights look. I mean, I should have given you some scratches or something. Maybe take off your shirt so you look the part of my whore."

My mouth falls open with utter shock as a wicked grin spreads over his lips. "Over my dead body."

"We need to play the part. It's just a few gropes between us."

I'm not sure if I want to laugh at him or slap him. He's definitely enjoying this and making the most of it by being the ultimate asshole. "Well, let's make one thing straight. I am not taking my top off for any demons."

"Oh yeah? You didn't really follow that rule before in Dorian's room."

My face flames. What a freaking prick!

"How about I'm the one whoring you out? I prefer that role-play," I suggest.

He barks a laugh, throwing his head back like that would never happen, which infuriates me further.

"Okay, stop cackling like a hyena."

"You forget one little detail, Aria. Everyone knows me down here, and the Greed Demon is *not* a prostitute."

I grind my teeth. "Fine, I'll play the damn part, but let's just get this shit done fast."

"Eager, huh?" He laughs again.

I exhale, trying to ignore my rapidly growing irritation, then glance around to see where we are. It's an empty street lined with black stone buildings, each dilapidated with broken windows, some sporting holes in the walls, and one is even covered in that transparent goo. But considering a woman—who could have just walked out of *The Grudge* movie—steps out of a front door and is holding hands with a miniature version of the kraken, well, I'm guessing this is a residential part of town.

"Let's move," Maverick growls under his breath, his hand slapping my ass, grabbing it, and not letting go. I'm plastered to his side regardless.

"You're a real dickhead today," I hiss under my breath.

"Only today?"

Thankfully we're on the opposite sidewalk of the terrifying woman and her child, but they're watching us like they'll fly in our direction and rip my face off any second.

I try to keep my head low as we hurry down the street. Once we pass them, I glance back to find the little kid staring at me. He knows something is up.

"See, that wasn't so bad," Maverick says as he turns me down the next street which has more homes, but right at the end stands a tremendous castle. Not even sure I can call it that.

It's like a medieval cathedral with a pointy tower so lofty, it might very well be touching the clouds. It's made of black and gray stone, dark windows, and surprisingly the front yard is perfectly cared for. A long driveway with manicured shrubs in the front. They're trimmed in the shape of... I squint to get a better look. Yep, I'm right. It's people being tortured, one looks like a person on their knees with their head by their side, another is lying on a bed of spikes.

Just lovely!

"I'm getting major Freddy Kruger and Edward Scissorhands vibes here," I mumble.

"Who are they? Kings from your land? Exes?"

I almost choke on my next breath. "Ha, no! They are fictional characters from old movies that my friend and I would watch growing up."

"The witch," he answers, and I nod.

"Yeah, the one who you tried to steal the soul from."

"Hey, I ripped up that contract."

True. "*Anyway*, what I was trying to say is that those movies have this same Gothic, creepy feel to them too."

"Good, then you're familiar. This should feel like home." He drags me forward by my arm.

We power-walk the rest of the way. I catch the movement of curtains in the homes we pass, the crack of doors

Upon reaching the building, I'm still utterly mesmerized by this weird-ass castle. "So, Lorcan lives here, you say?"

"Can't you see the lofty tower? That screams insecurity. The prick had to make sure his house was the tallest in the land. One time, Valdim started building a worshipping church—as he called it— with the intention to make it taller than Lorcan's. It mysteriously burned down two days later."

"So, which sin demon is Valdim again?"

"Gluttony."

I nod, remembering. "There's definitely no love lost between all the brothers."

Maverick shrugs and guides me outside the edge of the home, keeping the broken fence between us and the castle. "It's how Father brought us up. He's always encouraged hatred and competition between us."

"Yeah, but if you got along, you might all turn on him. It makes sense. Have you guys fight each other instead. It makes you weaker."

He stares at me, impressed. "Exactly."

We quickly march past the house, hoping we can get the relics and the heck out of here. On our walk, I finding more of those disturbing shrubs around the lawn.

"Feel anything with your toe?" Maverick asks.

"Not a thing."

His mouth thins, and he yanks me forward again. We circle the entire building, which turns out to be not as big as I first thought.

And aside from sweating in my shoes, my toes don't react at all.

When I shake my head at Maverick, he sighs.

"Well that fucking sucks. Maybe we should go inside?"

"If I can't feel it here, then I doubt the relics are here."

He looks over at the house again. "Fuck. This was meant to be a fast job. In and out, then you're back with your precious Cain."

Of course he'd bring up Cain again. The sibling rivalry between these two is getting annoying fast.

"Oh, sorry to disappoint," I begin. "Trust me, this is the last place I want to be stuck with you."

He ignores me.

"So, where would a jealous prick hide his stash?" I ask, staring at Lorcan's castle.

"Good question," he replies.

"Would he give them to Lucifer, you think?"

"Maybe, but I doubt it. He won't hand them over until he's sure it's going to benefit him majorly, so he'll be assessing all his options first."

"So, then what? We trail through Hell until my toe reacts?"

"That's our backup plan. For now, let's go to my place. I need to get you dressed in something more suitable that won't attract unwanted attention, then we might pay Lorcan's lover a visit. He tells him everything."

MAVERICK

"The dark decor is an interesting touch. I thought it was just your bedroom, but you've gone with the theme all over your house," Aria says, turning on the spot, and taking in the third dining room. I have six of them, but this one has always been my favorite, which may be due to the arched windows that look out on the Scorched Woods. I don't have many windows through the rest of the house; I like to keep my privacy from my family, but sometimes even I crave light.

Aria walks along the dark stone walls, circling the room. Part of me wishes she'd stop talking. I'm still fuming after watching her with Cain and his two demon nitwits. It shouldn't fuck with my head as much as it does, but each time I remember the scene, it's like poison bleeding into every fiber of my being.

I hate that Aria has made me care when I shouldn't give a fuck.

She pauses in front of a painting above the fireplace and draws my attention. "What's this about?"

I glance up at the image of me riding a two

headed fire-breathing horse. I frown, as I unfortunately remember the day too easily.

"Get on the fucking fire-horse," Father bellows, even though I'm standing right next to him, so now my ears are ringing with his voice. I can smell the whiskey on his breath, fury vibrating through his body, and he's clenching his fists.

One of the maids had once told me that parents were meant to protect, love, and cherish you. Of course, she had been a recently dead human forced into labor for Lucifer, but her words have always stuck with me. For a long time, I waited for Father to treat me that way, but when all I received were beatings and ridicule, I learned quickly that the maid's words were a delusion.

Demons like me don't get happy endings. We receive endless punishment for merely existing.

The animal neighs, shaking its heads and digging the acrid ground with its front hoof. It gives a sudden snort and flames shoot from its nostrils.

I flinch back but Father shoves me forward. "Don't you dare embarrass me. Grow some fucking balls."

I pause within striking range of the animal's flames and turn on Father. "Why the fuck do I need to take an image with this thing? They spit poison and hate being ridden?"

"And you, my son, need to change your reputation

from a weak-ass sin demon, to one everyone will be terrified of."

I blink at him, my entire body tensing while rage burns through me. I loathe everything about him, and how all he cares about is others' perception of him.

"Now, get on that fucking horse and look like you've conquered the beast for the painting. Or I'll get the thing to burn the flesh off your bones over and over until you do as I say."

And that's the truth right there, isn't it? At the core, Father only cares about how I make him look. At the end of the day, he never cares about me.

He waves for his marble soldiers to come for me, and the horse rears up in their presence, hating them. The scorching heat of the animal's fire strikes my back, and I start bellowing. Then my world goes dark.

I exhale loudly, driving the memory away. The only reason I keep the hellish painting is as a reminder of who Father is and the devil I'm dealing with. To never become complacent around him or believe he'll ever have my back. No matter his promises, he's a snake.

Aria's by the long mahogany table now, staring at the bowl filled with black grapes. "They're edible," I tell her.

She laughs. "You think I was born yesterday? There's no way I'm trusting anything in Hell."

She's smart then. She shouldn't trust anything Hell-made.

Including me.

"They are probably the equivalent of the pomegranate seeds that got Persephone stuck with Hades in the myths," she adds.

"You know that stuff's not real?"

She shrugs. "And for a long time, I had no idea Sin Demons or Archangels or Leviathans existed, but here we are."

A loud bang at the window sounds and she jumps in fright. Growling under my breath, I turn and wonder who what the fuck it is.

All manner of creatures roam these woods, but surprisingly, the person standing outside my window is my brother, Nix. A different kind of psycho.

I roll my eyes. "Go home," I yell at him, unsure if he can even hear me. "No one wants you here."

He's nodding and pointing at the only secret entry that I have that I was stupid enough to show him on a drunken night. It was meant to be used as an escape route if anyone decided to ambush me in my own home, cloaked by magic, but now he thinks he can use it to pop over whenever he wants.

He marches in that direction.

"Shit, he's coming in here?" Aria murmurs.

My shoulders tense. "Looks like it."

Maybe it won't be all bad. Nix is known to be one nosey SOB, and usually knows all the gossip in Hell. He might know where Lorcan has been stashing things lately.

Aria nervously licks her lips as she stands behind one of the tall black chairs.

Nix struts into the room, his long dark hair fluttering over his shoulders, those sharp eyes finding Aria instantly. He's dressed in a black double-breasted jacket with glinting red buttons that run from his throat to his waist.

His tongue flicks over the small smudge of blood at the corner of his mouth and he smiles wickedly. Looks like he's just come in from a grand feast. Maybe with Father.

Nix never misses the opportunity to stick his nose in my business—or anyone's business for that matter. Father's no different.

"Oh, Brother. Why do you never tell me when you're having fun so I can join?" He purrs for effect and drifts to the opposite side of the table from

Aria. "Hello again, beautiful, mysterious human. Or do we have a better name now for what you are?"

"Hey to you too, demon," she responds cheekily.

"What do you want, Nix?" I growl, my patience thinning by the second.

He swings in my direction and rubs his fingers along his baby-smooth jawline. "You've been gone for so long, is all. I've missed you."

I snort. "Liar. Why are you sneaking around my home?"

He grabs one of the chairs from the table and flops down before crossing one leg, placing his ankle across his thigh. "You're the one who's been gone all this time. Playing house with Cain and his..." He glances at Aria and reevaluates his next word. "*Plaything.* And now you're suddenly back. Call me curious."

"You're a drama queen."

"Yes, I am. I'll admit that. But how else is one supposed to occupy his time? Torturing, hunting, and fucking can only satisfy me so much." He clicks his tongue. "Besides, what I really want to know is what is *she* doing back here? A human with a soul returning to Hell? Is the place really growing on you, sweetheart?"

Aria rolls her eyes.

"We have a job to do," I say, and hope that'll be enough to quench his thirst for information. Of course, it doesn't.

He leans forward, hands on the table, eager for me to go on. "A job, you say? For Cain?"

"For us all. Will you just drop it?"

"Does that include me as well?" he asks, genuinely interested now. "Have you discovered something helpful in Lucifer's diary?"

Ah, shit. I had forgotten I'd agreed to tell him what was in the thing after we'd translated it as payment for getting me out of Cain's demon trap.

"Yes and no," I say vaguely. "The diary was useless. Only contained the scribbled descriptions of creatures he suspected Aria to be."

His eyes narrow. "So then, what's the helpful part that you found out?"

"We found out how to take down Lucifer," Aria says bluntly.

I curse. That's definitely not something we want circulating down here. Especially while we're looking for the relics.

Nix's eyes glow a brighter shade of green. "Oh?"

"Aria," I warn. "Shut your mouth."

"Come on now, Brother. That's no way to speak to a lady. Go on, Aria. Tell me."

Her gaze flicks between us, debating. Then, she lifts her chin. "We're supposed to be getting your brothers all on our side anyway. How can we do that if we don't tell them what we know?"

I pause, taken off guard. That's a damn good point, but still. It's safer the fewer people know—while we're searching for the relics, at least.

"Our job is to get the relics back. That's it. When Cain, Dorian, and Elias get down here, they can handle that part." And the mess that I'm sure will follow.

"Relics?" Nix's head perks up. "They're gone?"

"They were stolen," Aria explains.

Nix rakes his fingers through his hair, his normally confident expression faltering. "He did it, didn't he? Lorcan."

"You knew?" My eyes widen.

"He's been talking about it for a bit now, going up there and taking them so that Cain can't return. He's delusional, thinking he'll be next for the throne, but if Cain returns, that screws up the plan for him."

"Why didn't you say anything to me?" I press.

"I didn't because I didn't think he'd actually go through with it. Honestly," he says, "you know Lorcan. He talks a lot of shit but rarely does anything about it."

"Yeah, well, he did something. I chased him out of the house, but that fucker is fast," I reply.

Nix gets to his feet and meanders in front of the dark fireplace. A click of his fingers, and it ignites, roaring to life, flames licking the black stone in the hearth.

"Whatever it is you're planning, I want in," he says.

Call me a pessimist, but I don't trust him. "Fuck no," I snap.

"Maverick!" Aria gasps.

"We can't mess this up," I tell her. "It's our only chance at it."

His expression pinches as he takes a step closer. "That hurts, Brother. You know as well as me that Hell is breaking us down, bit by bit, until we'll be nothing but one of Father's fucked-up marble soldiers. I can't live an eternity like that. Cain couldn't, and neither can you or me. If you and

Cain are cooking up a way out of Father's clutches, I want to help."

For a moment, I almost feel pity for him, until I remember who I'm dealing with. He was one of the ones on board with Cain, Elias, and Dorian's coup attempt the first time, but then bailed when things got nasty. How am I supposed to know if he'll do that again?

But, to be fair, I hadn't been much help to them back then either.

Things are different now.

"I want in on the action. Let me help," Nix repeats, with a pathetically sad smile.

A familiar ache deepens in my chest, brought on by the desperate look in his face. I've been in his position, so I'm familiar with the overburdening terror of being stuck with Lucifer, knowing he has your balls in a vice and there isn't a thing you can do to change the fact.

"Fine, but the first step is getting the relics back from Lorcan. That's objective numero uno," I finally answer.

His eyes light up. "I can definitely help with that. I hate the fuckwit, so tell me what you have planned."

I glance over to Aria, who's watching us intently.

"We need to know where Lorcan's lover boy is," I tell him.

He steps back. "You're going after *him*?"

"He'll know where Lorcan's stashed the relics. It's the only way we find out without drawing attention to what we're doing."

"Okay, I think I can manage that. He's a slippery one but very predictable."

"So you know where he is?"

"I know where he could be. But, of course, that information will come at a price."

Annoyance prickles up my neck. "Your payment is having your freedom from Lucifer," I grind out.

He gives me a deadpan look. "That will take time, if we can manage it at all. If we don't, I need to be thinking about a plan B for myself, another way out. That'll require a lot of power. And a lot of souls."

My souls? "You're joking."

"Another option is to let me have a taste of the human girl."

Fury comes over me and instinct kicks in. I

throw my fist out, slamming it right into his face. Damn, that felt good.

Nix stumbles backward, blood dripping from his nose. He wipes it with the back of his hand, blood streaking his cheek.

"Fuck you, Maverick," he barks. "If I knew we were going to fight, I would have worn my battle clothes. This is my good suit." He scrunches up his face in disgust as he looks down at his jacket splattered with blood.

"If you keep wasting my time, then you can go fuck right off."

He heaves his next breath, his eyes squinting, and a harried look crosses his face. "Fine then. I'll settle for your demon contracts. All your pending souls. It's a fair exchange."

"What? No!" He wants me to hand over all the contracts I've made with humans, the ones whose souls now belong to me?

No way.

Nix watches me, tapping his toe on my stone floor, hands across his chest, and the temptation to hit him again grows within me.

"That's my final offer," he says. "Plus, I just saw Lorcan this morning. He told me where Lucifer's expected to be, so you'll need me to avoid him too."

When I lock eyes with Aria, she half shrugs. Of course, she doesn't understand how valuable souls are down here. Their lifeforce sustains us, gives us strength, so they're used as currency too.

I worked hard for mine, and to just give them up...

"Do you really need all those souls now?" Aria asks me.

"Yeah, do you, Maverick? With your new life on Earth, having them is a bit pointless," Nix tacks on.

As much as I hate to admit it, they're right. If I'm starting my life anew, do I really need all those souls?

"Fine, you have a deal," I answer reluctantly.

"Perfect!" Nix claps, then looks at me with a smug grin, revealing hundreds of tiny sharp teeth —part of his true demon form that people rarely get to see. It reminds me of who I'm working with here.

I really hope I don't regret this. I swallow the lump in my throat. "Get us to Lorcan's lover. Help us avoid Lucifer and any of our brothers, and then Aria and I will do the rest."

Nix doesn't respond right away, but his eyes drift upward as if pondering my plan. He gives a sudden clap. "I know exactly where we can find that information, and you'll need my help. But first, we need something more appropriate for Aria to wear so she blends in and doesn't draw attention. We need her demon-fied!"

Aria releases a small gasp, drawing our attention, and the fear on her face is plain as day.

6

DORIAN

*E*lias and I step out of my Ferrari to find Cain exactly where I knew he'd be—standing outside the empty lot where our club Purgatory once sat. Since Stephan and the Night-walker vamps set it aflame, nothing was salvageable. The little that was left standing had to be bulldozed but, of course, Cain refuses to give up on it. In typical Cain fashion, he's determined to resurrect the club from the grave and make it bigger and better than before.

We don't *need* the money it makes; we have plenty to continue our cushy lifestyle until the end of time. We don't *need* to use it for our reputation; it speaks for itself. So, why bother?

Cain won't say so, but I know him well enough

to know the real reason. Something was taken from him, so he's going to come back ten-fold. Sometimes the best revenge is success, even if that means rising from the ashes after a defeat. Literally, in this case.

So, since Aria went off with Maverick back to Hell, Cain's been keeping himself busy by overseeing the plans of Purgatory's rebuild.

He's standing cross-armed on the sidewalk, watching the construction crane lift a steel beam into the air, while the crewmen bark orders at each other as they work.

I glance over at the space next to Purgatory, where an old office building has been reduced to rubble, and pieces of it are finally starting to be moved by a backhoe.

Before I can say anything, Elias asks the question as we come to Cain's side. "What happened to the neighbors?"

Cain doesn't even look at us, only tilts his chin up. "I paid them well."

"We're expanding," I conclude. Again, not surprised.

He nods.

As the crane swings the beam to the top of the building's frame to start a second story, I realize that not only is he expanding Purgatory out, he's going up with it, too. "And two floors?"

Another subtle nod, and then he changes the subject. "Have you found anything out from Jamal?"

Jamal is the leader of one of our search teams located in Mexico where Gabriel placed the final relic to Azrael's harp. Cain tasked us with contacting him and making sure he found it.

Unfortunately, we had also come here to deliver bad news.

Elias glances at me with raised brows. It is his signal for me to break the news. I sigh. "So…we got ahold of him. He found that the coordinates Gabe gave us ended up being on top of the ruins of a temple. An Aztec temple. One that's long been excavated, turned tourist attraction…"

The muscles in Cain's jaw harden, but his expression remains smooth and unreadable.

"But—" Elias chimes in, "We found that it's a part of a traveling museum exhibit."

"Exhibit," Cain repeats stiffly. "Museum."

"Yeah. It's been on display at the British Museum for decades, but recently, it's been moved to New York City."

"Our plane is booked," I cut in. "We leave in an hour. You can stay if—"

"No, we'll all go," he says shortly.

"What about Purgatory?" Elias asks.

"It'll still be here when we get back," he explains. "And Gabriel wants us to retrieve the relics. No one else."

I clap Cain on the back. "Okay! Guys trip! Like the good ol' days!"

That gets a quirk of a smile across his lips. With my hand on his shoulder, I guide him back to my car, but Elias stays behind, looking less than pleased.

"What is it, big boy?" I call over to him.

Slowly, he makes his way over to us. "I'm not a fan of the city for obvious reasons."

I laugh at the absurdity of that. "But we're in a city. Right now."

He grumbles, "Glenside is small. New York City is a different animal entirely."

He's not wrong there.

"What museum are we going to?" Cain asks as he opens the car door and climbs into the back.

I take my place in the driver's seat, while Elias begrudgingly squeezes into shotgun. "The biggest one they got. The American Museum of National History."

As I turn the key in the ignition, my gaze flicks to Cain in the rearview mirror. He's peering out the window at the active construction. As if sensing my stare, he turns to meet my eyes in the reflection.

I know what he's thinking. Fixing Purgatory is just one checkmark on a very, very long and very dangerous to-do list.

"So, how are we doing this? Ambush? B&E after dark? The traditional distraction with some sticky fingers? Oh, or my favorite—murderous rampage?" Elias is practically salivating at the thought of how we're swiping the relic from this museum.

When neither of us answer, Elias glances between us in annoyance. "Is anyone going to tell me what the plan is? There is a plan, right?"

Cain shushes him sharply and takes the lead as we make our way through the throng of people and the many displays. The place is bustling with activity. Families, couples, older folks…and all on a weekday.

As we walk along, we pass a security guard who's dressed like a police officer, and is packing like one. Both a gun and a taser are strapped to his belt.

I tense. Not out of fear; more out of confusion and apprehension. Why does a security guard in a museum need a gun? I know we're in New York City, but damn. Is stealing artifacts such a common thing around here that they need to be locked and loaded? It doesn't help that we're here to do that very thing, *and* his gaze is locked on us as we cross the room.

Cain must've seen the same detail I did because he says in a harsh whisper, "Enough. We don't want to draw any unneeded attention to ourselves." His eyes flick the guard's way again, but at least it doesn't seem like he's following us as we enter the next room.

"I don't know if you noticed, Cain, but Elias is the size of a tree and I'm ungodly handsome. We stick out."

Elias snorts at the comment about me—of course. Jealous.

"At least tell me how we're planning on finding

the skull." Elias makes sure to lower his tone this time, but we're practically bumping into people with every step. No matter how quietly he whispers, someone's bound to hear if he continues. And he does. "Without Aria to track it down—"

Cain stops short, spins, and points to a sign directly above our heads that reads "Ancient Civilizations."

Glancing around, Elias realizes where we are. We're surrounded by exhibits about Egyptian pharaohs, golden and sculpted artifacts, and mummies of all shapes and sizes. Actual mummies, too. Not replicas.

The skull was found in Aztec ruins, so if Jamal was right and it was shipped here, this section of the museum is where it will be.

"Cain, did you forget?" I tease. "Elias can't read."

"Fuck off," Elias grumbles, his shoulders growing rigid with anger.

It's not my fault he makes it too easy to piss him off, and I enjoy poking the bear. Or hellhound, I should say.

Ignoring us, Cain takes the lead and weaves through the crowd to a section labeled "The Aztec People."

Elias looks extremely uncomfortable with so

many people around, and he tries to move quickly without bumping into anyone. There's a scale model of an Aztec temple, a few broken pieces of pottery, beaded necklaces, and…

A skull.

My pulse switches into overdrive as I spot it in a long glass case, surrounded by the other bits and pieces the archaeologists must've found during their dig. If you've seen any a skull—and boy have I —you've seen them all, and this one could be counted among the rest. The only difference I can see right out of the gate is in its size. This one is larger than the average human skull. But there is a good chance its owner wasn't exactly human, either.

Fascinating stuff for any other history buff, I'm sure, but we're here for one thing and one thing only.

As we stand in front of the relic, I notice the little plaque next to it labeled "Unknown Man - Date Unknown" and huff. Why even put the sign there if it offers no information at all?

But I digress.

"Okay," Elias begins impatiently. He's bouncing side to side, eyes locked on the last piece of

Azrael's harp right in front of us. "How are we doing this?"

I glance at Cain. Surely he has an idea. He always does.

His attention is pinned on the skull, too, and I know it's because he's itching to get to Hell. More specifically, to get to Aria. But he doesn't move or say anything as his brain works out a plan.

Peering down, I see Elias's fist clenching, and a thread of trepidation shoots down my spine. I know what he's thinking; I've seen that look on him before. He wants to take the quickest way to the relic, and that'd mean punching a hole through the display and stealing it, launching all the bells and whistles.

Although I appreciate the enthusiasm, it'd only make our job a lot harder. Especially the escape. This entire place could lock down. With one armed security guard, there is bound to be more, and that'd mean taking out whoever is in our way.

My follow-up thought is: why do I care?

A good question, considering I'm a demon and nothing should get between me and what I want. But Aria's voice is in my head, coaxing me to think about this another way. Avoid innocent deaths, and even though she's not here, my gorgeous girl is impossible to ignore.

I sigh and quickly scan the area for another way to solve this rapidly escalating problem. Smashing the glass and running is out of the question, so we have to be clever about this.

Lucky for us, clever is my specialty. Just like getting people to do what I want with a simple command.

Ah, yes, that's it!

Just then, a woman in pointed heels, a pencil skirt, and frilly blouse comes walking out of a nearby employees only door. There's a lanyard around her neck, one I'm sure would say something official about her working here.

Perfect. Just what I need.

I slide by Cain and Elias and make my way over to her.

"Dorian..." Elias starts to call, but Cain holds up a hand to stop him. He trusts me enough to know I can get this done.

Moving fast, I weave in between the many families, couples, and strollers, and manage to catch up to the woman I need. "Excuse me." I touch her arm, drawing her to a stop while using my power to push through our connection. "I need your help. There's something in that display case back there that needs to be taken out."

Her dimpled chin lifts as she looks at my hand on her arm and then meets my eyes. Her pupils shrink as my power slithers over her, taking control.

"I-I'm not sure what you mean," she stammers.

"Give me that skull in the display case," I command.

Her spine straightens automatically, the magic sinking its claws in and gaining full rule over her mind and body.

As she strides by me, I notice her lanyard says "Senior Museum Curator." So really, she's a pretty fucking important person. She pulls out a few keys from her pocket and finds the one she needs for the display.

Before she slides the key into the lock, her gaze finds Elias and Cain and apprehension passes over her face.

"Who…are you?" she asks.

Ah, shit. I forgot to add on the "Don't ask questions" part after my initial command. But luckily, a lie forms swiftly in my head.

"There was a mistake in the transfer of the exhibit. This piece needs to be returned to the

British Museum, and me and my coworkers are here to take it back across the pond." I push more power into my voice. "That is what you'll tell anyone who asks about what we're doing here or why the skull is missing."

Did that cover all my bases?

Wait.

"Oh, and walk us out of here through the back, won't you, lovely? My big friend here has a thing about large crowds." I slap Elias on the shoulder for good measure, but he jerks away.

"Y-Yes, of course."

I grin. Easy. Cake. And not a drop of blood spilled.

But then, when I look at Cain, he's pinching the bridge of his nose and shaking his head.

"What?" I whisper. "Took me a second, but I saved it."

"Barely," Elias snorts a laugh.

"Hey, you wanted a murderous rampage. This is easier. Cleaner."

"Yeah, and less fun."

"Dorian. Elias," Cain snaps our way as the woman opens the glass and carefully pulls the skull from its shelf. I hadn't even noticed before, but it was laying on a scarf or blanket of some kind.

Gingerly, the curator wraps it up, careful not to touch it, before passing it over to me.

"You must be careful," she warns us, her gaze deadly serious. "A lot of people think it's cursed."

Her words take me off guard and, not sure how to react, I laugh nervously. Cursed? She has no idea. As a part of Azrael's harp, cursed might not be the right word for it, but it does hold some extremely powerful and concentrated dark magic.

The curator's expression hardens. "This is not a ghost story, I assure you. Bad luck follows anyone who handles it. The worker who unpacked it from storage committed suicide the following day. We've had employees quit, go missing... Even the British Museum had similar problems..."

I peer down at the skull.

Yep. Sounded like relic magic to me. But suicides and missing people? That sounds a bit more intense than just some bad luck.

"We'll make sure to handle it with care," Cain assures her. I pass the skull to him, and he holds it close but with careful fingers. If it's anything like the foot or the heart, direct contact could unleash the magic it holds.

The crackle of a walkie-talkie radio sounds,

and I glance over my shoulder to see the security guard we'd pass earlier head straight our way.

"Shit."

Elias spots him next. "If we want to keep this clean, we have to go."

I whip back to the curator and touch her arm again. My magic surges. "Lead us out the back. And make it quick. We're going to be late for our scheduled flight back to England."

Blankness washes over her face and she nods. With my power of compulsion, she has no other choice but to obey. Taking the lanyard from her neck, she strolls to the employee door she'd come out of before, swipes the card, and holds it open for us to walk through. "This way, please."

We push our way inside and come face to face with a long stretch of hallway and many closed doors. Rooms for employees to take breaks or hold meetings, if I were to guess. Once we're cut off from the loud noises and many museum goers, we're drenched in a heavy silence. The curator's heels click against the titled floor as she crosses the hall and opens another locked door. This one has cold air rushing out of it and is clocked in darkness.

Like before, we follow her inside.

"Fuck." Elias gasps, looking around the massive warehouse-like storage room.

It's set up with shelves that rise close to two stories tall, all filled with priceless items on pallets, crates, and in bubble wrap. The smells of mold and dust saturate the air.

It's like Costco for history nerds in here.

Speaking of... I glance at Cain. He's looking up and down the shelves, lips parted in awe.

Well, what do you know? The demon may have just found his heaven.

"Hey, you may want to wipe the drool from your chin," I say, nudging him playfully with my elbow.

Unamused, he clamps his mouth shut.

"I know what you're getting for Christmas next year." I waggle my brows at him. "All access backstage passes to this place, compliments of my powers of persuasion."

When the sound of a metal door unlatching and opening echoes across the vast room, we all spin to see the curator at the end of the aisle, pushing the exit door open and waiting for us. At the same time, the security lock from the hallway clicks and footsteps approach the warehouse door.

"The guard," Elias barks, saying all our collective thoughts out loud.

"Let's go." Cain hurries away, and we follow at his heels.

As we rush past the curator again and step outside, I say with vigor, "Close the door and make an excuse to anyone who asks about the skull being gone. Tell them you don't know which way we went."

My power invades her senses, fogging over her own thoughts, and she hastily closes the door behind her. We walk down a set of cement steps into an alley that's full of more pallets and crates, these all empty, but we keep moving out of the empty back lot and towards more of the chaotic hustle and bustle of New York City.

As much as we hate the crowds, my power can only do so much; the woman can tell him what I instructed her to, but whether or not the guard believes it… That's a different story. The three of us know we're better off hiding among the masses, disappearing into the ebb and flow of people on the sidewalks enjoying the snow and left-over Christmas decorations adorning the streets.

"I *hate* running away," Elias grumbles. "Hellhounds weren't meant to run from a challenge. Especially a human. It's degrading."

He means his ego more than his hellhound.

"There's a time for everything, so keep up."

Spotting our car and driver looping around the corner, we head for it. Police sirens blare in the distance, and my chest tightens.

Looks like the nice curator lady wasn't convincing enough.

Even though this mission was rather easy, and we didn't have to dive into an active volcano, cross a frozen tundra, or fight off deadly Amazon village people, I don't want to be arrested either. Not how I want to spend my time.

We hop into the car and Cain gives the driver directions to go straight to the airport. No stops. We speed off.

Good thing too, because the streets light up blue and red behind us as police motorcycles and squad cars drive up and park in front of the museum.

"Cain," I begin, feeling a bit uneasy. He turns in the front passenger seat, the skull relic still wrapped in his lap. "Should we be... worried? They're sure to have cameras..."

"I'll handle it," is all he says, and those three

words ease my worries. We've been in a lot of shit over our century on Earth. Hell, we've been getting into a lot of shit since… forever. I don't know how Cain does it, but he manages to get us out of trouble every time. So, when he says he'll handle it, I know he will.

"Does anyone think this went a little *too* easy for us?" Elias asks, scratching at the stubble across his jaw. "No Black Castle of doom or Indiana Jones-like booby-traps."

At least I'm not the only one thinking it.

"Maybe we finally got some good luck on our side?" I shrug.

"Famous last words."

"Hey, I'm trying to be positive here. We've been through so much shit lately—"

"Lately? Try the last hundred years."

I'm about to argue but then realize he's right. "Yeah, so we deserve something to go right for once."

He rolls his eyes like a disgruntled teen. "At least we got the skull. Let's just hope Maverick and Aria are having luck finding the other relics."

Cain's muscles tense. He hates this helpless feeling a bit more than the rest of us.

I reach over his seat and touch his shoulder.

When his hard gaze flicks my way, it softens a tinge.

"She'll come back to us soon," I whisper, in an attempt to comfort him. And, if I'm being honest, myself as well.

Closing his eyes, he dips his chin in a nod and draws in a deep breath. "Yes. I know." Then, his jaw sets and when he opens them again, his eyes are black. "Or I'll take this entire world to Hell with me."

7

ARIA

"I feel ridiculous."

As I look down at myself, my stomach clenches. I'm wearing a jumpsuit with spaghetti straps and plunging V-neck. Completely transparent and all Nix's idea.

Good thing I wore a black bra and thong, but my entire backside is still on display. I'm pretty much in my birthday suit with all the see-through lace. Didn't know demon fashion could double as stripclub-chique.

"Got you some kick-ass boots that should fit," Nix announces, like he's doing me a favor. He drops the combat boots by my feet.

"Oh, thanks. They'll go great with the fuck-me-now outfit, drawing the attention of all the monstrous demons who want to kill me. Are you sure you know what you're doing?" I glance over to Maverick. "I think he's setting me up as bait."

Maverick stands up from the dining table and approaches me. He circles me, studying me like a predator.

"You'll be fine. Your tits are covered."

"Are you kidding me?" I grip my hips. "Look at me. I might as well be naked."

"Will you go naked?" Nix butts in. "I mean, I did propose it to Maverick but he said you wouldn't go for it."

"Fuck no is the right answer!" I snap.

"Then let's get a move on," Nix orders, already making his way across the room to the doorway he entered earlier. "Lorcan's lover is a fickle thing and doesn't like visitors in the afternoon."

"Wouldn't it make more sense that only you go?" I suggest. "You get the info and then let us know."

"Ha, I wish. He hates us sin demons, and last time I was alone in a room with him, he tried to skewer me with his chandelier."

"Wow, great. Who the heck is this demon?" I ask. "I never want to see him alone, ever."

Nix laughs wickedly. "He'll eat you on the spot if you do. We go as a team and stick together."

"Oh shit," I say, really not wanting to do this now.

"And what makes you think he'll talk?" Mavericks asks. "Seriously Nix, if you take us on one of your insane goose chases, *I'm* going to spear my claws through your heart."

"You're always so dramatic, Mav." He waves at the air between them as if he's swatting a fly. "Come on, let's go."

"Don't call me that," he snaps back.

Nix faces both of us. "Look, I have something he wants, and for it, he'll tell us anything. Now, move your fucking asses."

Maverick falls in line next to me and we head out as I lean in closer and ask, "Do we want to know what he's offering Lorcan's lover?"

"Nope. Not at all."

With Cain's ring still on my finger, and me in the company of two sin demons, no creature comes near us. If anything, I look like a hooker accompanying two men, and we're heading back to their place for a devious time. And while I initially thought my outfit might grab attention, I had it wrong. No one is even looking at me.

We're sticking to the suburban streets, which aren't too different from some of the run-down cities on Earth. Tall buildings, derelict houses, trash everywhere, steam gushing out from the cracks in the road. That's if you ignore the lofty black castles in the distance and the charred mountains surrounding us.

A man in a pinstripe suit strolls toward us, dragging a huge tail behind him. When he passes, I glance back to see the back of his pants are cut to allow the monstrous scaly tail to drag behind him. I'm not even going to ask.

But he doesn't bat an eye at us. So, flimsy, transparent fashion is the norm in Hell, apparently. The only good thing about it is that it keeps me cool, seeing as it's stinking hot in this place.

"We've been walking for ages," I groan. "Don't you have a carriage pulled by demonic horses we could use or something? You are sin demons for Hell's sake. I mean, why do you have roads when I haven't seen one car yet?"

They both cut a sharp glance at me, eyes narrowing, and for the first time I start to see a familiarity in their faces. Then they're howling with laughter.

"You've been watching too many movies,

sweetheart," Maverick murmurs. "And the roads are only for Lucifer to use when he's in the mood."

"It's not far," Nix adds, still chuckling to himself. "Carriage. That's fucking classic."

"Whatever," I groan.

After what feels like an eternity later, we finally turn down a side alley that reeks of death. I cover my mouth and nose with my hand and hurry after the brothers, stepping over puddles of more goo. It's disgusting.

Finally, Nix pauses in front of a narrow, two-story building where the front lawn had been burned to a crisp. A dead tree stands out front with animal skeletons hanging from the branches.

A thought strikes me. "Wait, can't Nix just shapeshift into Lorcan and talk to his lover? Get the info we need that way?"

"Ah, yes, that would be easier wouldn't it," Nix replies, sounding somewhat impressed I thought of it. "But unfortunately, I've tried to fool him before—you know, for a bit of fun—but they've been together so long, he's able to see right through the guise."

"Just means we're going to have to do this the hard way," Maverick adds in.

Hard way? Not sure I like the sound of that.

Nix knocks on the black door, and my stomach hardens in anticipation.

Maverick's glued to my side.

The door opens slowly, the hinges squeaking.

At the entrance stands a man, taller than me, and on the thinner side. Every inch of him is dark maroon, including his horns, which are curled back around his ears. Gold upside-down crosses dangle from his earlobes, and his expression is scrunched up in confusion at Nix.

"Sweet Lucifer, what do you want?" He glares over to Maverick and me, then scans the rest of the street. "Two sin demons in one visit. What are the neighbors going to say?" He snorts, and I can't tell if that's a laugh or an angry gesture. There's smoke coming out of his nostrils. "Is Lorcan with you?"

"It's just us," Nix answers. "I have something you want, and in exchange, I need a favor."

"Like I told you last time you thought we could be friends." He rolls his eyes, his upper lip curling over fangs. "Go fuck up shit elsewhere. I'm not interested."

He goes to shut the door, but Nix kicks his foot out, blocking it.

"Irnonoch, are you really going to say no to

this?" Nix stuffs his hand into his pocket, and I shift to get a better look at what he's offering.

Nix takes out an old-fashioned bronze key in his hand, waving it.

Irnoni…Inoch—fuck it, I'm calling the red demon Irno—gasps, his mouth hanging open.

"Is that what I think it is? Because if you're fucking with me, Nix, this time I will carve your heart out and eat it in front of you."

"Ouch," Maverick mumbles under his breath.

"What's so special about the key?" I whisper back, only to have him shush me.

"We got a deal then?" Nix counters, his chest puffed out.

"Come in. Don't touch anything and leave your germs all over it," he sneers, more smoke floating out from his flaring nostrils, and swings open the door.

If Lorcan's lover is this aggressive and terrify-ing, what the heck is Lorcan like?

Nix steps inside and waves for us to follow. With Maverick's hand on my lower back, I head in next. "Thanks," I say as I pass Irno, but he only leans in and sniffs me.

"You're a strange looking thing, and so pale, but you have a decent ass," he mutters to me.

I glance back and smile. "This is all natural." I grip my hips. "Men love ass." And I cringe hard on the inside, regretting instantly opening my mouth. I sound like a demon whore.

Shut up, Aria.

Irno huffs, snorting in the process. "Whatever, let's just do this quickly." He brushes right past me, nudging me into the wall in the process.

Maverick is quick to snatch me into his arms and steady me. His breath streams across my neck, his chin propped on my shoulder. "Best you don't engage. Lorcan may be the Sin Demon of Envy, but Irnonoch is jealousy incarnate."

Straightening myself, I walk down the long corridor. It's dark in here and we seem to walk for a long time, until we finally swing left into a dimly lit room.

We pass black stone walls and ceiling. There's a glossy chandelier with large fanged teeth hanging from it where there should be crystals, and a long wooden bench with spikes on the seat. Piece of furniture or medieval torture device? Take your pick.

"Take a seat," the demon sneers my way, then glances over at the spiky seat.

Is he joking?

"I'm fine. I love standing." I square my shoulders and attempt to look as comfortable as possible in a room that has my skin crawling.

"Suit yourself. Only being hospitable so you can rest your big ass."

Big ass? Bastard. I stiffen while Maverick sidles closer to me. "Don't let him get into your head. Plus, you have the most stunning ass."

I can't even deal with that right now.

The demon turns on Nix. "Okay, what do you want in exchange for it?" He juts out a red hand, palm up, long claws curling at the tips of his fingers. He's eyeing the key in Nix's grasp.

"I need to know Lorcan's hiding location. Where he hides his most precious possessions."

Irno barks a laugh, then lashes out and seizes Nix by the neck. He slams him up against the wall, and I flinch into Maverick.

"Are you mocking me? You come into my house thinking I will betray my lover?" He's squeezing Nix's neck so hard that I'm certain I just heard bones crack.

"He can't respond if you're choking him," I suggest.

Nix hisses at his attacker, his hand punching the demon in the face. It's enough to make him release him. That's when I notice scales materializing over Irno's skin.

Eww, he's a reptilian demon?

Maverick watches the two demons crouch low, appearing amused. "Are they going to fight?" I whisper to him

"Maybe. It's just an ordinary gesture when you visit someone to show your strength."

I tense up. "This is normal behavior?"

He grins at me. "You don't have such social etiquettes on Earth?"

"Yeah, bringing your host a bottle of wine perhaps, not choking and punching them in the face."

He looks confused. "That's strange."

I would almost laugh if I wasn't watching two demons in a power struggle. And, just as quickly as it started, the demons both stand, agreeing to a stalemate.

Nix straightens his jacket and lifts his gaze, still gripping the key like everything is normal. "I'm offering you your own castle, Irnonoch. No more living like a peasant with all the other wannabes in this part of the city." He lifts the key once more, and the fiery torches on the wall glint off the metal. "This is the key to the Castle of Souls, the most haunted building in Hell."

Irno has his arms folded across his chest, his lower lip between his teeth. He's blinking a lot too.

"And, did I mention, it's the second tallest building in Hell, with a direct view across the Field of Death, to Lorcan's castle? Do you really want him to keep lording over you that he owns a castle?"

Irno lowers his arms by his side, his chin rising, and huffs. "What is so important that you need from Lorcan?"

"He took something from me," Maverick states and steps forward, speaking strongly. "Nix is helping me retrieve it. We only want to retrieve what belongs to me."

Irno taps a talon on his chin. "So, you're saying I will own the Castle of Souls, all deeds given to me?"

"Exactly," Nix answers.

"And just so we make it clear, there will be no taking it back."

"Absolutely not." Nix grins widely. With a snap of his fingers, a puff of smoke erupts from his hand, along with a scroll. He hands it to Irno. "Sign this with blood, and it's yours."

Thick tension fills the air, but when Irno snatches the scroll greedily, I can't help but smile.

Instead, I wait, just like Maverick and Nix, in complete silence, as Irno unravels the scroll and reads it. From what I can see over his shoulder, the writing is tiny and there's a lot of it.

After what feels like eternity later, Irno cuts the tip of his index finger and uses the black blood to sign the contract.

"Done!" he snarls and thrusts out the rolled-up scroll at Nix. "Now, hand me the key!"

"Once you tell us Lorcan's hiding spot." Nix stands tall, shoulders squared, and I get the impression that if he really wanted to, he'd smite this demon in seconds. But he doesn't, which means he must hold some care for his brother Lorcan.

"Fine, but you didn't hear this from me." Irno lowers his voice.

"Absolutely not," Nix replies, green eyes shining with excitement.

Irno's lips pinch tight and he hisses the words. "In Lucifer's whorehouse. Behind the skull mirror. I hate it when he goes there."

"I know where that is," Maverick answers, and I cut him a narrow gaze, which he doesn't notice.

Who else goes to this whorehouse? Did Cain visit it when he lived here?

I'm still trying make sense of what he just said, when Maverick asks, "Why the fuck would he hide anything in there?"

"Because Lucifer still visits the place. Lorcan tells me it's the most guarded place, and as a sin demon, he has free access to go in anytime."

I want to call bullshit on behalf of Irno, because if Lorcan is hiding things in the whorehouse, it sounds like the perfect excuse to go there without him. Poor Irno, but that's none of my business.

MAVERICK

The walk to the whorehouse takes longer than I anticipated.

With Aria by my side, we stroll through the open gates to Father's spectacular fuck-mansion.

Nix lingers with the guards behind us, laughing and distracting them, while I keep my head low and get Aria onto the grounds. She flinches at any sound, and her eyes are huge, swinging left and right across the manicured land surrounding us.

Statues pepper the lawn in all manner of debauchery.

One statue is of a woman who is lifted off the ground by two men, while a third kneels and has his head buried between her thighs, devouring her. Another is of a man bent over, and a woman taking him from behind, while a huge horned demon claims her in the ass.

I used to love coming here to study the pieces of art, until I learned these were actual humans and demons who had managed to piss off Lucifer. So, his punishment was to place them in an eternal frozen state on the brink of ultimate pleasure… but never gaining the release they crave. Now that is fucking Hell.

"Are you okay?" I look down to Aria, who's studying a demonic goat with a hard-on chasing a girl who's running away, her clothes mid-way falling off her, her face in a panicked scream.

"I'm scared to ask what kind of whorehouse this is," she says.

"Anything goes here. Father built it to fulfill his every desire."

"And for sin demons too?" She arches a thin eyebrow at me, her voice croaky, like she doesn't want to hear the truth but still asks the question.

"Yes, you are correct. I won't lie, all my brothers and I have frequented the mansion many times, but we have also been around for a long time. Personally, I haven't visited the place in years."

When she doesn't respond, and there is unspoken tension between us, I focus on what I can control. Our mission. "You'll be my escort once we enter—just follow our lead so we can get out fast."

"Trust me, I want to get in and out of here as fast as possible too." She licks her lips nervously and turns her attention back to the dark building with lofty, arched windows, stone walls, and a pointy roof. *Three stories of depravity,* Irnonoch once called the mansion. And he wasn't wrong. The things I've seen within those walls would make even a demon blush.

Nix catches up to us, strolling alongside me. "Fuck me, but it's been a while. Last time I came here, Father had brought in those sirens from the pits of Hell. I remember they were so fucking horny, that we—"

I jab him in the ribs, which makes him groan, then he looks over to Aria who's watching with huge eyes, listening intently.

"Umm, yeah, I gave them a good fuck. The end." He smacks his lips, making a popping sound.

"Why'd you give one of your castles away to Irnonoch to help us?" I ask him, out of curiosity and to change the topic.

Nix shrugs and stuffs his hands into the pockets of his dress pants. "I can't do a good deed to help my brother?"

I laugh and roll my eyes. "Don't mock me, Nix. Everything you do is to benefit you."

Nix doesn't respond right away as we make our way toward the mansion down the long, winding path. Aria fiddles with Cain's ring, twisting it around her finger.

"I want in," Nix finally answers. "And for you and Cain to see I'm serious about this. So, if I have to give away all my castles, I'll do it."

"Yet you were quick to take my souls," I remind him.

"That's different, Brother. I needed to make sure you were serious about working with me."

"Do demons ever just help people out of the goodness of their hearts, instead of making everything a deal?" Aria asks.

"Think you just answered your own question

there, luv," Nix says. "Goodness and heart don't go with demons."

"Don't agree with you there," she rebuts, and I know she's referring to Cain. My brother has changed a lot since he was kicked out of Hell. He's settled down, more in control of his rage, and he's found love with a human girl. When I look at Aria, I can't blame him. She's fucking gorgeous and brings something out in me that makes me want to be a better demon.

But then I can only picture him buried deep inside her, forcing me to watch. I have no issues with watching...but only if I can also join. Not to have them just prove a fucking point.

We head up the front steps, and as we reach the doorway I swing my arm around Aria's waist. Nix stands on her other side. I wrap my knuckles on the door.

It opens in moments, and we're greeted by Chyd, the mansion butler. He's an old human with no soul after he ended up down here for killing half a dozen women.

"Masters." He bows his head at me. "It has been a long time since you have enjoyed our establishment."

"Yes," I respond and walk inside, taking Aria with me. Chyd steps aside, eyeing her carefully.

"Is the lady a new guest?" he promptly asks.

"She's mine," I growl and grab her ass, to which she flinches against me.

He reels back a few steps, bowing his head. "Of course."

Nix falls behind us and takes Chyd aside, which I can only assume means he's going to buy his silence about us being here.

Aria makes a small gasping sound as she lifts her head and takes in the grandeur of the entrance hall—the marble, the golden chandeliers, the paintings on the wall of males and females naked, posing in sensual positions. The sweeping staircase curling up to the next floor, railings made of pure gold, the windows tinted with a faint blue, casting everything with its hue.

"It's not what I expected," she murmurs.

"For Hell?" I answer and guide her quickly up the stairs along the red rug.

"Just for the house being what it is." She's busy studying a painting of a woman with heavy tits bound in rope, and when she glances my way, there's a light blush to her lips.

Fuck me, but that's a beautiful color on her.

Footsteps strike the floor behind us, and I glance back to find Nix marching to catch up with us.

He gives me a wink, which I take as him having dealt with Chyd.

In silence, we hurry down a dimly lit hallway, then take the next set of steps to the third floor, where we finally come to a stop in front of ornate black doors that reach the ceiling.

"What's in there?" Aria whispers.

"Lucifer's fuck room," Nix answers. "Are you excited to see it?"

She scrunches up her nose. "Not in this lifetime."

Nix snorts a laugh, and I push open the doors. Bright light from the window drenches the oversized four-poster bed that is completely black and made to fit at least twenty people. It swallows most of the space in the room. The carpet is pitch black, as are the walls, the only color coming from the arched windows.

Aria rushes ahead of us, turning on the spot, her mouth hanging open almost in awe. "My toe is tingling. They're in here."

"Toe?" Nix asks.

"Don't ask," I snap in response. I wouldn't even know how to explain it if I tried.

Nix strides across the room and throws himself on the bed, and I can only imagine how much fucking has taken place there. Knowing it is all with Father, I avoid touching anything.

Aria screams, and I literally jump in my boots, then twist to find her staring into the skull mirror. I let out a long breath.

The thing is, the actual mirror is a simple long piece the length of her body, with a black decorative frame. Except, it's not the design that gives it that name. But its reflection.

"What the fuck!" she cries out, running her hand over her face, her head and body shown as a skeletal form dressed in her lacy number. Hollow eyes stare back at her, her bony jawline moves as she opens her mouth then closes it.

She glances over at me. "What the hell is this thing?"

"It's an illusion," I say, stepping closer, except I fucking hate the thing. It freaks me out to look at myself in skeleton form.

"It's one of Father's fetishes," Nix pipes in. "He likes to watch himself *boning* someone while looking like that." He waits, clearing hoping we'd get his joke and laugh. But when I only snort, he climbs off the bed to stand next to Aria, both of them now looking ghastly.

"This is just some freaky shit," Aria replies, striking different poses regardless.

I step behind the mirror, figuring the relics have got to be back here somewhere. Lorcan would have hidden them somewhere out of sight. But there's nothing obvious, so I peer around the tiny space. Except, all I can see are the flat back of the oval mirror and its clawed feet. The relics are too large to conceal anywhere behind it.

"Fucking shit," I snarl. "If Irnonoch lied to us, I am going to murder him."

Aria and Nix pop their heads around the mirror and look at me. "They've gotta be here," she suggests. "My toe is going crazy right in this spot."

"Well, unless they're invisible, I don't see where anywhere they could be hidden."

She steps around with me, as does Nix, and that's not helping us one bit. We can barely move now, caged by the mirror and wall behind us.

"It has to be here," she insists, her brow furrowing, scanning the floor and the mirror. On either side of us, there's nothing. "I feel them. They should be here."

"You keep saying that," I insist.

Nix shrugs and steps out from behind the mirror, while I suck in a deep breath. I can't fail at this. I made a promise to Cain, to Aria. Though, after his asshole act, part of me would love to make him suffer somehow. But that means harming Aria…and while I'm still pissed, I have other ideas of how I'd prefer to bring her pain.

The door opens abruptly, and I jut my head up, shoving Aria behind me because I expect it to be Father. She hits the wall or something in the process, because a creak sounds. But my gaze is locked on Chyd rushing into the room, his breath racing, and panic scribbled across his face.

"Lucifer has arrived at the manor," he gasps with terror. "You must leave his room immediately."

"Fuck!" Nix races across the room to Chyd.

My lungs freeze, and I whip around, reaching for Aria. "We leave now!"

Except my hand swings through the air because Aria isn't standing, she's crouching down and her hand is half buried in an open compartment in the wall.

"Is it there?" I whisper and kneel down as she draws out a black box with a metal lock on the front. She holds it easily in two hands and looks at me with a smile.

"This is it. I can hear its song now. This box is holding back their power." She shuts the secret compartment and scrambles to her feet.

I get to my feet. "Good, now we need to get the fuck out of here."

Nix is by the doorway, waving for us to follow.

Aria tucks the box under her arm, and we run, my pulse thundering in my veins. Her smile has faded, and now a dark fear crawls over her face.

At the doorway, I peek my head out, and see it's clear. "We can't go the way we came, so we head out the back way."

"Agreed," Nix whispers, and Aria tenses against me.

We rush outside, shutting the door behind us, then I swing left, in the opposite direction of the staircase.

Aria stays close, not making a sound, while Nix lingers behind us as a kind of protection. He knows as well as I that if Father finds Aria, we'll both be punished for sneaking a human into his whorehouse. Not to mention what he'll do to her.

Voices rise from behind us. Aria stumbles on

the rug as she tries to look back. I catch her while she clings onto the box of relics.

Shadows appear at the top of the steps.

We're exposed, and the end of the hall for our exit is too far away.

Nix looks at me with horror, and panic slams into me. I glance around and spot a door several feet from us. I flick my hand at him and we all scramble inside like the devil is on our heels.

I shut the door hastily, my breaths ragged, and I place my ear to the door to listen for sounds.

Aria suddenly gasps, drawing my attention to the room, and I sigh because of course I had to pick this room of all places.

Three bodies hang from the ceiling by their ankles. They're not dead…nothing truly dies in Hell unless Lucifer makes it so.

Nope, this is the storage room for his play toys when he's in the mood for fucking something close to death. Truly, Father is a vile creature.

I collect Aria by the waist and twist her toward me, my chest clenching. "Don't look, sweetheart. I hate that you even have to see this filth," I whisper.

She clutches onto that box and nods, while Nix is beneath a woman, staring at her face. They're all out of it, placed under a sleeping spell until Father has use of them.

When I place my ear back against the door, the loud thumping of footfalls sounds near...too fucking near, like they're coming this way. As though they've walked right past the bedroom.

Shit. Shit.

I swing around, my gaze whipping across the room, and I settle on our only option. A chute door in the wall.

"They're coming this way," I growl, to which Aria's face whitens.

"Fuck," Nix mouths, but I've snatched Aria's arm and we're speeding across the long room to the back corner. I pull open the silver chute door.

"Are you fucking kidding me?" Nix hisses, standing in front of the window. "We go this way."

"And then what? Have him watch me fly away with Aria in my arms and you crash to the lawn down below?" I whisper. Nix isn't like me and Cain. We were the only brothers to get the perk of wings.

To hell with that. I don't even wait. I just collect Aria into my arms.

"Are you sure about this?" She's trembling in

my arms as I push her feet-first into the chute. "I don't want to die here."

"Oh, Aria, I would throw myself onto a blade before I let anything touch you. Trust me." As angry as I still am, this is about saving all our lives.

She looks at me for a short pause, like she's still determining if she can trust me, but then she nods. And I push her into the shoot that dips diagonally from the room. Her small squeal has my heart squeezing.

Footfalls stop at the door. My stomach hits the floor, and Nix literally flies right past me and into the chute, head first. I throw myself in there too, grabbing the latch and shutting it just as I hear the door swinging open.

Putrid air rushes past me as I slide down in pitch darkness. Next thing I know, I'm freefalling and, out of instinct, my wings snap out, beating them just once to glide down to my feet.

The basement around us is dimly lit, and we're alone.

Nix groans, clutching his shoulder. "I think it's best if we split up for a bit," he says. "So Father doesn't think we're up to something." He dusts off his clothes.

My gaze swings to Aria, who's kneeling in front of the box that's snapped open from her fall.

"Shit," she grumbles, quickly placing the relics back into the box and shutting it. I cross the space between us in two long strides.

"What is it now?"

She glances up at me, blinking like she's lost. "There are only three pieces in here. Where the hell are the others?"

"That fucking *sonofabitch*!"

8

CAIN

The second we walk through the mansion's door, I head straight for my office with the wrapped skull still tucked under my arm. Dorian and Elias follow close behind.

"We can't hide it in your bedroom again," Dorian says as we enter the library. "Lorcan knows that hiding spot."

He's only stating things I already know. "I'm aware."

My bedroom and the basement are the safest places in the house, and since both places were breached, I'd rather keep it close to me for protection. And since I'm either here or at Purgatory, and the club is temporarily out of commission, this is where I will be spending most of my time while waiting for Aria to return. This is where I'll store the skull.

After striding inside, I place the skull on my desk, pull back my chair, and kneel before it. Dorian comes in and leans over to watch while Elias stands in the doorway, arms crossed. I wrench open the drawer and feel around the inside for the secret latch at the back. Moving around the other items in there blindly—a stapler, pens, some ink pads and stamps—I find the small groove in the wood and push it. There's a small pop and a panel opens underneath the desk.

"Woah, that's impressive. Is that where you hide your diary?" Dorian asks, and I glare his way. "What? Your father has one."

I ignore him and reach into the compartment. There are a few important papers in there, such as the deeds for our properties, some spells I've acquired over the years from some powerful spell-casters, etc., but luckily, there's still enough room for the skull.

The sound of soft, heavy paws signals the entrance of Cass, the tiny lynx kitten turned massive domestic house cat, thanks to Aria's attachment to the creature and an unknown magical potion. Like any feline, Cass is curious and, at times, a menace.

On cue, he jumps onto my desk, the wood creaking under his enormous weight. To our horror, he swats at the skull, sending it flying off the edge.

"No!"

Dorian tries to grab it, but he's a millisecond too slow.

Panic surges as I watch the last piece of Azrael's harp plummet to the ground. If it shatters, that means the end of our chances of getting back to Hell.

Suddenly, Elias is there and snatches the relic right before it meets the floor.

I release my held breath and rise from under the desk.

"Fuck, that was close," Dorian snarls.

Narrowing my eyes at Cass, he responds by growling at me. I growl back even louder, and the lynx hops down and leisurely strolls out of the office, bushy tail swiping side to side.

"Good catch, man. Those fast animal reflexes really came in—" Dorian stops abruptly. When I look over at him, I realize why.

Elias is standing there with the skull sitting on

his bare, open palm. The scarf covering it must've fallen off during the drop, and he is frozen in place, eyes wide and mouth slightly agape.

"Oh no." Dorian and I move closer. "Elias…"

When he doesn't respond, Dorian looks at me, fear clear on his face. "The magic has him. He's been rendered catatonic. How do we get him back? What do we do?"

During his rushed questions, a flare of power zaps across our bond, taking us off guard.

"D-Did you feel that?" he asks and rubs his arms.

Goosebumps rise on my arms, horror rising as the realization crashes down on me. "It's like it was with the foot relic. Because of the bond, it's going to affect us all."

"Shit, Cain! What do we—"

Another surge shoots through the magic tie, but this time Dorian stiffens in place, the same blank and lost expression as Elias.

Fuck. I've lost him too.

That only leaves me.

I have to get that skull out of Elias's hands.

Moving as fast as I can, I grab the scarf and hurry around the desk. I reach for the relic just as another wave of magic hits me, striking me like a hammer to the head, and everything goes black.

I blink. At least, I believe I do. I can feel the brush of my eyelashes against my cheeks every time I do it. But I can't see anything. Even with my demon's advanced eyesight, I can't seem to penetrate the darkness.

Where am I?

My entire body tingles with static electricity, almost to numbness, and even though I command my limbs to move, I can't tell if they're actually doing as they're told.

Elias? Dorian? I call into the abyss, but like my sight, the words are swallowed up by the void. I hear them echoing in my head, but they never touch my ears.

I remember the moments before I arrived here. Cassiel knocking the final relic off the desk, Elias catching it, and the magic radiating across our bond and freezing first him, and then Dorian.

It must've gotten me too.

That's what this must be. I've been captured by the skull's dark magic.

My feet touch solid ground, and instantly the numbness dissipates. The darkness lifts, and I find myself surrounded by stone walls, wet with condensation. The air reeks of mildew, sulfur, decay, and fear, and I recognize the place instantly.

I was a frequent visitor of Lucifer's torture rooms in the lower levels of his castle. Ever since my conception, he'd bring me down here to brag about his handy work and preach about it being my responsibility to oversee the torture of captured souls. And I was damn good at my job, too. Unquestionably so.

The screams of the damned penetrate the walls, begging for a death that can never really come. I take in the heavy feelings of despair, desperation, and pain saturating the air. There was a time when I got nothing but sick satisfaction out of being here, but things are different now. *I'm* different, even if part of me gets excited over the idea of reliving this part of my life again.

But the other part of me knows better. I am under the skull's dark charms. This isn't real—it can't be. I'm still banned from Hell. So then…what is the relic trying to show me? Is it like the foot? A possible flash into the future or the past?

A moan comes from the shadowy center of the

room, and I hesitate. I didn't know someone was in here with me.

"Hello...?" I step closer slowly, allowing my vision to adjust to the darker spots. There's a metal table there, similar to an autopsy table, and even under the matted dark hair and dry blood painted across pale skin, I can tell it's a female. She's naked and seems to be unconscious, which isn't an uncommon occurrence for the torture rooms, but what takes me by surprise is the glimmer of gold around the woman's neck.

My heart hammers, trepidation prickling up my spine.

No. No. It can't be.

Terror seizes me, my breaths speeding up.

It can't be her. It can't.

With shaky hands, I reach out and gently brush the hair away.

The single wing pendant...

Aria.

My mind blanks. Her face is bruised and swollen, almost unrecognizably so. But I know it's her; I can feel it in my very soul. My Aria. My love.

"No... Aria... Wake up. Please." She doesn't stir. Not even when I brush my knuckle across her cheek, avoiding the nasty gash marking it. Her lip is split too, and she's so thin and pale… Like she's been down for days. Weeks.

"Aria, p-please." My voice trembles. "It's me, Cain. I'm here. If you can hear me, please open your eyes. Move. Something."

She looks dead, and just the thought has me panicking. Souls can't die down here, but then why can't I feel her through our bond? There's nothing there. Just emptiness.

I have so many questions; they bombard me, torture me. How did she get down here? Did Lucifer capture her? Where's Maverick? Did he betray us?

Then comes the anger. It rips out of me, snapping my demon to the forefront. So much fury and grief whirl within me, all I can think about is finding whoever did this and unleashing hell on them. My wings whip out, filling up the entire room.

"Put those puny things away. You'll poke an eye out."

Every muscle in my body tightens at the familiar smug voice.

Father.

Folding in my wings, I whirl on him and cross the room in two great strides, my rage fueling me.

He doesn't even flinch, which only angers me more.

"You did this!" I roar.

His black brows knit together. He stares at me and then huffs a laugh. "What is this? Some kind of joke?"

My insides tremble, and I'm doing all I can not to punch a hole through his chest or let the thought of Aria being gone sink in and cause me to collapse onto the ground.

"My son, I'm only here to admire your work. As you asked."

My...work?

He walks around me to the table, where Aria's unmoving body lays still. My chest clenches. "Don't touch her!"

Rubbing his chin, he circles her, his hungry gaze roaming over her body. My stomach tightens as more anger tumbles through me.

"She is quite the specimen, isn't she? I'm a bit envious you got to play with her," he says as he continues to walk about the table and look her over like a hungry predator. I have no idea what he's talking about, but seeing Aria practically unconscious in front of me tears apart my soul.

"Although, I'm surprised you chose to have her

unconscious and not begging you to stop. I know how much you like to hear them beg."

My fists clench as heat rushes over my skin. Unable to contain it any longer, my hellfire ignites.

"Shut your fucking mouth," I snap.

"I don't understand why you're getting so upset," he says calmly. "You're doing good work down here. Why can't you take the compliment?"

Good work?

"You think I did this?"

"Who else? None of your other brothers have the precision, patience, and skill of torture like you do, Cain. Why do you think I picked you? You get it from me."

"I'm nothing like you."

Again, his gaze sweeps over Aria. "Oh, but you are. Just. Like. Me."

Terror claws up my throat. I know what he's implying. He's saying I did this to her. I hurt her, tortured her close to death.

Impossible.

I would never.

Would I?

I step back, chest heaving.

Extinguishing my hellfire, I lift my hands to see that they're covered in blood. Her blood.

No…I…I wouldn't. Not Aria.

Not her.

My knees give out and I collapse.

No!

DORIAN

Hands slide across my torso. One, two, four… They run along my shoulders, down my arms, across my waist. Teasing. Stroking. Making every hair on my body stand on end.

Power sizzles across my flesh. My power. And it's growing rapidly by the second.

As the sexual intensity around me heightens, I'm charged, like a battery struck by a lightning bolt. As an incubus, this is what we live for.

It's been a long time since I've felt such power, bathed in it, relished in it. When I finally open my eyes, I am temporarily blinded by the kaleidoscope of colors dazzling me—part of my power manifesting as it gains strength. There is so much red, the coloring for the highest level of lust a person can feel, that I'm drowning in it, dizzy from the euphoria it leaves me with. I can hardly think straight.

I try to grip onto any solid thought that I can find. Like… Where am I?

It's a good start, but when one of the hands dips past my waist to stroke my cock, I push my head back into the pillows and lose myself to the delicious sensations crashing into me. There's heat—someone's breath, I realize—whispering across my cock's tip. A warm tongue circles around one of my balls and then draws it into their mouth, sucking gently, and I'm struck dumb on the spot.

I can't make sense of it still, but while part of me is drunk on both the magic and the sex, another part wants me to refuse it. To rip myself away and see this as wrong. But the demon in me growls with a vicious need to fuck and feed, so I let these strangers do whatever they please, leaving me to become more lost in the fog.

Weight presses into me as someone straddles my waist. Lips press onto mine for a scorching kiss that sends bolts of desire straight to my cock. Nails rake through my hair and pleasure-filled moans fill my ears.

Unable to resist, I find the person's hips and help slide them down where I want to feel them most. They begin to rub themselves against my raging hard erection. Teeth nip my shoulder, and the deadly combination of pain and pleasure is almost too much to bear.

A voice in the back of my head keeps telling me to stop. This is wrong. But, fuck, it feels so good.

Over all the panting, grunting, and moaning, I barely make out the creak of a door opening.

Another person to join the party?

"Dorian?"

That voice. The pain in my name.

Oh shit. Aria!

Realization spears through me, and as if cold water had been thrown on me, I'm thrown out of my sex-crazed stupor. When I sit up, I find that I'm in bed—my bed—with four women. Naked women.

Oh no.

Everything stops.

"Aria... It's not what you—" But I stop myself, because it is *exactly* what it looks like, isn't it? But I don't know how I got into this situation. I don't know how this even happened.

As I spiral down from cloud nine, I crash and burn, my body sluggish, my limbs feeling like a ton of dead weight. I can't even move in the bed to get out of it, and boy do I try. I want to run to her, hold her, and plead for forgiveness, but my body doesn't respond.

The look of immense pain and betrayal on Aria's face murders me.

I did that.

She trusted me, and I hurt her beyond repair.

I destroyed her after I swore to her I would never. That she was the only one my heart and body needed.

"Aria… Please. I'm sorry…" I don't know what else to say. Nothing is good enough.

Tears glisten in her eyes, angry ones, and her body grows taut. "I shouldn't have expected anything less from a sex demon." She spits the last word like it's poison on her tongue, then she spins and storms out of the room.

Stomach plummeting, I use all my strength to haul myself out of bed, but it's no use. I'm paralyzed until my power balances out again.

All I can do is watch her walk away and disappear down the hallway, and I know, deep down, I've lost her forever.

Hands glide up my chest again, pushing me back into the pillows.

"Get off me," I shout, as the women begin to

kiss my stomach, neck, and legs. "No! Stop!" But I'm helpless, unable to move or fight.

"Leave me alone!"

My power flares again, building and building the more they caress me, their fingers exploring every inch, and their kisses becoming more demanding on my flesh. Different shades of red dye-out my vision, and it's not long before I'm lost to the intoxicating feeling of the moment.

It's like a drug, and I'm an addict.

After all, like Aria said, I'm a sex demon. An incubus. I'm a slave to my baser urges. Nothing more. That makes me a glutton for sex and the power it gives me. I can't control myself, and that means I can't commit myself to only one person; I can't truly love someone.

My eyes sting with tears, and the stabbing in my chest is immeasurable.

I love her. I know I do.

I love her.

And now she's gone.

Forever.

ELIAS

When I hit something solid underneath me, I land on all fours and start running. The frigid wind whistles past my ears, combs through my fur, and stings my nose, and when my eyes finally catch up with the rest of my senses, the blur of the forest rushes by me.

I don't know how I got here. The last thing I remember is being in Cain's office, looking for a place to store the last of Azrael's relics, but somehow, I've made it to the woods.

Strange… Things aren't adding up.

But, before I can think harder on it, I burst into a clearing and spot the last person I expected to see standing in the same place I'd found her the first time. Serena.

Like last time, I skid to a halt, changing midstride into my human form. She has some balls, showing up here again after what she did with the hellhounds breaking into our house. Her cocky smile never wavers though. Has she come here to gloat?

Anger whips through me. I don't think I have an ounce of love left for her. All that love has turned to pure hatred, and I have no problem keeping good on my promise and strangling her where she stands. Our bond be damned. I'll do it.

As I trudge over to her, her face changes before my eyes. Dark eyes, equally dark hair, an innocent face, but a look that says she's hardly an angel.

Aria.

My Aria.

I shake my head, confusion making me stumble. How could I have thought she was Serena?

Am I losing my mind?

"Elias," she says, and the voice belongs to Aria. A smile brightens her entire face. "You've been out here for days. Are you going to come back inside?"

My heart beats a little faster, like it always does when I'm around her. "Do you miss me?" I tease.

She chuckles. "I was just wondering if I'm going to have to build you a doghouse outside or something."

What a little shit.

I hurry over, wrap my arms around her, and lift her off the ground.

"Hey!" she shrieks, laughing.

She weighs practically nothing, so I spin her around for good measure.

"Elias! Stop! I'm getting dizzy!" But she giggles and throws her arms and head back, giving in. I keep spinning us, around and around.

"Elias! Let me down."

This time, the voice speaking doesn't sound like Aria.

Confused, I slow down.

"Fuck! Enough, Elias! It isn't funny."

No, definitely not Aria.

I stop abruptly and let go. Serena stumbles back, angrily readjusting her jacket and brushing down her hair.

"You never know when to stop," she snaps.

"Serena?" I stare at her, dumbfounded. I was just holding Aria; I know I was.

"What's with you?" She glares at me. "It's not funny."

What the fuck is happening?

I scan the clearing and sniff the air. I don't know *what* I'm looking for, but I can't help but feel like someone is trying to play some kind of fucked-up trick on me.

When I don't see or smell anyone lurking in the shadows, I turn back to Serena. "What are you doing here?"

"Just wanted to see how much you're fucking up your life." She smirks, and my hellhound bristles.

"Fuck you," I growl. "I told you I'd kill you the moment you stepped foot in my territory again."

"So, then why haven't you?" She holds out her arms, challenging me. "Here I am. Still very much alive."

My hellhound shoves against my restraint, wanting out, and at this point I may just let him. Why haven't I ripped her apart?

I can't answer that.

Not wanting to even deal with her and her nonsense, I spin on my heel and march away. If this is another one of her tricks to distract me, it's better to ignore her. I'll send Cain to finish her off later if she's still trespassing. He'll be more than happy to do what I can't.

"Oh? Is that it?" she shouts to my turned back. "You're just going to leave? Walk away like the pussy you are?"

A mighty roar rips from my throat and I whirl around again, fury blazing, only to almost bump into Aria standing there, right in front of me.

"Shit!"

"Sorry..." she mumbles bashfully. "I thought it was impossible to sneak up on you with you hellhound senses."

I look across the clearing where Serena had just been, only to find it empty. When I glance back down at Aria, her brows are pinched in worry. Her gaze searches my face, and her hand comes up and touches my cheek.

"Elias, are you okay? You're scaring me a bit."

Terrified she'll switch on me again, I pull her into my arms and bury my face into her neck. I inhale deeply, taking in her unique smell, the one my animal recognizes and loves. The one that I know is mine.

She hugs me back just as hard, and I relish the way her body presses into mine.

An excruciating sharpness jabs into the center of my chest, paralyzing me and making me backpedal. Looking down, I see a dagger handle, its blade embedded into my chest.

Rapidly, I lose feeling in my arms and legs, and my knees buckle under my weight. I crumple, my mind a fog from the pain. She pierced my heart.

Rolling into the fetal position in the snow, warm blood covers me, but I'm cold. Too cold. And suddenly I'm so tired, I can barely keep my eyes open. My vision blurs, but I can see someone standing over me. A dark figure among the white winter background.

"Ser-Serena?" I croak out. It has to be her. She must've been using some kind of spell to change her identity.

But as she crouches closer to me and her form comes more into focus, it's Aria's beautiful face smiling down at me. Not Serena.

I can't believe it.

"You're an idiot," she spits with venom. "You actually believed I cared about you?"

I can't believe what I'm hearing. The words sound like Serena's, but the voice and person saying them is Aria.

"Cain and Dorian were right. They said you're the weakest of them. That you'd be easy to kill. I just didn't think it'd be *that* easy. Pathetic really."

Cain? Dorian?

But they are my brothers. They wouldn't plot against me.

The pain is overwhelming. Every inhale feels like there's glass in my lungs. But I don't know what's more debilitating—being stabbed in the heart or Aria's deadly confession.

Keeping my eyes open takes much more effort than it should, but I refuse to die easily. "I don't know who you are, but you aren't my little rabbit. She loves me, and I love her."

Throwing her head back, she barks a laugh. "Will you die for her then?" She kicks me hard in the side, making me grunt.

"Yes, and I'd kill for her," I begin, my voice cracking from the pain. "I'd destroy worlds for her. Raise Hell for her. But you aren't her."

As the words flow from my lips, the pain in my chest ebbs and breathing becomes less of a chore. I'm not sure how, but I keep going. "I don't know who you are, but you aren't Aria."

Her eyes widen, and when I follow her gaze, I realize the dagger is gone from my chest. Even the wound is healed over.

I touch it just to make sure.

Yep, nothing. The blood's gone, too.

It has to be a hallucination or some other kind of magic.

I knew it.

I start to get up, the weakness slowly draining from my limbs. Racking my brain, I try to think back to what I was doing before running and winding up here.

On my feet, I search the clearing for anything amiss, or for something to trigger a memory. When my gaze lands on Aria again, she backs up with a look of panicked horror on her face. I wobble on my feet but square my shoulders as I walk toward her.

"Who are you?" I demand.

"I-I don't know what you mean."

"You're not Aria," I say, and the words make me stronger. "This isn't real. Where am I? Where're Cain and Dorian?"

At the mention of their names, I get a flash of an image of Dorian, Cain, and I in Cain's office. Then Cass knocking over the skull and…

Wait a fucking minute. The skull.

That's what this is. The relic's magic.

"It's the relic!" I shout at the sky, and as if triggering something, the scenery around me spins, taking the impostor Aria with it.

M y eyes fly open.

Breathing quickly, I take in the room—the desk, the office's Victorian style decor, filled bookshelves, giant paintings of mythical battles…

Yep. This is definitely Cain's office.

To my left is Dorian, and in front of me is Cain, both suspended in time and locked mid-pose. Cain's holding the scarf, and by his frantic look, he had been hit with the skull's magic just before reaching me.

I snatch the scarf from him, wrap the relic up, and put it on the desk. The moment it's out of my hands, both Dorian and Cain snap out of their trance. They gasp for air as if they'd been holding their breath for hours.

"Holy shit. What happened?" Dorian half-chokes.

Cain's gaze jumps all over the room, unsure if the magic's truly been broken. When he spots the skull, his tight muscles ease.

"The relic… We got trapped in its darkness," he says and swallows uneasily. "I… I was in Hell. In Lucifer's torture rooms. I had… hurt Aria."

Oh shit.

"Aria had stabbed me in the heart," I explain. "At first she was Serena, but then she changed to Aria, and told me she never cared about me."

"Stabbing you and saying that shit to you? That has Serena all over it," Dorian replies and runs a shaky hand through his hair.

"And you?" Cain asks him wearily. "What did the relic make you see?"

Dorian hesitates, his gaze dropping to the floor.

"Let's hear it," I tell him.

He sighs heavily. "Just me… in an orgy."

I blink. "Excuse me?"

He holds up a hand so he can finish. "And then Aria walked in. The look on her face… I had ripped her heart out."

I don't know. It seems like Dorian got the best one of us three, but the heavy regret and distress on his face says otherwise.

He glances at Cain. "That may have been me at one time in my life, but after we found her, I…"

"I know what you mean," Cain finishes for him.

"The look on her face, Cain… It damn near killed me." Pain strains his voice. "Not being able to control myself like that, hurting her like that, it's one of my biggest fears."

"Mine as well," Cain says. "In mine, my father was praising me for being like him and torturing her close to death."

"Sounds like the relic gave us all nightmares," I suggest.

Staring at the skull, Cain shakes his head. "Not nightmares. It showed us our greatest fears."

Dorian's eyes widen. "Fuck, I think you're right."

Making the same mistake I had with Serena and being literally and figuratively stabbed in the heart classifies as my greatest fear.

Yep. Checks out.

"Now we understand why those museum employees thought it was cursed and went loco bananas," Dorian says.

Cain nods, then picks up the skull, careful to touch only the scarf, and places it in the secret compartment under his desk.

"One thing I don't quite understand though," Dorian begins when Cain remerges, "how did we manage to break free of it?"

"I think I was the one who did it somehow," I admit. "I was able to see through the magic's ruse, and once I realized it wasn't real, I was able to snap out of it."

"It's lucky you did, otherwise who knows how long we would've been stuck in our own fears," Cain says.

Dorian squeezes me on the shoulders and shakes me. "Go Elias! I'm so proud."

I shrug his hold away, and he bursts into a fit of laughter.

Just then, Cass strolls back into the office, and jumps on the computer chair. Like always, he's got an air of smugness to him whenever Aria's not around, almost like he's proud of knocking over the skull and sending us into a fear spiral.

The fucking furball.

To my surprise, Dorian glares at him. He's always been on the sweeter side to Cass than me or Cain, but right now, he looks like he wants to throttle him.

"Guys, let's all take a moment to realize that we—three of the most powerful and handsome demons Hell's ever created—were almost killed because of a fucking cat."

Cass responds by lifting up his leg and licking the underside of his fur. Not a care in the world.

9

ARIA

hy did we think getting the relics back would be that easy?

I never met the demon, but Lorcan's a sin demon—he's smart enough to know someone may come looking for the relics, and if he can't stash them in seven different places all over the world like Gabriel did, then he's going to do what he can to make it difficult.

That means hiding them separately as much as he can.

Maverick is fuming and cursing out his older brother so fast, it sounds like he's speaking in tongues. Rightfully so. But we need to worry about getting out of this basement, especially now that Lucifer's mucking about upstairs.

"We need to get out of here," I say, searching the darkness for a way out. I spot a small, barred window two feet above us, a strip of Hell's red sky beyond it. If we manage to take out the bars somehow, we can shimmy our way through. "There. Do you think either of you take out the bars?"

"Easy." Maverick steps up and uses his wings to lift himself off the ground. With one hard yank, the entire grate comes off, and he tosses it to the side.

"Age before beauty," Nix says and throws me a wink over his shoulder.

Maverick rolls his eyes. "Just scout the yard and let us know if it's clear."

"Right." He leaps up, grabs onto the window, and pulls himself out with ease. Then, he scrambles to his feet and disappears.

Maverick and I exchange looks.

A tense moment passes by.

"You don't think he'd leave us, do you?" I ask.

"We're demons, so yes, I do."

When there's still no sign of Nix, I curse.

"Should've known better than to trust him," Maverick groans.

"And you should know that I like to keep you on your toes, Brother." Nix's face appears in the window. "The yard is clear now. But I'm sure we don't have much time. Let's go."

Maverick's hands are suddenly on my waist, and I'm rising toward the window, where Nix's waiting hands are. When I'm close enough, he seizes me and yanks, while Maverick shoves me from behind, palms full of my ass.

I can't help but think he'll be teasing me about this later. When we're not in serious trouble.

Relic box in hand, I flop onto the grass at Nix's perfectly polished shoes but quickly hop to my feet and wait for Maverick to follow. He folds his wings back into his back and hauls himself through.

He stands and shakes the ash and god knows what else out of his silvery blond hair. With a hasty look around, he snatches me by the hand and starts to tug me down the path at a brisk pace. Nix stays close behind, glancing over his shoulder every now and then to check if we're being followed. Luckily, we aren't.

Once we're far enough away, Lucifer's whorehouse nothing more than a blip in the distance, Maverick whirls on me. "So, we only got three," he says, running a hand down his face as he thinks. "Only three…"

Is there an echo here?

"Yes. Only three," I repeat.

"Which three? Did you see?" Nix asks eagerly.

"The eye, hair, and heart—because they've been connected," I reply.

"Connected?" Maverick asks and starts to lead us back toward Hell City.

"Um, yeah. The hair and eye accidentally connected before I was kidnapped by a werewolf biker gang. And I guess the heart locked on during our tumble down the chute."

Nix clears his throat. "Excuse me. Did you say werewolf biker gang?"

"They called themselves the Full Mooners."

"You're kidding," Maverick says, close to laughter.

"Can't make this shit up if I tried."

Nix's brows shoot up in surprise. "I guess Earth is more exciting than I thought."

I want to say that when it comes to my life, it's a three-ring circus, but I refrain. Our mission was a success for the most part. We may not have gotten all the relics back, but we have three. Hopefully there is only one more stop for the others and we can high-tail it back home to the living plane.

All the sulfur and close encounters are making my stomach hurt.

After some time, we reach Maverick's castle, if you would call it that. As we approach the massive building, Nix stops and starts to walk back the way we came.

"This is where we part, my dears. It'll be too suspicious if we're together for too long," he says, saluting us. "I'll ask around and see what I can find about the other relics. I'll come back when I can."

I give him a short wave, and Maverick guides me around the back of the house to his secret entrance. He opens the door for us to step inside, and I ask, "Does he do that all the time? Just pop in and out like that?"

"Yes, he does it to everyone. It's kind of his thing." As we walk along the corridor, he unbuttons the cuffs of his shirt and begins to roll up the sleeves to his elbows. I try not to stare at the way his muscles flex or how the simple clothing change makes him look even more sexy than he already does.

My mouth's suddenly dry. "He seems to have taken a special kind of liking to you though."

He side-eyes me and his lips quirk up at the corner. "He's probably the closest brother I have."

"But you don't trust him?"

"Nope."

How weird.

"You can't trust anyone here," he goes on. "Sometimes, not even yourself."

What the heck does that mean? Probably best if I don't ask.

Instead, I say, "Do you think he's going to snitch on us being here and hunting for relics?"

We begin to climb a grand staircase to an upper floor. "There's a good possibility. But do I think he'll tell? No. Not right away at least. Not when I've promised him all my soul contracts in exchange for his help."

Even he doesn't sound certain, and that makes me nervous.

"So, what do we do now?" I ask and hold up the box. He takes it from me and goes over to a large grandfather clock in the hallway. Like everything else is this damn place it's black but with what look like tree roots weaving through the other pieces of wood and brass. When he presents it with the relics box, the roots slither away from the face, as if they are alive, and reveal a hollow opening inside. He slides the box inside and the roots crawl back into place, perfectly concealing it from view.

"Woah," I gasp.

That gets a chuckle out of him. "Lorcan's not the only one good at hiding things. This entire place is full of secrets."

After seeing what the fireplace in my old room could do, I believe that a hundred percent.

"*Now*," he says with emphasis to circle back to my original question, "we're going to get some rest. Tomorrow, we will go and hunt down the other relics."

"Rest? You mean sleep?" I glance around to find a window, but there barely are any in this place. "How do you know when it's night here?"

"Night doesn't exist in Hell," he replies smartly. "It's one smoky, burning red sky forever and ever. But our bodies know when it's time to shut down, and mine is saying I need to feed and regroup if I want to be strong enough for what's ahead."

"Hopefully nothing crazy," I whisper, my heart beating a little fast.

"Aria, this is Hell. Or did you forget?" He turns and strides down the hall again, forcing me to run to catch up. We walk along in silence for some time, and when he stops in front of a door without warning, I almost bump into his back.

"You can stay in here," he says and opens the door for me.

Stepping inside, I'm shocked to find it's not the same one he'd imprisoned me in last time. This one is full of paintings, some displayed on the walls and some on easels half-finished. They range in size, color, and subject, but all of them are extremely detailed. Even more surprising is that this room has huge glass doors leading out to a balcony and, with the curtains drawn back, light floods inside.

There's a modest size bed, a couch, a few book-shelves, and paint-splattered canvases haphazardly stacked on the floor.

I'm in complete awe. It actually looks some-what...normal.

For a medieval doom castle, that is.

Maverick hovers in the doorway, unrolling and rerolling his sleeve, but now almost as if he's fidgeting. "I'll try to find some...edible food for you to eat. Although I can't promise anything. It's been a while since I've been home, and as I'm sure you know, demons rarely eat regular food."

I wave his offer away, my gaze still dancing over all the paintings decorating the walls. Most of the hanging space is gone; every inch is covered with a framed masterpiece.

They're all renditions of earthly things, too. A swan in a lake surrounded by a lush meadow, two horses running across a grassy plain, spindly trees covered in snow with the full moon shining through the clouds…

Then a thought hits me. "Wait…did you paint all these?"

"Hm?"

I turn to face him fully. "All of these. Did you paint them?"

His gaze drops like he's wondering if he should tell me the truth or not. But then he nods. "I did."

I don't know what to say.

"As you know, demons have eternity to waste, so I've taken up a few hobbies to keep me sane." He's trying to brush it off like it's no big deal, but I'm still having a hard time believing it. These paintings aren't just 'meh, okay.' They're actually good. Really good. Like…should be hanging up in some exhibit or museum, good.

"Hunting, killing, fighting…" he goes on, rattling off his list.

"And the arts apparently."

He shrugs. "When I would go to Earth to

see you or do Lucifer's bidding, I'd see some interesting things. And I wanted to remember them."

I stare at him, wondering who the hell he really is.

"I'll wake you in a few hours," he says, taking the door handle. "Sleep well."

When the door shuts and the lock clicks, silence overtakes the room. I take another full look around, still marveling at the secret talent Maverick possesses. It makes me wonder if Cain knows about it, or Nix. It definitely doesn't seem like he wants to boast about it, even though he should. The attention to detail and coloring are amazing. Lifelike.

That's when my gaze comes across something interesting in one of the paintings. It's of a woman standing in a fog, part of her face obscured by it, her dark hair wet and stuck to her face. The half of her that you can see is dripping wet, and even though only one eye is visible, her gaze pierces you.

I get closer, familiarity striking me.

Is that supposed to be…me?

And the haziness surrounding me… Is that meant to be the hot springs Maverick had taken me too? Where we'd kissed back when I'd thought he was an angel.

Holy shit! It is!

Another painting, not too far off, is of a woman laying on a large four-poster bed and colored as if the viewer is peeking in through a stained-glass window.

Like my bedroom's window at the mansion.

I glance to one of the unfinished canvases on an easel and see myself there too, half-painted. A dark womanly figure against a white, snowy background.

"When I would go to Earth to see you or do Lucifer's bidding, I'd see some interesting things. And I wanted to remember them," he'd said.

Interesting things, like me?

I should be weirded out that he was stalking me for so long, watching me from the shadows, but my stomach tightens for a different reason. Flattery? I'm not sure. But the fact that it doesn't freak me out only confirms how fucked up I am.

It's so hard to peg Maverick down. He's a wild-card, and I never know what he's going to do.

Shaking my head, I cross the room and climb into the bed. The mattress is surprisingly soft, and once my head hits the pillow, the exhaustion really sinks its claws into me. Even with the constant wails of Hell creatures outside the castle, it doesn't take long to drift off to sleep.

***

*T*he booming knock echoes through the stone walls, amplifying the sound. I leap up in bed, my heart hammering.

We've been found out! Lucifer knows!

My mind is going a mile a minute, nausea and panic rolling in the pit of my stomach.

The bedroom door shoots open and Maverick stands on the other side, eyes wide with terror. I'm off the bed and rushing over to him in a flash.

"Someone's here," he says in a harsh whisper.

"Who is it? Nix?"

He shakes his head. "Nix never knocks. This is someone else."

My heart is hammering against my ribs. "What do we do? What if it's Lucifer?"

He pauses. Obviously all of these thoughts have been going through his head as well. "Stay here. Do not leave this room. Whatever happens to me," he commands.

"Whatever happens to you? What the fuck are

you talking about, Maverick?" Does he think the person behind that door means to hurt him?

His voice booms. "I'm not kidding, Aria. Fucking stay here. If things get bad, get yourself out. Go to the gate."

I can barely process what he's implying before he spins and hurries down the hall and jumps down the staircase. Seconds later, the echoing creak of the big front doors opening breaks the eerie silence.

My entire body tenses, bracing for the worse.

"What the fuck are you doing here?" Maverick sounds angry, not scared, but I'm not sure if that's better or worse.

"Hello to you, too."

It's a woman's voice. One I don't recognize.

"I said fuck off," Maverick growls.

Whoever it is, he doesn't want them around.

"Cool it, Mav. I can't just stop in for a visit?"

"No."

"Come on, I just want to chat."

"When was the last time I saw you, Serena? Over a century ago? And now you just want to pop in for a *chat*?"

Wait, Serena? Elias's bitch of an ex, Serena?

Fury scorches through my veins, and my feet

are walking me toward the voices before my brain can register what's happening. But I need to see this bitch; I need to know who betrayed my demons and broke my hellhound's heart.

When I reach the landing, I lean over the railing to get a clear look of her through the sliver of open door. Blonde hair cut in a sharp bob, emerald-green eyes, and dressed head to toe in motorcycle chic.

She's gorgeous, of course, with a badass edge that I'll never have. Super skinny, long legs, and a model's height.

So, naturally, I hate her.

When Maverick tries to slam the door in her face, she grabs it and shoves it open a little more. "There's been a lot of talk throughout Hell that you were back. Chyd said you visited your father's whorehouse of all places," she begins, trying to grab his interest.

"Needed to release some frustration," he replies blandly.

"I had money on Cain killing you while you were up there." A smirk twists her ruby-painted lips.

The mention of Cain has Maverick's shoulders stiffening. "Yeah, well, he didn't."

"Lucky you," she says. "You know Lucifer's ticked you weren't able to bring back more information about the shadow girl. I'd expect a visit soon, if I were you."

Fear weaves up my spine. There goes our cover. Or Maverick's. But if Lucifer comes to see him, there's no doubt I'll be figured out, too.

He must be considering the same thing because he says, "Well, I better start preparing. Thanks for the warning."

Again, he tries to close the door and she shoves it to keep it open. "One more thing," she says, and my annoyance prickles across my skin. I can feel my temperature rising along with it. "Did you see Elias? How's he doing?"

Hearing his name on her lips sends my anger spiraling and Sayah darting to the surface. Silently telling her to wait in case I need her, I practically fly down the steps, Serena's gaze quickly finding me, and her cocky smile wavers. Maverick's expression is a mixture of fear and aggravation, but I ignore it.

"Oh, Mav, you didn't tell me you had a lady friend over," she purrs, and for some reason, the way she says the nickname even grates on my nerves.

"I visited the whorehouse. What do you think I did there? Check out some library books?"

His comment doesn't even touch me. Neither does the fact that she's looking down at me like I'm below her in every way, with her lip curled up in disgust. Like I am nothing more than one of Hell's sex slaves.

I'm breathing hard, my body shaking with rage, unable to think about anything else but the pain she put Elias through, how she ripped out his heart and stomped on it repeatedly.

"You totally could've gotten someone prettier, Mav," Serena says, out of the corner of her mouth. "This one looks like she was crossbred with a horse."

"Why don't you go lick Lucifer's balls some more? After all that time in the whorehouse, I'm sure they'll need a good cleaning." The words fly from my lips, my voice not even sounding like mine.

But there, I said it. And I'm not taking it back.

Serena leans forward, eyes narrowing. "Excuse me?"

"That's what you're good at, isn't it? Doing Lucifer's dirty work?"

She glances at Maverick, the shock clear on her

face. "Are you going to let this slug in fishnets talk to me like that?"

He cocks a brow. "But is she wrong?"

She scoffs and then points a long fingernail in my face. "Listen here, you little trollop—"

My fist shoots out and connects with the side of her face before she can finish her sentence. Something tells me Sayah put some strength behind it, because it sends Serena stumbling backwards, tripping down the front steps, and holding the side of her cheek, which is now bleeding and split open. I look down at my hand and see Cain's ring glistening with blood.

I smile.

Who knew this thing would come in handy in more than one way?

Serena looks up, cursing, but Maverick's fast to shut the door and lock it this time.

An apology hovers on my tongue, but Maverick holds a finger to his lips to silent me before moving to a peep hole in the door and looking through. When he confirms she's gone, he turns back to me.

"You know that was really fucking stupid, right?" he bites out. "You could've been found out."

"I know. I know," I reply, looking at my bloody

ring again. Even though I know all that, I still don't regret it. "But damn, did it feel good."

I expect him to bagger me more, but instead, his mouth twitches as if he's holding back a smile. "Serena deserves much worse, but socking her like you did is a good start."

Oh, well then, I'm glad he approves.

Unfortunately, his mild cheeriness doesn't last long. "Bad news is that her visit means we're in a lot of trouble. Now that word's out that I'm back in Hell, she's right that Lucifer is going to want to meet with me."

"So, what does that mean?" I ask as worry wiggles its way through me.

"It means time's gotten cut shorter. And we can't stay here. It's the first place he'll come."

That's not good.

"Any ideas?"

He pauses, thinking.

After a long moment, he says, "One…"

One is better than nothing, right? "Whatever it is, let's do it. I'm in."

10

MAVERICK

"This place is safe, you say?" Aria asks as she cautiously steps through the door. We walk into the palace's empty foyer, our steps echoing loudly in the silence.

"Yes. No one comes here. It's been abandoned and some think it's cursed, so it should be left alone. Lucifer won't check for me here." The sweltering heat is unbearable today. Father must be pissed—the demons working underground always torture twice the number of souls when he's in a foul mood to attempt to cheer him, and as a result, everyone suffers.

A hellish gnat swarms around me, a pesky thing with six fangs, and I swat it out of my face. Another side-effect of increased heat.

Aria glances over her shoulder at me, gaze narrow. "Like a witch's curse?"

"It's not hexed. But rumors spread like wildfire in Hell, and many of these fake tales are cast out intentionally." I shut the door behind me and lock it.

She studies me carefully. "So, you've made yourself a safe house where no one would find you? Clever."

"Don't sound so surprised," I respond. "I may be the big bad demon in the room, but I'm not a fucking monster. Now, keep going straight ahead, past the staircase," I growl.

Her eyes flare with defiance, but instead of snapping back, she turns away from me, and I follow her deep into the main room.

"I see you're still in your shitty mood," she mumbles.

I bite my tongue hard at the fact that we're here after her confrontation with Serena. The coppery tang of blood coats my tongue. With it comes a fire that scores my chest while my mind fills with images of Aria being fucked in front of me by my brother, and me being unable to join in. It's been in my mind endlessly and it's driving me nuts.

Cain can be such a bastard when he's jealous. I

nearly lost my mind watching them…

I stuff my hands into the pockets of my pants and trail close behind her, my gaze on her tight body, her curvy ass in her fishnet jumpsuit, and dark hair I'm craving to wrap around my fist as I fuck her. My cock twitches at the thought.

The thing about Cain's stunt is that it made me jealous as fuck, and the image is imprinted in my mind of her body, her curves, her moans, her scent. It's all stuck in my head, torturing me.

She pauses a few steps ahead and tilts her head up to take in the monstrous main room. The walls shine like polished black glass, and our distorted reflections stare back at us as we move. Even the flooring has the same translucent, ice-like effect, and every one of our steps echoes against the suffocating silence of the place. It speaks volumes to who my brother was when he lived here.

Broody. Arrogant. A recluse.

"Wow. I thought your other house was over the top. This is the epitome of a bachelor pad for a serial killer. Did this home once belong to Lucifer?"

"Father has never lived here," I say, which is true. She doesn't need to know who did. Not yet, anyway.

That'll be my little secret.

I turn to take in the vaulted ceilings, the space lacking any furniture. Everything in the room guides your sight to a set of elevated steps against the far wall, traveling to a black throne.

Two pillars flank it on either side, and a lofty wall embedded with skulls rises up from behind the seat. There's a window located over the throne, casting bright light from above giving the impression that whoever sits in the spot is somehow divine.

I roll my eyes. I've always hated this fucking eyesore.

Aria's staring at the seat, then looks at me, and back again. "This is so you." She waves her hand toward the throne as if anyone could ever miss it. "Very over-indulgent."

I bristle, squaring my shoulders. "What's that supposed to mean?"

"You're a sin demon, right? Figure it out." She turns from me abruptly and walks deeper into the room.

I exhale an exasperated breath. "I'm surprised you think so little of sin demons. Espccially since your loverboy, Cain, is one," I snap, strolling toward the doorway leading into the hall. "Guess now that you've let him fuck you, he's no longer a horrible demon like the rest of us."

"You asshole!" she bellows, her jawline clenched when I grin back at her. Oh yeah, that got her all riled up.

"Such language." I tsk and keep striding across the room, loving that I've roused her anger.

Her footsteps strike the hard floor, her breath quick. "You've been in such a pissy mood ever since we arrived in Hell. I'm sorry you didn't like what you saw with Cain and me. That's your problem, isn't it? But don't take your family issues out on me." She's shaking, but her expression is firm, and it seems she's not finished.

But I don't give her the chance. I grab her arm and haul her with me into the hall and up the grand staircase.

"What the hell? Let me go, Maverick," she warns.

"You think I'm an asshole, then fine, I'll be that asshole for you."

My jaw ticks as I grind my back teeth. I wrench her to a door that I kick open, and then shove her inside.

She rips free from my hand, stumbling. The

room is dark with barely anything visible except for the light pouring in behind me from the hall.

"What is this room? What the hell are you doing?" Panic streaks her face.

As anger flares over me, she glares my way.

"You want to know the truth? I am fucking livid at the stunt Cain pulled. He knows what you mean to me."

Her expression softens. "Yeah, and what's that?"

I huff and step inside, shutting the door behind us with my foot, encasing us in darkness. Good thing the dark is my friend.

"If you can't work it out for yourself, then there is no conversation to be had," I snarl, while an excitement rises in me at watching her stumble about blindly. Her arms are out in front of her, waving about, trying to find a wall or something.

"Seriously, Maverick. You're really starting to piss me off."

"Welcome to the club." I step toward her, and my hand falls to the blade I keep in my boot. There's something just so delectable about the scent of her fear, to see her frantically trying to find the door. Something in me wants to make her hurt.

I sneak up behind her and blow a breath into

her hair.

She snaps around and I slide out of her reach. "Fuck you. I don't like this game," she yells.

"Yeah, and I didn't like being the observer either."

She swings in my direction, following my voice, so I sweep to my left, but not before I nick her on the arm and across her cheek with my blade. I want so much more, but that's coming.

Her cry is music to my ears.

"What the fuck is wrong with you? Did you just cut me?"

"Does it feel good? Figured we could have our own party. How does that sound?"

"Like you're a lunatic."

"Then it's safe to say you like them crazy."

"You're such a prick today. Boohoo, you got blue balls and now you're being a baby. But if you want me to play along while you keep being an ass, then fine. Make it a fair playing field. I need light." Even in the dark, I see her gripping her knife.

With a smile, I silently move across the room to the window covered in a cloth. I rip it off, light stealing the dark, my eyes momentarily blinded… just as something zips past my head. A sharp bite of metal grazes my ear. I hear the dull thump of it striking something behind me, and I twist around to see a knife embedded in the wall.

Savage.

"I adore how volatile you are." But I'll admit, underestimating her might be my undoing. I touch my ear and my fingers come back with blood.

She lifts her chin confidently and grins. "You're not the only one with surprises." Just as she grins my way, I hurl my blade for that pretty little face.

She ducks, a gasp on her lips, but then swings around just as fast and lunges for the weapon I threw at her.

I snatch the one near the window while she scrambles up on the bed and leaps at me, releasing a war cry.

Be still my heart and cock—which just hardened—at the beautiful sight. That brief pause is all it takes for this gorgeous creature to crash into me, shoving me to the ground, my blade falling from my grasp. She straddles me and something sharp pierces my shoulder.

I wince.

"Oh, oopsy." She acts coy as I glance at the blade sticking in the meaty part of my shoulder. It's not deep but stings nonetheless.

She starts to shift off me, but I snatch her hips

and rock my erection against the heat burning between her thighs.

For a moment, she moans, her eyelids fluttering upward, but just as quick, she slaps me across the face.

Not that it hurt, but it catches me off guard long enough for her to lunge off me.

"Clever," I say as I yank the knife out my shoulder with a groan, blood drenching my shirt and dripping down my chest and arm.

I twist back up on my feet. "You're good. Must have had a hell of a teacher teaching you to use knives."

She snorts a fake laugh. "He was mediocre. Too busy caught up in his own petty jealousy to really focus."

I arch a brow. "Petty?" I blow out a breath. "Is that so?"

She comes at me, my pulse racing at her insult, my chest bursting to prove her wrong. All the while, my cock pulses because seeing her in fight mode, makes me fucking wild for her.

At the last second I swing out of her path, snatch her hand with the blade, swing her around to face me, then drive her backward.

I lean toward her face. "Maybe the problem is

you weren't paying attention and were too busy flirting with your teacher, wishing he'd just fuck you already."

She gasps, the sound of my obsession. Her ass hits the bed and she rips her wrist from my grasp.

Swiftly, I snatch her by the back of her neck, holding my knife to her throat.

Just as quick, the cold steel of her weapon presses to the base of mine.

"Stalemate," she coos, though she's frozen on the spot, her chest rising and falling quickly. The cut on her cheek pebbles with blood, and it looks spectacular on her.

My hold on her nape never relents, and I push forward, her bite of her blade razor sharp against my skin. "If you intend to cut me, then do it."

She trembles. "Y-You're always so dramatic."

I inhale deeply, taking in her perspiration, her fear, and the sweet scent of her arousal that would drive any man to insanity. Nudging my knee between her thighs, I force them farther apart and push myself between them.

"It's tempting, isn't it?" I whisper. "One swipe, and my throat is sliced. Is that what you want?" I press my bent leg forward a bit more, my thigh wedged between hers, her heat flooding through the fabric of my pants. I wriggle my leg slightly to make sure she feels me. "Or do you prefer this?"

"Seems you're projecting your own fantasies on me," she mutters, her chin high, but lust swims behind her gaze. She's not fooling anyone.

"Then why is your pussy so hot and drenched?"

Her eyes narrow on me with hatred, and she bites the side of her lip when I rub her once more. *Fuck me.* My cock is throbbing.

Aria sets my pulse on fire with her body and that wicked look, like she wants to fuck me, then murder me, in that order. She's the kind of woman that any man would desire. I can see why she's reduced my brother to a love-struck mess.

"I'm not afraid of you," she says brazenly.

"Good," I reply and release the back of her neck, but she doesn't go anywhere while I have the length of my blade pressing into her throat. "I hate pushovers. I want a fighter." Lowering my free hand to her waist, I grab a fistful of the lace jump-suit, my nails extending into claws, and I tear the fabric roughly off her, shredding the material.

She cries out, and I glance down to where I've accidentally cut her across her hip. "Oops." I grin deviously.

"You're a real bastard, you know."

"And I love it when you flirt with me." I tear more of the material from her, leaving a gaping hole across her middle and lap, her skin so tempting. The black thong needs to go. "I prefer this look on you."

I reach down and hook a claw into the elastic of her underwear.

Her free hand is on mine, nails digging into skin, her glare warning me.

"Don't think about it," she raises her voice.

"Oh, I've thought of nothing but having your pussy bare so I can see exactly how much I'm turning you on." Before I can even give her the chance to respond, I flick my claw, slicing through the elastic and her underwear pulls apart at her hip.

"Bastard!" Her eyes grow wider.

"You know you love it."

Sharpness cuts across into my throat, and I know she's sliced skin. Her bulging gaze says it all. Her hold softens as the warm trickle of blood rolls down my neck and under my shirt.

I smirk, loving the sensation of my cock swelling, while the sting on my neck hums as if it has a heartbeat of its own.

"Did it feel good to cut me?" I retract my claws.

My normal fingers now crawl higher up her thigh, and this time she's not pushing me away. I skirt across her bikini line, and the temptation to shove her down and bite into her, fuck her, is unbearable.

Except, this isn't just about me, now is it?

She gasps while spreading her legs for me shamelessly.

I push aside the rest of the torn fabric of her underwear and run my fingers across her slit. She's so wet, so beautiful, it undoes me. Her eyes flutter upward as I spread her lips with my fingers and plunge two into her warmth.

My dick strains for release.

"This doesn't change how angry I am at you," she promises, as a trickle of blood rolls down her cheek and onto her neck. The urge to lean in and lick it grows by the second.

"Aria, I am the one angry, not the other way around." I finger her faster, and it takes her moments to look at me. She watches me as if barely holding herself together. It's exactly how I've always wanted to see her... on the verge of losing control, me the one who pushes her over the edge.

"And now I will hurt you in the most delicious way," I promise.

Her mouth curls into a smile that begs for more.

I pull out of her, much to her protesting moans, and I wrap my free arm around her lower back, holding her in place. She reaches for my pants. A hard tug of her fingers at my pants and zipper, then she has them dropping down to my feet.

There are still blades at each other's throat, and I sure as fuck won't be the first to put mine down. I've seen the savagery in her gaze, and as much as I'd love her to cut me rougher, to make me feel the biting agony of steel on flesh, I want something else first.

She palms my cock, and I hiss as I step closer.

"That's it, gorgeous."

"Maybe you should let go of your blade," she suggests. "It'll be easier."

"You'd like that wouldn't you."

She shrugs with an adorable grin. But the hunger coursing through my veins is killing me. The desperation to finally have this girl all for myself is becoming too much.

I push her hand away and guide my cock to her swollen pussy, my mind thrashing with hunger. She lifts her legs, spreads them wider, rocking her hips, and I push into her.

She cries out, her breaths quickening, her free hand on my arm, and I drive deeper into her while staring into those gorgeous dark eyes. Her pussy sucks down on my dick, squeezing, wanting more.

"Is this better?" I ask, my voice breathy.

Neither of us have relented on lowering the blades. I push against the one in her hand, and feel her softly pulling back. She doesn't want to hurt me, so I lower my blade and set it to the bed next to us.

But she holds hers still, and I reach up to grab her arm. "If you wanted to kill me, you'd have done it already." I push her hand aside and the knife tumbles from her gasp and onto the floor.

Then I push myself closer, slamming my cock harder into her tight cunt, and our mouths clash. We kiss like hungry wolves, lips and tongue, her hands yanking on my shirt.

I wrench the fabric up and over my head, then grab her hips and lift her ass off the bed with ease, ramming into her harder.

She moans, her fingers digging into my arms as her legs curl around my hips. At this stage, I'm only interested in fucking her, not caring what clothes I'm wearing. But hers... oh, they need to go, and fast.

I tear at them with one hand as she holds onto me, the sound of material ripping echoing around us. The whole time she's groaning, rocking her sweet hips to meet each slap.

"Drag me to the dark side, Maverick." She lets go of me and falls onto her back on the bed, her legs still strangling my waist. She's slowly peeling away the shred of her clothes, her bra sliding off.

Her breasts bounce with each thrust, and she's tugging on those perky nipples, her back arching, her cries fucking beautiful.

"You're going to ruin me," I growl.

I reach over and collect my knife, pausing my assault on her tight body, my cock deeply rammed into her.

She cranes her head up to look at me with an arched brow, finding me holding the weapon. "Maverick."

She tenses against me, I set a hand on her chest, pushing her back down. "Relax."

Then I place the flat side of the blade across her stomach and she flinches at its coldness. She's frozen in place, her skin covered in goosebumps.

"You like this?" I move the cold metal under her collarbone and she moans as I trace the valley between her tits with the dull side of the knife. I pick up my pace of fucking her once again, pulling and pushing into her. Her lips curl up with her moans, her gaze lost in arousal.

Then, I make a tiny incision just over her left breast.

She flinches and cries out, her eyes huge, while blood beads instantly. "What the heck?"

The drop races around her breast and runs down the middle, leaving a red path across such perfect skin.

"It's beautiful," I say, then I lean forward and run the flat of my tongue over the wound, licking up her blood. Coppery, slightly warm, and sweet. An excited shiver runs down my spine. "This is how I want you. Naked, spread for me, and covered in blood."

She blinks at me, drawing her full lower lip between her teeth, then reaches over to cup the sides of my head. She draws me down on top of her.

"My turn," she purrs.

Her mouth latches onto my bleeding shoulder where she'd stabbed me earlier, her tongue lapping at the blood. My cock hardens, my balls constrict, and I hammer into her hard, my world spiraling around this girl... This human.

When she releases my shoulder and peers up at me, she licks the blood from her lips like I've given her the most incredible gift. Part of me twitches, and I tighten my hold on my hilt as I place it across my other shoulder, relishing in its cool touch.

I take a fast swipe across the skin, the sting deep. But the way she stares at the blood is worth it. I bury myself in up to my balls and groan, so damn close to the edge.

She's so tight, so fucking amazing.

She wipes her hand across my cut and comes back with blood dripping from her fingers. With a grin, she smears it across her tits.

"Don't stop fucking me," she orders.

And I don't hesitate to plow into her, thrusting so hard the entire bed rocks with us. I drop the blade to the floor and lower myself over her once more, the sticky wetness of blood gluing us together. Our mouths crash together, like this is where we are meant to be, bound to each other.

I flash her a smile and jackhammer into her tight core as I reach down between us, two fingers rubbing on her adorable little clit.

It's only seconds before she stiffens under me, her eyes squeezed shut, a scream singing on her lips.

Her expression is beautiful as she orgasms, but the way she's constricting my dick, she unleashes my own climax. Together we're writhing, bellowing, drowning in the most insane orgasms.

"Fuck, keep squeezing my cock. Take it all."

I don't know how long we've been lost to our bodies, but when I finally come up for air, I'm staring into the deepest eyes. At the most stunning smile. Her body painted in blood.

"I've underestimated you," she breathes heavily.

"Yeah, how so?"

"Here I thought you brought me to a creepy Gothic castle, but instead, this room, this bed, is starting to grow on me. It actually feels comfortable." She stretches her arms out on either side of her, throwing her head back on the blanket. "And hell, you can fuck well." She almost blushes, and the sight has my dick swelling again.

I lean forward, covering her body with mine and pressing my lips against hers. "As they say, best for last."

She smirks while I pull out of her and stand up. I hadn't expected to feel such a strong draw to her, or how much I wish we could curl up and stay in this bedroom for a week so I could fuck her brains out.

My gaze dips to her swollen lips between her thighs, at my seed starting to seep out of her. The sight is glorious.

"Now this is the kind of fucking you should use to measure every other that will follow." I grin and lick my lips.

She blinks at me, seeming stunned at my words.

I pull my mouth into a harsh smile, then yank up my pants.

"Why are you looking at me with that strange smile?" she asks, propping herself up on her elbows and closing her legs.

Collecting both our blades, I can't stop staring at her naked. "I find it adorable that you like this room. Maybe it's because it belongs to Cain. And I just fucked you in his bed."

Her eyes narrow with that earlier feisty fire I'm used to. "Wait, what? This is his home? And you had sex with me here on purpose, just to spite him? You bastard."

I smirk. "That's where you're wrong. I've been aching to fuck you. It just so happened that our first time was in Cain's abandoned home."

And I can't wait to rub it in his stupid, arrogant face. It may be even better than the sex.

11

ARIA

For an abandoned palace, Cain's residence still has all the amenities: running water, power, and a lack of spiderwebs. But I did discover he has a walk-in closet with all manner of clothing, like I'd walked into Macy's. Men's and women's clothing, shoes, jewelry.

I'm not sure if I should be worried that Cain is secretly a cross-dresser or that he kept these in his home for all the women he picked up in Hell.

Except the Cain who lived here and sat in that intimidating throne downstairs is not the same man back on Earth waiting for me.

I get dressed in the most modest thing I can find. Leather pants, that must be one size too small and a black tank top that creeps up over my stomach.

Running my fingers through my wet hair after the hot shower, I head back into Cain's bedroom, where I find Maverick lounging back on the bed with eyes closed and hands behind his head. His legs are crossed at the ankles, and he's freshly dressed in black pants and a button-up shirt.

I'm still annoyed at him for not telling me this is Cain's place, but I'm so used to the brothers being competitive that it doesn't surprise me.

When Maverick cracks his eyes open, he pushes up to sit on the side of the bed. He eyes me head to toe. "You look ready to go into battle."

"Maybe I am." I slide up next to him and flop down onto the mattress. "To kick your ass again for lying to me."

A devious smile spreads his lips. "I never lied to you. I just withheld information."

"Tomayto, tomahto."

He shakes his head. "What's that mean?"

"It means you're splitting hairs and making excuses. It's the same thing."

He twists around to look at me, his leg bent between us. "I wanted to see your reaction to the castle without knowing who owned it, so it was the truth."

I roll my eyes hard. Why don't I believe him? "So, have you got all the jealousy out of your system?" I ask.

He shrugs, locking gazes with me. "I may need more time with you to make up my mind."

"I think you got your moment to stick it to Cain, which is plenty enough."

He watches me intently. "Do you still not realize what you do to me? How much I want to be with you?"

Everything about Maverick screams gorgeous and dangerous, and he brought something out of me that I never knew I liked…knife play, tasting his blood, letting me see the beauty in darkness.

Does the desire he stirs within me stem from Sayah, or is it purely me craving dark things? I don't want to think too deeply on it because I don't know if I'll like the answers I find.

I shouldn't be embarrassed after what we just did in Cain's bedroom, but talking about feelings has me blushing. Go figure.

Maverick smirks in acknowledgment. He knows how I feel, even if I struggle to admit it. Loving three demons took me a while to accept, and now to find myself falling just as hard for a fourth—Cain's brother of all demons too—well, my brain and heart are having trouble keeping up.

"So, where to next? We need to find the rest of the relics and head back home."

He studies me for a long pause, and I can't help but wonder if he's pondering my words. I realize what I implied, *our* home.

"While you showered, I flew back to Irnonoch and threatened to take his new castle from him if he didn't spill more on Lorcan and his other hidey-hole."

"And?" I get to my feet and tug down on my pants, since they bunched up and are strangling my lady V.

His eyes follow my hands and he goes silent.

"Focus," I say.

"Right." He raises his gaze to meet mine. "Lorcan had gone to the hellhound ring just yesterday. It's not a place he'd ever visit. Father goes there often, but not my brother. So, that's strange, right? And I know the guy who runs the joint. So that's our next stop."

"Okay. What the heck is a hellhound ring?" It doesn't sound good.

"I'm assuming Elias told you hellhounds are

used as soul collectors from Earth. The hellhound ring is a fighting pit and tavern in one. It's where the furry bastards congregate and bid on the winners."

"Okay, well that sounds like a fun place," I say sarcastically.

"And we should head there before it gets too late."

With new determination, I nod and look down at Cain's ring on my finger. "You think this will be enough to keep me concealed?"

"It has so far. Though your clothes are rather bland, which might draw attention."

I sigh. "There must be something I can throw over the top of this for dramatic effect. If we're going to a hellhound tavern, I don't want to draw attention."

"I'll find something." He doesn't look concerned. Instead, he takes my hand in his and leads me out of the bedroom. Worry curls in my gut. All I can think about are all those hellhounds that had been sent after me on Earth, how terrifying and feral they'd been.

A hot breeze swishes past us, tugging at my hair and the black cape I now wear over my sexy demon ensemble. After our run in with Serena, I thought more coverage was needed in case we ran into anyone else familiar down here. And for my own sanity, honestly, since I still don't feel completely comfortable wearing clothes this… *tight.*

"This is it," Maverick states.

I glance up at the words above a door of a stone building—'The Ring' painted in red. And I swallow the boulder clogging my throat

"Anything I should know before we go inside?" I ask, just as a beefy man struts past us, grunting with each breath, and—shit—he's three times my size. "Geez. I'm going to die in there," I mumble under my breath.

Maverick grins. "You'll be fine with me. Just stay close, and like before, you're my escort. All you need to focus on is picking up on the relics in there."

I nod, and he takes my hand in his, then we stride into the establishment. The moment I step inside, my toe give a faint twitch. Yep…we're on the right path.

It's dark inside, stuffy too, and it's hard to tell what I'm looking at first. The dark ambience unnerves me. But the deeper we walk in, the more my eyes adjust, and the more my toe buzzes.

"This is definitely the right place," I whisper to Maverick.

"Perfect." His arm loops around my back and he hauls me tightly against him, as if he wants to make it clear he owns me. And I'm perfectly okay with that when a huge monster of a bald man leers in my direction, his grin revealing missing front teeth.

I cringe hard on the inside.

Then I swing my attention to an empty boxing ring in the middle of the enormous room. Around the edges of the crowd are tables and chairs, half filled with demons. Both male and female by the looks of it. Though, to be honest, I try my hardest not to stare and draw attention. Against the back wall to our right stands a bar that stretches the width of the room. Several bartenders are serving drinks to the masses pushing to get served.

There's no music playing, just the loud hum of voices, growls, and laughter.

Maverick looks over to me, his eyes shining from the spotlights over the stage. "We're going to walk around, and you can tell me if there's one location that has your toe going crazier than others."

"Sounds good." And we're off, doing the round. Me keeping my eyes low, Maverick, holding me tightly. I feel gazes on me, studying me. It doesn't take long before sweat pools between my breasts.

A shadow falls over us, and Maverick unleashes a thunderous growl, to which the demon with pointy horns backs away. Then we keep on walking. This place is feral, demons establishing dominance by means of growling. Another reason shivers keep racing down my spine.

After a round, Maverick pauses and looks at me, expectedly.

"Nothing. No matter where we are in the room."

He sighs heavily, then guides us to an empty table at the edge of the room. "Stay here, I'll be back."

I grab his arms. "Wait, you're leaving me alone?"

"Just getting us some drinks so we don't look so suspicious. You've already drawn the attention of several mutts. Let's fit in." He unpeels my fingers from around his wrist. "Won't be long."

I take a seat quickly and lick my lips, hating how uncomfortable this tavern makes me feel. I let my gaze roam the room, and notice two men looking my way, their stares dark, shadows over their faces. The other females in the room are dressed like the men...in heavy leather pants and jackets, lots of buckles and weapons on their belts. It would have made more sense to dress like them rather than like a fucked-up mix between an escort and a magician.

Shit.

Part of me can't help but wonder if this had been Elias when he lived in Hell. Partying, fighting, bidding for jobs...

Someone suddenly sits in front of me, a bulky man with muscles rippling down his arms. "You are a small thing. I might break you, and that excites me. I'm the strongest hellhound in here, and I will destroy them all if you want me to."

"Um, okay?" I look over my shoulder to Maverick, who's chuckling with one of the bartenders. I clench my teeth, glaring at him to get his ass back here.

A loud bang on the table has me jumping in my seat, and I turn back around to the brute with squinty eyes and a huge jaw.

"I understand," he growls. "You need more proof that I am the toughest. Leave it to me." He shoots to his feet, sending the whole table rocking. I grab hold of it so it doesn't topple over as the guy takes several steps to the next table and grabs the first guy by the throat. He lifts him out of his chair so fast I gasp.

With ease, he slams him onto the table in some swift wrestler move, and with his second hand, he twists his head hard. I hear his neck snap.

A small cry slips from my throat, and I shuffle back in my seat. The others at that table scramble away. Then the beefster glances at me, head high, with an awkward smile that shows way too many sharp teeth. It's like he's waiting for me to confirm he's the toughest.

Fuck. Fuck. Fuck.

When the hellhound sneers, I freeze. But instead, he whips away from me and stalks deeper into the crowd, leaving a trail of screams and dead bodies.

Fuck me.

Sayah's lingering just below the surface, nudging me to release her so she can show this hellhound a good time her way. While that's the opposite of keeping a low profile, I'm tempted to do it if that gorilla comes back my way.

I slip out of my seat and get up, bumping right into Maverick. He's not even carrying any drinks.

"Shit, we need the hell out here," I whisper. "Why'd you leave me alone? I told you not to." Shaking, I glance out over the room just as the beast tosses two men off him.

"Is that you're doing?" Maverick states, not looking the tiniest bit concerned.

"Shut up unless you want your neck snapped too," I snarl and fist his shirt. "We gotta leave, now!"

"Well, lucky for you, I know where Lorcan might have hidden the relics."

I can't stop staring at the hellhound, my heart pounding in my chest like a storm. "As long as it's far from here."

"Come with me," Maverick says, his hand in mine, and we move quickly toward the door next to the bar.

A terrifying growl comes from behind us and I flinch, twisting around and half expecting that monster to be chasing after us.

But instead, he's in the boxing ring, beating his chest. Oh, shit!

I shove past the door with Maverick and shut it behind us. I can't calm my breathing.

"It's okay," Maverick reassures me. "I could have taken him."

"Really? He is double your size and he killed six hellhounds out there in just a few seconds. And I'm not like one of you. He could have killed me for real."

Maverick leads me down a long passage, right past the kitchen, and then we're rushing down the steps. "Brinkus didn't want to kill you. He wanted to fuck you."

His response has me stiffening, but he doesn't relent and keeps hauling me down the dusty steps. "Wait a second. You know that crazy beast out there?"

"Not personally. But here's always here, trying to pick up any girl when she's alone. He's an insecure bastard."

"You dickhead," I cry out. "You knew he'd try to pick me up and you left me to him?"

He chuckles. "Hey, I needed to get the eyes off us, and now everyone up there is entertained by his theatrics."

I'm shaking, unsure how to feel, but I want to strangle Maverick. "You're a real prick sometimes, you know that? It wouldn't have hurt to let me in on the plan."

He shrugs. "Yeah, I suppose, but then you would have given it away. You don't exactly have a great poker face. Your emotions are so easy to spot. So it had to look real."

Once we reach the bottom of the steps, I kick him in the shin.

"Ow."

"Don't ever use me as bait again." Then I turn to really take in where we are, considering my toe is going berserk. "Okay, relics are definitely in here."

The basement resembles an endless maze with several passages spearing out from the main room. Darkness yawns from within each opening.

"It worked out, didn't it?" Maverick states. "We found the relics."

"Yeah, by taking a risk. What if he kidnapped me while you were too busy blabbering with the bar guy?"

"Don't worry. I had an eye on you the whole time."

I exhale loudly and stomp away from him. Following my twitching toe, I stop in front of the first tunnel to my right and it responds by going even crazier in my shoe. "Okay, it's down there." I point into the pitch black. "Do you have a flashlight?"

He swoops toward me. "I'll go first. I have great night vision." Then he slips inside, and the darkness swallows him.

"Hey, wait for me." I rush in behind him, and I can't see a damn thing.

I pat the wall and move swiftly, when suddenly there's a hand on my breast, squeezing. "Hmm. Mine," Maverick whispers.

"Stop fucking around," I snap, pushing his hand off me.

Next thing I know, he snatches me by the waist and lifts me off my feet, pinning me back to the wall. His breath is on my face.

"Doesn't the dark just make you want to fuck?"

"Not really."

"It does for me." His mouth is suddenly on mine, our lips crushed. I should shove him off me, but call me weak. I kiss him back, adoring the way he takes me with such possessiveness, how he licks my mouth, attentive to my needs.

My pulse races for a very different reason now.

His mouth is at my ear. "Just give me the word and I'll strip you, lick that sweet pussy of yours, and fuck you until you scream for me to stop."

My stomach jumps at the thought of him going down on me here of all places. I chew on my lower lip, hating and loving how easily he's broken me.

When I don't respond quick enough, he releases me and I collapse back against the wall. The tingle of nerves pulse between my thighs. A kiss and a few words render me completely flustered.

Goddamn him.

My chest rises and falls quickly as his hand trails down the side of face. "Your choice."

The magnetic pull between us is unbearable, but the constant hum of my toe brings an air of logic into the decision.

"Relics," I breathe, then clear my throat. "We focus on the relics; no distractions."

He chuckles. "If that's your preference. Not that we can't do both if you change your mind." He pulls my hand into his and we move swiftly through the darkness.

A faint orange glow appears up ahead. We pick up speed, soon emerging into a cavern where the walls and ceiling are carved out of stone.

My toe is in a frenzy. We're in the right spot, and I veer to the left where I sense my toe pulling me.

There are wooden boxes all over the room, most filled with bottles, so I guess this is where they stash their liquor, or whatever they drink. Human blood? Baby tears? Something gross, I'm sure.

Maverick is on my heels as I close in on several empty crates. With haste, I move them out of my way. And behind them, we discover one wooden crate with black fabric covering it.

"What do we have here?" Maverick quickly pulls it away and lifts out a black box. It's identical to the one we found in Lucifer's whorehouse. He hands it to me. "Want to do the honor and check if the rest of the relics are all in there?"

I turn and pull open the latch. It isn't locked. At once, the overwhelming buzz of their power swarms over me. It's intense and has me swaying, so I take a quick look. Three items are all there—from what Cain told me, they are the spine, intestine, and foot of the harp. I shut the box with a thud and the energy fades.

Their intensity is crazy. I can't even begin to imagine what this box is made of to contain all their power.

"All there. Let's collect the others from your place and get back to Earth." I tuck the box under my arm, and we practically run out of the basement.

"As much as I like being back in Hell, part of me misses Earth," Maverick mutters as we race up the steps.

"Maybe because it's awful down here."

"Yeah, perhaps." His voice is almost strangled, and part of me feels bad for saying that about the only home he's known most his life.

Once we emerge into the main tavern, my senses snap to high alert. The entire room is in chaos. Half the patrons are at the tables, and the other half are in a brawl. No bouncers are kicking them out, so I'm guessing this is a normal event.

I'm frantically scanning the room for that brutish hellhound, while Maverick drags me toward the exit, when a filthy growl erupts from in front of us from the shadows.

I lurch backward, Maverick does the same, taken off guard by the lunatic hellhound lunging in front of us. He has half a dozen mates on either side of him, all staring at us.

"Do you see now why using me as bait was a shit idea?" I hiss.

"Yeah, hindsight is a bitch," he says quietly, then

pushes me behind me. He steps forward, shoulders broad, a growl rolling within his chest.

"What business do you have with me, mutt?" Maverick booms, drawing the attention of those nearby.

Great idea. Insult the big demon.

"You don't scare me," the hellhound snarls. "I've been wanting to sharpen my teeth on one of you ass-wipe sin demons."

The demon has barely finished his insult when Maverick lunges at him, his horns and wings out. Someone screams, and I'm pretty sure it's the hellhound. They slam into a table, bringing it and those sitting at it down.

Utter chaos breaks out. I can't tell who's who, but there's blood spurting and something just got thrown across the room...oh shit, is that someone's tail?

"Maverick!" I call out, hugging the box under my arm, worried for him as two of the brute's buddies have jumped into the battle.

But the others have turned toward me, leering over my body.

One of them slurs, "Slut, want to show me your whore pocket? You can sit on my fuckstick."

"Eww. And your pickup lines are shit," I blurt,

while my mind races with a way to get away from them and get out with Maverick intact.

In a flash, the big beast with a long biker's beard comes at me fast. I swing away from him, but he seizes my cape with his meaty hand. I desperately tug at the ties around my neck to loosen it.

I leap out from his reach and twist around as he tosses the cape to the ground.

"Where will you run to?" He mocks me with a disgusting grin.

"Only one reason a soulless person like you comes here," his friend mutters. "To be fucked, and you haven't had a real demon until you've had a hellhound, or three, in you." He barks, his buddies joining him.

I roll my eyes at how cringe-worthy they are.

"Sure, whatever you say, Tweedle Dee, but one of my boyfriends is a hellhound, so how about you three go fuck yourselves elsewhere." I don't even know where my brazen confidence comes from, but I've had enough.

Another demon is suddenly thrown across the room from the battle, then Maverick slams into the back of the huge hellhounds in front of me. They all crash forward, and he rolls off them, and comes to me. He's in bad shape. Bleeding and coughing up blood, his shirt ripped to shreds. His wings are retracted. So much for sin demons having any kind of authority in Hell. Yet he smiles like this is a walk in the park.

Behind him, half a dozen demons make their way in our direction.

Panic hits me hard, and I tremble.

"I'll be fine," Maverick slurs.

"Are you so sure?" But as the hellhounds descend upon us on all fronts, terror rattles me.

The monsters shove one another to be first to get to us…to me.

The pounding of my heartbeat in my ears is all I can hear.

So, I do the only thing I can…I reach deep within me and my lips curl with the command. "Sayah, come out."

There's no hesitation. She rushes out as though she's been lingering, waiting for my call. Like suddenly she only follows my command.

Her dark shadow rears, extending taller than any of the hellhounds in the room, rising up before us like a monstrous horse.

There are so many of them now. Fifteen, maybe

twenty. But her presence doesn't seem to scare them.

A howl bleeds into the background, and suddenly the demons are charging toward us.

"Sayah," I call out as Maverick drags me behind him.

Immediately, her dark shadow snaps outward in a circle, slamming into each beast, throwing them off their feet and onto their asses. She completely excludes Maverick, which tells me she knows he's with me. She watches everything, after all.

I grab Maverick by the arm but he's too busy gawking at the sight of Sayah.

"We need to leave," I yell.

At my words, Sayah retracts and carves a path for us toward the door, knocking out anyone in our path like a wrecking ball.

We rush past the hellhounds groaning on the floor, and as we pass the dickhead with the beard, I can't help myself. "Fucking cocknose. There's a new word for your vocabulary."

We shoot forward, lunging toward the exit, when I glance back to ensure no one follows.

That's when I see him… Lucifer.

His steely gaze slips over me, his mouth twisted

in hatred.

My blood runs cold.

Hell, why is he everywhere?

He's watching us, taking a step after us.

Terror squeezes my chest and I can't breathe, so I do the first thing that comes to mind. I unleash Sayah at him. "Stop him," I command.

She rushes toward him like a giant black mass.

"Move your ass," Maverick yells behind me, pulling me by the arm to leave the tavern.

Sayah throws herself at Lucifer, and she must have caught him off guard, because one second he's coming for us, the next he's flying across the room. He crashes down in the boxing ring.

The room explodes with growls and bellowing shouts.

"Sayah, back to me," I call out, and I'm already running outside on the street with Maverick as she zips back into me so fast, I barely sense her sliding within me. There's no resistance from her and I can't thank her enough at this moment.

The echo of howls fills the tavern behind us, escalating.

"Fuck." Maverick's wings snap out from his back, and he sweeps me into his arms. We're suddenly airborne, the wind crashing into us, and I wrap an arm around Maverick's neck, the other clutching the box of relics.

Down below, demons spill out of the building.

"We need to go get the other relics, then head to Earth urgently," I say.

"I know. Now, hold on." He picks up incredible speed and we're suddenly shooting through the air so fast I can barely take a breath.

My heart clenches, and I squeeze my eyes shut, praying with everything that we get home before Lucifer can grab us.

12

ELIAS

Morning light bursts past the horizon, painting the inky black sky a brighter shade of gray. I sprint through the forest on four paws and circle around the mountains, like I've done every night since Aria and Maverick left for Hell. Just in case they decide to pop up during the late hours of night.

I pass Hell's gate, which has no signs of the door opening. Not even a hint of sulfur in the air, so with dawn approaching, I decide to turn around and hightail it back home.

As I swing around to change directions, the sound of rock grating against rock splits the silence and the strong caress of magic strokes my fur. I stop just as molten cracks split the mountain-side and slowly melt away.

Sulfur is the first scent to assault my senses, and then the unmistakable smell of my mate. Aria.

My hellhound instantly rejoices at her return, and I tilt my nose to the sky and let out a loud howl.

Aria stumbles through the gate first, gasping for breath, eyes wild with panic. Maverick soon follows, and the moment he passes through, he glances over his shoulder to watch the rocks reform and seal shut.

Sensing the tension and fear between them, I command the power of the change into my bones and within seconds, I'm standing on two feet again, buck naked in the snow.

The moment Aria spots me, she runs over and leaps into my arms. Squeezing her tight, I lift her off the ground, inhaling her sweet, sweet scent.

"Holy shit, I missed you," I say, swinging her around.

"Ditto." She presses her lips against mine for a much needed kiss. My hunger for her ignites instantly, and I sweep my tongue into her mouth.

Maverick clears his throat to cut our make-out

session short. Aria and I break apart. "Sorry to interrupt this little seven minutes in heaven, but we need to get out of here. The devil's on our tail."

My heart falters, and I drop Aria onto her feet. That's when I realize she's holding a box.

The relics. Has to be. "Wait, Lucifer?" I ask, realizing the severity of the situation.

"No, the fucking Easter Bunny. Yes, Lucifer." Maverick's silvery wings snap out of his back and he grabs Aria around the waist. "Let's move it!"

He leaps into the air as I race back toward the mansion, shifting mid-way to increase my speed. When I reach the tree line and spot the lights of the house on top of the hill, I change back. I see Maverick and Aria touching down and hurrying through the back doors.

I follow them inside.

"Isn't Lucifer bound to Hell? I thought he couldn't leave often," Aria says, still breathless as Maverick tugs her along.

"You want to risk this being one of those times he can?" he replies.

At the sound of footsteps and voices, Cain and Dorian pop their heads out of the library. Seeing Aria, their eyes light up with relief.

"You're back." Dorian beams.

Cain's gaze drops to the box in her hands. "Was it successful?"

"Yes, yes. Hi, hello. We're here. We have the relics, but the excitement's not over," Maverick explains quickly as he pulls Aria deeper into the room.

Cain's face turns serious. "What's wrong?"

"Lucifer and his demons were chasing us in Hell. We barely made it to Maverick's place for the rest of the relics and then out of there," Aria says.

"So, if Father isn't on his way for an unexpected visit, then there's no doubt he'll be sending friends to knock on your door." Finally, Maverick lets go of Aria. Walking to one of the tall windows, he peers out.

Dorian heads over to his side and looks out, too. "We need to protect ourselves. Cain?"

"Then we'll prepare for a fight," he says. "I don't believe Father will be strong enough to pass through the gate a second time, but he'll send legions."

"Is there an echo in here?" Maverick huffs.

"Wait," Aria chimes in. "What about Gabriel?"

"The angel? What about him?" Dorian answers.

"Can't he do something to help? This is his problem, too."

"She's right," Cain replies. "We have the relics. He needs to help protect them if he wants us to keep Lucifer out of Heaven."

"Well then, summon the halo-wearing ballerina," Maverick snaps. His attitude is really getting on my nerves.

Cain tilts his head up to the ceiling, and when he speaks, his voice booms with power and command. "Gabriel, archangel. Appear."

The air around us charges with electricity and grows heavy, like the feeling right before a huge thunderstorm. There's a flash of light that burns my eyeballs and dries my mouth, but when my vision adjusts, Gabriel is standing in the center of the library, hand on the hilt of his sword and massive wings spread wide. His menacing gaze sweeps over all of us but lands on Aria last. Seeing her makes his lip curl in a silent snarl.

A warning rolls over the animal in me and my muscles tense. My hellhound can sense the danger, and I immediately cross the room and become a barricade in front of Aria. His desire to end her burns in his stare, and I have no doubt the angel would kill her the moment we looked away.

Cain knows it too, because he shifts closer to us and addresses Gabriel to reclaim his attention. "Gabriel, I summoned you here because we have retrieved the relics."

That makes him turn to Cain fully and his brows lift in surprise. "You possess all seven pieces of Azrael's harp, then?"

"We do."

His mouth peels back, exposing perfectly white and straight teeth. Too perfect. Serial killer perfect.

Aria steps back, while I hear Maverick breathe "Holy shit" nearby. And I don't blame them. It may be a smile, but it's eerie as hell.

"It seems you're good for something, son of Lucifer," Gabriel goes on. "You must pass through the gates, enter Hell, and defeat the Hell king immediately."

Cain only shakes his head, appearing bored more than anything else—his specialty. "We need to rest and feed to be at our strongest before doing this herculean task. We will go tomorrow."

"Tomorrow," he repeats, his voice gaining volume with his anger. He's about to argue further, but Cain stays in control of the conversation.

"If we are to win, we need to be at our best. We get only one chance at this."

Slowly, Gabriel's shoulders ease and he leans back on his heels. His hand even falls away from his sword. "Fine then, demon. Tomorrow. But why summon me now?"

I catch movement at the corner of my eye and glance over to see Maverick bouncing on his toes. He's dying to say something, to put in his two-cents, but he's also trying to be respectful of Cain's position. It's something I had a hard time learning myself when joining him and Dorian. I'd gone from a commander of a hellhound army, Alpha, to taking orders from someone else. But that's the way our dynamic works best, so even I have to sit back sometimes.

Realistically, the fact that Maverick's even attempting to let Cain lead says a lot in itself, doesn't it? I definitely didn't expect him to comply —not this soon at least.

"It was with purpose," Cain explains. He pauses, glances at the angel's expanded wings and waits. Finally, getting the hint, Gabriel folds them against his back. "Lucifer knows Aria and my brother were in Hell. It won't be long before he discovers why, and he knows exactly where to send his legions to find us. Here."

It takes a moment, but as the words sink in, realization passes over his face.

"We are asking for your protection. I have this house warded by magic, but you and I both know it can only do so much. We need something stronger."

He looks over us all one by one again. It's obvious he's debating whether it's worth helping us or not.

I'll tell you what, the moment this is all over, if he ever shows his ugly angel mug here again, I'll spare him the torture and fight him myself. Then we can really see who's stronger—a soldier of Heaven or of Hell.

After some time, he says, "I can shield the house in Heaven's light. No one, Hell-made or Earth-born, will be able to get in or out during that time."

"But then how are we going to get to the gates?" Aria quips behind me.

His piercing stare latches onto her again, and his hatred seems to radiate from him. "I will relinquish the light at midnight. Then, the danger will resume and it will be up to you to make it to the gates alive. I will not be able to assist any further."

Not be able to, or just doesn't want to? I'm thinking the latter.

"That'll be plenty of time," Cain says, to steal his attention away from Aria once more. "We can work with that."

Gabriel nods once, pulls his shoulders back, and steps more toward the middle of the library. Then, pulling out his sword, he holds it straight above his head. The air becomes charged with power, making every hair on my arms stand on end. White light swirls around the blade and shoots through the ceilings, cloaking us all in brightness. My skin prickles and burns as if I've been laying in the summer sun all day, and that's from inside the light bubble. I can't even imagine what it'd be like to touch the outer edge. As demons, we'd probably get zapped into oblivion.

Maverick rushes over to the window and peers outside again. "It's lit up like the Fourth of July out there," he says. "Nothing's getting past that."

Cain turns back to the angel. "Thank you."

Gabriel sheaths his sword. "Don't make me regret this alliance, demons." Then, he pops out of existence with another blaze of light.

I grunt and rub my eyes furiously to stop the itching and burning. "Fucking angel."

"He has a serious attitude problem," Dorian

says. "But at least he was good for something this time."

"Do you really think this light shield thingy is going to keep out whatever Lucifer is trying to throw at us?" Aria asks.

"We have to hope so," Cain answers. That's really all we can do.

Then Cain holds out his hand to her, which she accepts with a small smile, and he leads her over to the couch to sit. "Now, tell me, my love. I want to know everything that happened in Hell."

She tenses slightly, but it doesn't go unnoticed by me.

"We all do," I say and throw myself onto the chaise. And now that we have some time…"

Dorian perches himself on the back of it. "I see Maverick has you wearing the latest Hell-whore-chic."

At the mention of his name, Maverick glances over his shoulder and snarls. "She had to blend in."

"Riiiighhhttt." Dorian winks. "But go on, gorgeous. Story time."

With everyone's eyes watching and waiting, she draws in a deep breath and then starts weaving the adventures that the three of us missed out on in Hell. Nix, the close encounter in Lucifer's whorehouse, the run-in and much-deserved punch with Serena—which is my favorite part for obvious reasons—and the fight at The Ring…

When she ends, her gaze passes over each of us to gauge our responses. I'm just glad she's home, in all honesty. My hound hates being away from her for so long. And her punching Serena? Icing on the cake. I don't know why, but just the thought of it has my cock hardening. My little rabbit defending me, wanting to fight for me… It's hot as hell.

Dorian's lost in his thoughts, tapping his chin, while Cain's silently processing it all. I'm sure there were some parts to her story he didn't like, especially how close they came to being caught by Lucifer not once, but twice, and maybe even his other brother Nix's involvement, but after all that, Maverick had done what he'd asked. Aria is safe, and we have the relics now. Even I have to give him credit for that.

"The most important thing is we got the relics back," Aria says, finishing. "All of them. And you said you found the last one?"

Cain nods. "We have the skull, it is true."

Her face scrunches in disgust. "Of course it's a skull. Of course."

"Azrael wasn't the type to make it into something desirable, like a pair of fuzzy bunny slippers." Dorian laughs.

She smiles at his stupid joke. "He should have."

"Maybe you should write him a strongly worded letter."

"Maybe I will."

Maverick snorts, unimpressed with their banter.

Get in line, buddy. Can't escape it.

"Can we focus here?" Maverick snaps in annoyance. "We have everything to build the harp and get you into Hell, but we need to figure out what we're doing once we get there."

Aria presses her lips together and tries to look more serious. "He's right," she says, but another chuckle slips out. She covers it up with a cough. "We need a plan. Even with the five of us and Sayah, I'm not sure we can take Lucifer down."

"I know. That was one of our mistakes the first time," Cain says. "We thought we could do it on our own."

"And any back-up we did have bailed. The people want to be free of him, but their fear outweighs anything else," Dorian adds.

"We have Nix," Aria says and turns to Maverick. "He's proved himself so far. Right, Maverick?"

He dips his head in a subtle yes.

Aria continues, "So, what about the other sin demons? What if we can recruit more to our side? We'd said before that the brothers are all pieces of Lucifer, and killing them would make him weaker—"

"In theory," Cain reminds us.

"Yes, true. But that also means you're stronger together. If all the sin demons work as one, your collective power equals his," he says.

"Holy shit. She may have something there," I reply, glancing around the room.

Unimpressed, Maverick rolls his eyes. "You forget one teeny-tiny, important detail. Our brothers are complete and utter assholes."

"But we got Nix to help," Aria says.

"Yeah, but Nix is a kitten compared to the others."

"I wouldn't go that far," Dorian replies. "Every sin demon is a hellion of their own right. I think we can get some others on board with this. Valdim would be my next ask. And I can see Raziel being down for a little payback."

Val is a glutton of all things—including revenge, and Lucifer's done some shit things to

Raz in the past. He hates his father as much as we do.

"Yeah? But what about Lorcan? He stole the relics from you. You think he's just going to agree? Just like that?" Maverick throws his hands in the air, exasperated. "Come on, Cain. You know better than all of us. There's no way Lorcan will agree to any of this."

Cain, though, doesn't say anything. Only stares, too lost in his own thoughts to give an answer.

"Don't forget Torryn," I chime in. "He's the most stubborn one out of all of you."

"But he loves a fight," Dorian quips.

Very true. "That he does."

"We just need to word it a certain way to all of them. You know, tell them what they want to hear, kiss three-horned babies, *schmooze*." Dorian waggles his eyebrows in a suggestive way.

"Schmooze." Aria laughs. "What is this? Politics?"

"Pretty much the same idea," Dorian replies and then looks at Cain. Like usual, something silent seems to pass between them, but this time, I have a pretty good idea what they're both thinking. Maybe it's the magic linking us or maybe I've finally gotten on their same level of friendship, but I'm almost positive they're both thinking about Cain's vision after grabbing the foot relic and his idea of killing the sin demons to make Lucifer weaker.

Of course, none of us want to do that. Dorian and I flat out refused to even acknowledge it as an option, but Cain's willing to do whatever it takes to boot Lucifer off the throne. And if that means making the relic's premonition come true... Well, he doesn't care.

Personally, now that we have this other idea on the table of uniting the brothers instead, I'm liking it more and more.

"Cain, what do you think?" Aria asks him, breaking the silence. "Do you think it's possible? Getting all your brothers together?"

He pauses as he contemplates his next words. We all wait because it's near impossible to ever read his expression or know what is going on in that head of his.

After a long moment, he says, "It's worth trying."

That's good enough for me, Aria, and Dorian. Maverick, though, looks a bit dumbstruck. He wants to say something more—I can see him itching to argue his point more—but he backs down, deciding against it.

Well, would you look at that? The kid's finally getting it. He must've realized the other option wouldn't end well for him either.

CAIN

I begin to undress, unbuttoning my dress shirt and glancing at my reflection in the standing mirror. I look worn—even I notice it—like I'm holding the weight of my world on my shoulders.

And maybe I am. Heaven and Hell certainly depend on us winning this fight. There's no doubt Lucifer will be coming for the living plane too, if he's to succeed in his plans.

This is critical.

I may have appeared calm on the outside, but Aria and Maverick's return, coupled with the sudden danger we were in, rattled me. Even now, I can see the shadows of Lucifer's Hell creatures stalking the perimeter of the bubble Gabriel put us in, and I wonder if it'll crumble at any moment.

My hope is that Gabriel's loyalty to the cause and his god is stronger than his hatred of us. It's all I can do at the moment.

Although I instructed everyone to rest before we face down the hellions and use Azrael's harp at the gate, I won't be taking my own advice tonight. With my chaotic thoughts running amok, sleep would be impossible.

We need to feed to gain strength for what's ahead, but with the light shield, no one can get in or out of the mansion. It's not ideal, but we'll work with what we have. We have no other choice.

Soft footsteps outside my room make me pause. It's Aria. I can feel her presence through our link before anything else. She's like an extension of me now. Parts of one entity. We are all.

"Cain?" Her timid voice has me looking up. I can see her reflection in the mirror hovering in my partly open door. "C-Can I talk to you for a minute?"

Her look of worry doesn't go unnoticed by me, so I wave her inside. She steps in.

"Close the door," I whisper, and she obeys. But she continues to stay close to it, almost afraid of coming any closer to me.

The hideous memory of her laying in Lucifer's torture rooms, cut up and bloodied by my own hand, comes to mind, and nausea rolls through me. I quickly cross the room and wrap my arms around her. To my relief, she presses into me, burying her face into my chest, and I relish in the feel of her close to me again.

I would *never* hurt her. Never.

Damn that skull and what it made me see. There's no doubt in my mind its dark power made me, Dorian, and Elias live through our deepest fears—mine still haunts me. It may very well haunt me forever.

We stay like that for a while, holding each other, saying nothing. And this time, when Aria tilts her head up to look at me, a smile touches her lips.

"I missed you," she says.

"I've missed you, too."

"Would you say…you've missed me like hell?" Her smile widens at her poor attempt at a joke, and I feel my own mouth lifting at the corners.

"You're spending too much time with Dorian. His poor sense of humor is starting to rub off on you." I chuckle.

She steps back and shrugs. "Maybe so, but you didn't answer the question."

Ah, she's going to make me say it. "Like Heaven, Hell, and everything in between."

"Good." That seems to satisfy her. For now. "I'm not interrupting anything, am I?" She starts to walk across the room but stops at the mirror I'd just been in front of and glances at herself in the demon get-up. Her nose scrunches.

"No. I was getting ready to relax before midnight."

"You mean obsess over what we need to do until midnight," she corrects me.

I can't even argue. She knows me too well.

"Yes," I confess with a sigh. "Exactly that."

She touches her arm and glances at the floor. There's something she wants to tell me—I know it—so I wait.

"Cain… I…" she begins, the words not seeming to come.

I come to stand behind her and run my hands down her arms. She glances at me through the reflection.

"What is it, my love? You can talk to me," I encourage.

"Promise you won't be mad."

Never a good sign.

My stomach flips with worry. It's clearly something that's been troubling her. Maybe something that happened in Hell that she didn't want the others to know, and that worries me even more. Does it involve my brother? It must. Did he harm her in some way? If so…

I tell myself to settle down. My thoughts are running away from me again.

I keep it all off my expression and reply, "I will say I'll listen first and process before reacting."

Her troubled look says she doesn't care for that answer, but it's all I can give. Which she knows. Instead, she lets out a breath.

"Okay… So…in Hell, Maverick took me to your home. Well, your old home. The black castle."

My spine stiffens. That is certainly not what I expected her to say.

I don't know what Maverick's motives were when showing her my castle, but when I assess her face, it still weighs heavy with fear and uncertainty.

"I haven't been there in a century," I explain. After being banished, I missed the place I called home, but recently it hasn't even crossed my mind. I could even dare to say I've forgotten about it. "I'm not the same demon I was when I lived there."

"You're right. Your style has definitely changed." She gestures to my mahogany four-poster bed with deep blue curtains and gold accents. Dorian likes to tease me for my love of 19th century decor, but it's the century we first walked onto the living plane and established ourselves anew, so I have a fondness for it.

"Is this really about my style preferences, Aria?" I ask her. I can't imagine that it is.

She shakes her head. "No, of course not. I didn't know it was your place. Maverick kept that from me when we…" She trails off and meets my eyes in the mirror.

I hear the next words loud and clear; she doesn't need to speak them. She and Maverick fucked.

To my own surprise and credit, no anger stirs. Why? I'm not really sure. I suppose it's because I expected it in a way. Maverick did pledge his loyalty to me *and* Aria after our tussle in the hall, which means he'll do anything for her as well. She is his master.

At first, this confused me, but then I realized it's simply Maverick's way of saying he cares about her. More than he wants to admit it. To me and himself.

The "picking my house to do it in" was his attempt at revenge for making him watch us fuck her earlier. His last jab at me. Does it bother me? A little, but like I told Aria, I've moved on from that part of my life. Our house in Glenside feels more like home.

When I meet Aria's gaze again, I realize I haven't replied and she's been waiting anxiously.

"You're mad. I knew you'd be. Don't kill Maverick. He didn't force me to do anything. I wanted to, too. Cain, please. I'm really sorry. I'm—"

"Do you care about him?" I cut off her ramblings.

Not expecting the question, she blinks at me.

"Do you care about Maverick?" I repeat.

Her large brown eyes lock with mine. "I do."

Said with such certainty. Such truth.

I sigh. "Then that's all I need to know."

She spins and peers up at me in disbelief. "Really?"

I rub my thumb down her cheek and over her upper lip and then her lower. "If you truly care for him, then I will not get in the way of your happiness. He will be welcomed here."

As my words take their time to sink in, she continues to stare at me.

I keep tracing her beautiful mouth, watching the way her tongue presses against her teeth in anticipation. My muscles tense with the sudden urge to kiss her, to claim her again as my own.

"It's about time I let go of my past and look to my future." This time, my voice comes out huskier and full of need. "One I hope you will be a part of forever."

"Cain…" she breathes.

I can't stand it anymore. The distance between us feels too great. I lean forward and taste her lips for myself. She instantly pushes up onto her tiptoes and deepens the kiss, her tongue wrestling with mine. My body vibrates with hunger, my demon's reaction to her closeness immediate and too powerful to ignore. As it snaps to the surface, my wings shred through my shirt and hellfire ignites under my skin.

I pull away briefly so I can peer at her beautiful face. Desire sparks in her eyes, even with me in my demon form, and my pulse picks up speed. I love seeing her this way, hungry for me. The real me. I don't have to hide who I am when I'm with her.

"You are my world, Aria. My everything," I say.

"I don't think I'll ever get tired of you talking like that," she whispers.

Good, because as an immortal, she is going to hear it for the rest of eternity.

"Stay with me tonight," I tell her.

I don't want to dwell on what's waiting for us in Hell anymore, and you help me forget.

She replies by tilting her head up and kissing me again. Her entire body presses against me, and I can feel Sayah's power hovering close to the surface. Our coupled darkness makes goosebumps rise on my skin, and the energy passing between us ups the urgency tenfold.

Kissing her hard, my wings fold in around us, caging us in and drowning us in shadows. I grab the waistline of her tight pants. One hard rip and they're in two pieces dropping to the floor. At the same time, she's tugging off her top, unable to get it off fast enough. My hands are on her gorgeous breasts, nipples between my fingers, and I pinch them just a bit so she moans.

She's so petite against me, and yet so fierce.

I shrug off the shreds of fabric left of my own shirt and yank my belt out of the loops of my pants.

A sharp nip of pain shocks me temporarily, and

I realize she's bitten my lip. When the metallic twang of blood hits my tongue, my demon roars.

Fuck the foreplay.

I'm desperate as I inhale her delicious smell, run my hands over her perfect body. And the way her soul calls to mine... I can't resist. I had intended to take my time with her, but I can't wait a second longer. I need to bury myself inside her.

The moment my wings open up, I toss her onto the bed and flip her onto her stomach by her ankles. That curvy ass calls to me, and I lean over, then take a mock bite. She winces, and I love the sounds she makes.

Pulling myself back up, I run my large hand over her ass, and she shivers under my touch with her need.

"Get on your knees," I demand with a growl. I want to consume every inch of her. Everything about her is so soft and delicious that I can't keep my hands off her.

She obeys, lifting her ass into the air, giving me a perfect view. Her pussy is glistening wet, just begging to be devoured. My cock strains to plunge into her.

"Beautiful." I grip her ass cheeks, spread them wider. I bury my face in her, opening my mouth, covering her clit, giving her firm strokes of my tongue. Tasting. Savoring. Teasing. I can't seem to get enough.

"Cain," she breathes my name, begging for more. Her body trembles against me, but my fingers dig in to hold her in place. There is nothing in the world that can explain the exhilaration of having my face buried in between the thighs of the most gorgeous girl. My girl. My love.

"You're so perfect," I say and lap at her clit.

Her body shudders, her back bowing as her orgasm starts to crest.

"Come for me, Aria. I'm going to fuck you through it." I turn my attention to her swollen clit and suck on it mercilessly. Her body rides the orgasm, and I never let her go.

She cries out. "Fuck! Cain!"

"Mmmmm…"

"Fuck! Fuck! Fuck!"

She grips handfuls of the comforter as she hits that delicious high, and I quickly reposition myself behind her. There's no time to fully undress, and my pants are wet from leaking, so I yank them down and then push the head of my cock into her pussy.

I sense her tensing against me at my girth. "Let

me in, beautiful." I kiss her neck and shoulder, sensing her relaxing.

And I press into her, her body squeezing me.

"Shit, you're tight." I suck in a sharp breath as her muscles clamp down on me the deeper I go, but the demon in me wants more. He wants the pleasure to come with pain.

I slam into her so hard, she collapses on the bed. She's too weak to hold herself up anymore, but that doesn't stop me. I slide my arm under her waist to help tilt her ass up and ram into her again until she screams.

Then I lower my body over her, never relenting as I fuck her. I nuzzle her neck and whisper, "This is how I want you, so I can control you, fuck you, love you."

Her response comes in the form of a moan as I drive into her, picking up speed. Together, our bodies slide against one another, igniting a fiery friction that could burn the world if we let it.

She's so swollen and needy. I absolutely adore her this way.

She pushes her hips back and forth as much as being pinned under me allows her. The sounds she makes are so fucking sweet. So primal at the same time.

"Cain!" she gasps, barely catching her breath, and yet I know she demands more.

With a growl, I keep thrusting into her, burying myself deep, to the hilt. Her cries fill the room entirely. I fell hard for Aria from the first time I saw her, and fucking her is beyond my wildest dreams. I bounce against her ass, making her cry out for more.

"I'm close again," she says, her hips rocking to meet each slap as I plunge deep into her. "Make me yours."

Every inch of me is on fire, my balls tight, and I rush to the edge myself.

I growl. "Oh, fuck!"

She tenses suddenly, howling her scream, which in turns triggers my own climax. My dick throbs inside of her and stars dance behind my eyes as everything shatters and realigns.

She thrashes under me, her pussy squeezing around me, sucking on me. The fire between her thighs is an inferno. We're both breathing heavily.

When I finally slow down, I pull out of her and crash down on the bed next to her. I wrap her in my arms, her heartbeat still thumping wildly.

We're both gasping for air.

Hell, that was everything I needed.

She turns her head over her shoulder to look at me.

"You fuck like a demon possessed, you know that?" She presses her ass against me, and if she keeps wiggling that way, she won't see me coming.

My wings fold back into my spine. "Is that a problem?" I ask.

"Do I look like I'm complaining?"

I laugh as a wave of exhilaration flares over me. She curls against me, and I spoon behind her.

"Might be a good idea to get some sleep with what's coming up," I suggest.

"Mhmm…"

After a while, she whispers, "Cain…" but when I look down at her, she's sleeping. I hear her heavy breathing.

She's dreaming of me. Of us.

Completely beautiful.

I wish more than anything I could freeze this moment in time and keep her safe in my arms for all eternity.

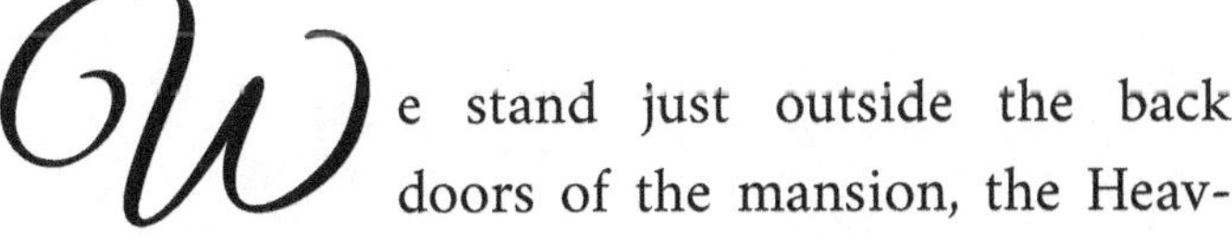

e stand just outside the back doors of the mansion, the Heaven's light shield over our house still in place but gradually dimming the closer the seconds creep to midnight. Just beyond the brightness, hundreds of shadows of Lucifer's Hell creatures twist and pace restlessly, waiting for their chance to pounce.

We're going to be cutting this close.

My gaze passes over the group. Everyone's attention is pinned on the danger in front of us, a look of determination on their faces. Dorian is crouched low, horns curling out of his silvery hair and symbols glowing across his bare chest. Elias has already changed into his hound form and is snarling at the monsters beyond the barrier. Maverick and I both have our demons freed, our wings spread, and our charges in hand that we are to guard with our lives. Maverick will fly with Aria out of harm's way to the mountain, while I'm to bring the box with all the relics to the gate.

"Are we all ready?" I ask.

Dorian glances at the watch on his wrist. "We better be. T-minus thirty seconds."

The light shield continues to dim, the magic waning in and out. I begin to count down silently.

20...

19...

18...

I glance at my brother. Aria turns and wraps her arms around his neck. He hoists her legs around his waist and holds her close. When he glances at me, surprisingly, I see no hint of smugness in his expression. Only understanding and certainty.

He's ready to get this done just as much as I am.

10...

9...

8...

7...

The barricade flickers, and the yellow eyes from Lucifer's hellhounds shine menacingly. There are demons among them this time. Known as imps, they're lowly, spindly creatures that look more like giant spiders mixed with rabid, hairless dogs than anything else. Hideous things with unhinged mouths and scaly gray skin. They're known for not being the brightest, so they aren't the best in most missions, but since they like to kill and not think, they add bulk to an army where it's needed.

"Shit, he sent the imps," Dorian says.

"Stick to the plan," I order. "Nothing changes."

Maverick's wings begin to beat against the air, lifting him and Aria off the ground.

"Lucy, baby, we're coming home!" Dorian lets out a battle cry.

3...

2...

1...

The second Heaven's light extinguishes, the monsters charge.

13

DORIAN

I leap into the air and hop off the backs of two hellhounds. Jaws snap my way. I twist just as the talons of one of Lucifer's imps slash the air. I dodge it, barely, the pointed tips slice the surface of my skin.

Dammit, maybe I should've worn a shirt.

Oh well. If I learned anything from Elias, it's that women dig scars, so maybe some more battle wounds will get Aria in a tizzy.

Not that I need any help in that department.

The whoosh of wings beating against the wind sounds, and as two dark shadows pass over me, I peek up to see Maverick, Aria, and Cain flying above the trees. According to Cain's plan, it's my and Elias's job to lead the hellions away from the mountain so that they can safely put the harp together and open the gate.

So, in other words, we're the bait.

Elias's shadowy form moves left, bulldozing through more imp creatures and tearing out the throat of other hellhounds. When we have a somewhat clear enough path, we zigzag through the masses. I let out another battle cry and Elias howls, tongue lopping out of his mouth in excitement, as we rush toward the driveway and gravel road leading to town, as far away from the mountain as possible. Luckily they follow, and only a few hellhounds break off to chase Cain, Maverick, and Aria's shadows.

As long as we got most of them off their tail, that's what matters. I have no doubt Cain can handle the stragglers.

The next question is, how are we going to shake all these monsters and get back to them in time to step through the gate?

Elias seems to have an idea. He's leading us closer to the main road where cars and trucks are zooming past, their headlights cutting through the pitch blackness.

Oh! I see where this is going.

He picks up speed, and so do I.

We're going to have to time this just right for it to work.

I see the beams of light growing brighter from the distance, hear the rolling of eighteen tires and the rumble of a diesel engine getting closer. Louder.

Together, we dash into the middle of the main highway, the hounds and imps right on our asses. A horn blares, so loud my ears pop, the bright lights of a semi-truck blinding us. I hold my breath as Elias and I jump for the ditch on the other side of the road, and then there's the boom of the collision. The tires are still screeching and I can smell rubber burning from the driver's attempt to hit the brakes on time.

Black blood smears across the ground and paints the truck's hood, but the creatures themselves have disintegrated with their death.

A fast and terrible way to go. But efficient.

I glance at Elias and he gives me a satisfied snort.

The truck blocks our view of the other side of the street, but from the shadows moving underneath, it's a good guess the surviving hellhounds and imps are retreating back to the house. Or worse—to the gates.

"We need a shortcut," I say.

Elias's ears perk up and his snout whips to the right. He knows the way.

He's off and running, a speck of darkness against the wintery backdrop. I push my demon hard to keep up with him, sprinting further up the road then down into a small ravine with a partly frozen creek running underneath a bridge.

We follow the curves of the water, trying our best not to freeze our feet—or paws, in Elias's case —and when he finally guides us out, I can see the rocky face of the mountain through the naked trees. We've come up on the opposite side of it.

The echo of fighting sounds from not far off, accompanied by the snarls of attacking hell-hounds, and we're off and running towards the commotion.

A blaze of hellfire ignites the night, the heat smacking me in the face even at this distance. And a dark figure zooms in and out of the shadows, swallowing up hounds and imps, like a phantom of death.

Rounding the mountain, the scene unfolds in

front of Hell's hidden entrance. Cain is in full fight mode, ripping apart imps with his bare hands, spearing them with his talon wings, and blazing any approaching hellhounds with his inferno powers.

Maverick is kneeling in front of all the relics, scrambling to get them connected before any of Lucifer's monsters descend.

The most amazing sight is Aria, who is standing in front of him, hands out, black tendrils shooting from her feet and across the white snow. Each line connects to a mini Sayah, each zooming in and out of the trees and bushes, taking out anything in their path. An imp will be there one second and then swallowed up by one of the shadow monsters in a blink.

Utterly horrifying.

I catch movement out of the corner of my eye. One of Aria's Sayahs and it's coming right for me.

My stomach plummets.

Aw, fuck. I can't fight a shadow.

"Sayah, no!" Aria's voice booms. "Back."

Right before it engulfs me, it shifts right, just missing me, and zips back into Aria.

That was too fucking close.

Elias has joined the fight, helping Cain take out

the rest of the creatures. I hurry over to Aria and Maverick.

"Sorry about that," Aria says sheepishly. "She didn't know who you were in the woods. And when she's given free rein to kill…well…"

"Explanations later," Maverick snaps, then waves for me to join him. "Make yourself useful and help me get this thing together."

I drop to my knees beside him. "What do you have done so far?"

He gestures wildly to the pieces, all scattered except for the eye, hair, and heart, which had bonded previously with Aria.

"So, nothing," I say dryly.

"Look, asshole, I'm trying here, but they aren't sticking for me."

"Sticking."

"You know, connecting."

"Please tell me you aren't touching them with your bare hands," I say.

"Of course fucking not." Then he clamps his mouth shut. "Well…yeah actually." He points to the intestine or "snake." The one that made us all panicky as hell in the Amazon.

"No wonder you're spazzing." I glance around, looking for something to grab the relics with without having their dark magic affect me. I'd use my shirt like before, but I voted to skip it for this trip.

I start to undo my pants.

"Woah, buddy. Not the time or place," Maverick says.

"I don't see you coming up with any ideas. We need to get them together, but we can't touch them."

"I told you. That doesn't matter. The intestine wouldn't even connect when I handled it. It's like something's missing. A key or something."

"Or glue?" I huff a laugh.

"This isn't fucking funny," he bites out. He points to the heart, eye, and hair. "How did you get these to stick together?"

I hesitate. "We didn't."

"Will you two stop bickering like an old married couple?" Aria chimes in, gaze still focused on the other mini shadows helping Can and Elias fight.

Aria. That's right. She was the one who linked the other three. During her tussle with the werewolves and Sir Surchion.

Shit.

"Aria!"

Her head whips our way.

"You need to be the one to link the relics and form the harp!"

Her brows pinch. "Me?"

Maverick grabs her shirt and yanks her to the ground with us. Every tendril and Sayah creature wiggles back to her and disappears into her actual shadow.

"We need you to do whatever you did before," he growls, annoyance growing.

"I-I didn't do anything really. They just… clicked together," she replies.

"Well, do that again."

Reaching out, her expression falters, unsure.

Then she sits back on her heels and whispers, "Sayah."

Instantly, the shadow re-emerges, this time at full size and mimicking Aria's shape.

"Do you think you can put these relics together to form Azrael's harp?"

"How is this shadow going to know what Azrael's harp—" Maverick's cut off by Sayah darting over the relics, moving them in a blur of speed, and aligning them. They begin to vibrate, gradually shifting closer and closer. Sparks fly and pop, like a damn firework display, and we leap back to dodge the rogue cinders.

I push Aria back and Maverick protects his face, but the moment all the relics connect, a wave of magic explodes outward, making us all stumble back and fall onto our asses in the snow. Even Cain and Elias lose their footing as the harp's power cascades over the earth in a massive wave. The pungent scent of sulfur wafts through the air, strong enough to make a person gag.

When I peer at the ground again, a small harp of tarnished gold lays there with all the relics in place. Like some kind of morbid and grotesque trophy. The skull sits at the very top, mouth open as if it'd been paused mid-scream. Inside, the eye sits, and the water from Styxx's river shines bright inside the jeweled orb. The hair, heart, and intestine have been unwound and pulled tight at the strings, the spine arched as the back of the piece, and the foot as the base.

Then Sayah retracts back into Aria, and we both stare at Maverick.

"You were saying?" she teases.

"That's your smarter-than-average shadow," he mumbles.

"Leviathan, remember? Sayah's been around

since the beginning of time or some shit," I reply and stand, wiping the snow and ice from my pants.

I help Aria to her feet, too, and Maverick follows.

Cain and Elias walk over, Elias now on two legs instead of four, and both of them covered in Hell-creature blood.

"Who's going to play the thing?" Elias asks, wiping his bloody face with the back of his hand.

"*Play* it?" Aria asks.

"It's the only way to open the gates," Cain replies.

"But what if it backfires?" Aria glances at him nervously.

"She's right. If each relic held its own curse, I can't imagine the impact they all have together," I say.

"Ask the Leviathan again," Maverick suggests. "The relics don't seem to affect her."

Aria closes her eyes briefly and draws in a deep breath. When she opens them again, she looks concerned. "She's refusing to come out."

"What! Tell her to get her shit together and—" Maverick shouts.

"Maverick," Cain warns, and he shuts it.

"Yeah, didn't you just see Sayah suck up all

those hellhounds? I wouldn't piss her off," Elias says.

"I'll play it." Cain pulls his shoulders back, taking control of the situation, as usual. "Hopefully the darkness won't be too overpowering for me."

Aria's eyes widen. She doesn't like the sound of that plan. "Hopefully?"

"I'll do it," I offer. "What's a little more excitement after tonight?"

"Fuck it. Give it to me." Elias steps forward.

Aria reaches for it first. "No, I'll do it."

"No!" We all yell in unison, but that doesn't stop her. She's about to swipe it when Maverick grabs it first. He strokes the strings a few times, a terrible thudding sound coming from each of them.

No one moves. We wait, gazes dancing over Maverick and then the spot in the mountain's face where the gate is supposed to open.

When nothing changes, Maverick holds out the harp and frowns. "Did we do something wrong?"

"Maybe it needs to be tuned?" I suggest. "It did sound a bit...dead."

But then again, how much music can a bunch of body parts make?

The ground shudders beneath our feet. We all freeze in place.

"You all felt that too, right?" Aria squeaks.

Another quake, followed by a low rumbling sound.

Maverick looks around wildly. "What the fuck?"

Another rumble, louder this time.

"That sounds like…drums," Elias says.

Then the ground opens up beneath our feet and music erupts from the earth—an eerie but melodic tune with a choir of voices singing an ancient language even I don't understand. The music hums across my very being, and my bones rattle under my skin.

Aria covers her ears, and Cain quickly pulls her against his chest.

Damn, was this the type of music Aria's been hearing when searching for the relics? It's hauntingly beautiful but way, way too loud.

"Look!" Maverick shouts, pointing to the mountain, where cracks of glowing magma line the rocks. "It's opening!"

Slowly, the stones melt away to reveal a massive cave, cloaked in darkness.

Holy shit. This is it.

After a hundred years, we're going home.

Suddenly, a powerful wind pushes pass us, strong enough to lift our feet off the ground. Cain holds Aria tighter while we all lock our knees, trying to fight against it. But it's no use. It's drawing us closer to the gate.

"We're being sucked in!" Maverick tries to yell over the deafening music. I read his lips more than hear him.

Do we fight it? Do we let it take us? I have no idea.

I glance at Cain for guidance, but he's more concerned about Aria. He's wrapped his wings around her to protect her, but it makes the pull of the magic too great for him to withstand.

A second later, the wind swoops them off their feet and they both spin through the air, plunging toward the gate at a deadly speed. The moment they pass through the entrance, they disappear behind the veil of darkness, and panic crawls up my throat.

Fuck!

Maverick's next. He's lifted off the ground and flies into the cave feet first, the harp still in hand.

The only ones left, Elias and I exchange fearful looks.

What do we do?

Then certainty passes over his face and I understand what he's thinking. If one of us goes, we all go. We're in this together. Until the end.

At the same time, we jump into the air and let the forceful current take us, too.

My ass hits something so hard my teeth rattle in my mouth. Pain laces up my spine, and I let out a loud oomph.

The ground. I hit the ground.

Looking up, I see I'm surrounded by tall grass in every direction.

I push to my feet, rubbing my aching butt cheeks. Is it possible to break your ass? Because I just might have.

The sharp scent of rotting flesh assaults my nose, making my eyes water, and when I look above me, red streaks burn across the sky, as if it's made of smoldering embers.

Yep. Definitely in Hell.

Some things I could never forget.

But where in Hell am I?

I spin in place, seeing nothing but rolling hills of more and more of this high grass.

Dorian's head pops up on my right, not too far away. Like me, he looks around to search our surroundings. "Where are the others?" he asks, brushing off dirt from his arms and chest.

"No idea." I scan the hills, seeing nothing again at first, but then I spot three dark figures sprinting right for us, the grass swaying behind them as if moved by the breeze.

Dorian follows my gaze and squints his eyes. "There they are. They must've spotted us, because they are running like bats out of Hell." He chuckles to himself at his stupid joke.

As Cain, Aria, and Maverick get closer, their fearful expressions become clearer, and my pulse gallops with the sudden sense of danger. They're not running toward us; they're running *from* something.

Dorian must notice it too because he freezes and says, "What the—oh shit!"

"What?" I gasp.

"Griyns!"

Griyns…Why is it not ringing a bell? But Dorian's hopping on his toes, ready to bolt out of there.

I peer across the hill at Cain, Aria, and Maverick again, who are closing the distance between us rapidly, and then the strange wave of the grass behind them.

But that's not from a breeze. The air is dense and stiff here.

Dorian doesn't waste any more time and makes a run for it too.

The field behind him moves frantically now, narrowing in a funnel right behind the gang.

"Run!" Maverick's yelling like a big baby, holding onto the harp. He's a damn sin demon. They all sprint right past me. But I'm pissed that we are being chased by these small critters, screaming scared.

"For fuck's sake!" I growl, storming forward in the long grasses, having had enough. These freakish griyns have always annoyed the shit out of me. I clench and unclench my fists, ready to fight.

The grass around me sways wildly, clear where the suckers are.

"Elias, you idiot, just run. Stop being a hero," Dorian calls over his shoulder.

"Yeah, yeah," I crow back, and then I lunge, snatching one of the shitheads by the back of the neck. It's a scrawny thing, with pale, sagging skin, like those animals humans call monkeys. Except it has no hair.

The griyn wriggles ferociously in my grip, hissing at me, sharp teeth bared and used to slice the skin off their victims. It's their delicacy, and revulsion fills me at the sight of them. It's not the way these naked things look that bothers me. I'm more than used to hideous forms in Hell, but that they attack anyone. Even their own kind when they get hungry enough. Fucking vermin. Zero loyalty.

I grab its head in my other hand, then swiftly snap its neck, then dump the creature to the ground. It's been too long since I've really gone hunted, so I shake myself, unleash a howl from my hellhound deep inside and attack.

One after the other, I tear them apart with my bare hands, with my teeth. They're so small compared to me...only a foot in height, but their numbers are where their danger comes into play. I carve my way through them...they come at me in pairs, snapping out of the grasses where they hide, but I'm just as fast.

I've broken so many necks, and still there are more creatures.

Snatching one in each hand, I squeeze the life out of their necks, their screeches piercing the air, when something sharp bites in the back of my leg.

I groan and look over my shoulder. One is latched onto my calf, biting me, and I kick it off with my other foot. The high grasses in front of me sway like a stormy ocean, undulating savagely right toward me.

There are so many of them…the reality hits me like a hammer to the chest.

I've never seen so many of them together, and I've hunted in these fields before.

Crap. Maybe confronting them had been a mistake. They normally attack in small groups… half a dozen or so.

"Well, aren't you all a bunch of fuckers!" I toss their dead friends toward them and swing left, sprinting out of their way.

Dorian's yelling something at me from a distance, and I look up to him waving his hand as if I can't see his fat ass.

My mind races. That one bite in the back of my leg still stings like a bitch.

Aria's calling me too, and I glance back to find the grass has gone dead still…too still.

I don't stop, my chest is pumping, and I dart toward the crew, figuring I'd taken down enough.

The piercing bite of small teeth comes fast at my ankles, then so many more I lose count.

I growl and turn to shake them off, but before I can even make a move, a ball of them crashes into the back of my legs, sending me forward, and I fall, the ground racing up to my face.

Goddamn fucking weasels. There is no way I'm going to die at the hands of these hairless monkeys.

DORIAN

*A*ria screams at the top of her lungs at Elias being yanked under.

One minute, Elias is tossing dead griyns into the air like he's a fucking juggler, the next he drops and he's dragged away.

"Of course the idiot got himself taken," I snarl, giving the spot he stood seconds earlier a glare. So much for keeping a low profile.

"Let them have him if he's going to do something so ridiculous," Maverick mutters under his breath. "Better yet, why doesn't he just go to Father's front door and declare you're all back? Damn him."

"We need to help him." Aria turns and sprints after Elias, pushing through the tall grass that swallows her up to her waist.

"Aria," Cain calls out, going after her, but she's not stopping.

So now, we're all busting our asses running through infested grass, and I'm not in the mood to have my skin razed off and eaten in front of me as I pass out.

Suddenly Aria yelps and she falls into the grass. Then she's gone.

"Fuck no!" My heart beats hard and fury bleeds through me. I thunder faster, all of us frantically searching for her where we'd seen her last, pushing grass aside, yelling for her.

"Aria! Scream so we can follow," Maverick calls out, clutching the harp while pushing the grass out of his way.

When her cry comes from across the field, not too far from where Elias had fallen, we charge in that direction.

The grass shakes viciously around us now. My

skin crawls, but I'm too damn scared for Aria to give a shit about what happens to me. Unlike us, she'll die out here.

Cain's wings spread out and he takes flight, blotting us in his shadow. He flies low, then he dive-bombs to the ground as if he's spotted something. Aria?

An explosion of grunts and hisses are all that we hear. I swing in that direction and glance over to Maverick, who wears just as much determination on his face as I have pumping through my veins.

But without warning, his drops and all I see are his flailing arms before he vanishes beneath the greenery. I lunge after him, but he's gone, along with his gurgled yelp.

Shit.

Fear coils deep in the pit of my gut knowing that if we all fall here, that's it. All those years of effort to find the relics, to not die at Lucifer's hands, are wasted if we lose Aria. Everything will be undone by some freaky skin-eating demons.

Anger burns through me at the thought, and I lunge toward a sound, only to find Cain wrenching Elias up by the arm. He's bleeding and covered in scratches, his clothes ripped, but he's growling for retribution like the hellhound he is.

The ground around us is littered with dead griyns.

"Where the hell is Aria?" I scan the area but she's nowhere, and my gut twists in on itself.

Another scream, this time sounding like Maverick. Seriously, he better not have lost the harp.

"Aria!" I yell and stare out across the field, catching movement up ahead in the grass.

I throw myself that way, my demon spilling out, horns and claws. I lunge and drop down on three of the little shits, which I shred to pieces, blood splashing everywhere. Their squealing hisses attract more of the fiends that rush toward me. And I go ape shit on them, tired of this crap.

Moving with lightning speed, I demolish every single creature that comes to me. When all I'm left with are dead carcasses and me splattered in their blood, I rise to my feet.

Sucking in scorching hot air into my chest, I scan the enormous field and find myself completely alone. My lungs are on fire as dread strikes. They're all gone!

"Aria? Cain? Elias?" Where the fuck are they?

I know, deep down, we are in huge trouble now.

I spear back through the field to where Cain and Elias had been last. Of course they're not there, and my mind blanks.

The grass is swishing in every direction when Aria's scream reaches me. She's farther to my left, and I sprint like a mad man.

I gulp. "I'm coming."

For the space of a heartbeat, time seems to stand still. My pulse pounds in my ears, while the weight of the situation drives down on me, drowning me.

Maybe ten feet from me, Aria bursts up from the field with a fierce battle cry on her lips, a creature in her grasp and bites all over her arms.

Sayah emerges from her chest, stretching outward. Her shadow is so immense, it's intimidating. Even to a demon like me.

And in a flash, Sayah surges outward across the field, flittering past me then vanishing down into the long brush. She spreads across the whole field, being in all places at once with unbreakable speed.

The sharp squeal of hisses and cries taint the air in seconds, the sound deafening. It confirms that there are so many more of those bastards than any of us realized.

Slowly, Cain and Maverick climb to their feet nearby, followed by Elias, stumbling and looking like they'd been run over by a truck. But they're alive. And by some miracle, Maverick is still clutching to the harp.

"Aria." I take quick steps to her side and she drops the dead griyn, then wipes her hands on her shirt.

"Talk about the worst welcome party back into Hell." She half laughs, while I reach over and wipe the drop of blood rolling over her cheek from a cut.

Then I collect her into my arms, a slight tremble within me is a reminder of how close I came to losing her. "You belong to me, Aria. And I would have died if anything happened to you."

She cradles her cheek against my chest for a moment, then pulls back. "I feel the same way. And that's why I had to run for Elias. Each one of you mean the world to me. I won't ever pick one over the other, so I just need everyone on board to protect one another." She almost sounds pissed that we didn't stop Elias pulling his dumbass stunt.

I kiss the top of her head and swallow my

words. They aren't for her. I also remind myself of promises I'd made—that we'd all share her. Even when Elias does stupid crap that endangers us all. "I know and agree."

Her laughter is like music, even in a macabre field with us both splashed in blood.

"By the way, you're glowing." She points at my chest.

I look down to where my incubus runes beam a bright blue through my clothes. "Always happens during battle."

"I like the look on you." Her grin is wicked and she traces a hand over my collarbone.

"Sounds like you want a private showing?"

She laughs even louder and turns to the others, who are just now joining us. We're all together again, alive, even if bitten and bruised.

Aria throws herself at Elias. My initial reaction is that she'd slug him one for being an idiot, but instead she hugs him. I don't like that it disappoints me.

"We're a team now," she reprimands him with her stern voice. "No hero stuff, okay? We fight or run together."

He offers her a lopsided grin, which I am

guessing is his attempt at being coy about apologizing.

"Can I punch him now?" Maverick pipes in.

"Fuck, first time you've said something I agree with," I mutter, and a sense of triumph flares through me that it's not just me wanting to smash my fist into Elias's face.

Except he's rolling his eyes, chuckling. "Can't believe you're so jealous."

I stiffen when Cain steps forward and collects her from Elias, showing us his possessiveness.

"Aria's right. We're a team. Sometimes we'll fuck up, but we help each other, no matter what."

"Fine," I finally admit. "Now can we get the hell out of here."

"About fucking time. Follow me, we're heading to Torryn's."

Good news, Cain and Torryn don't have a broken relationship. Bad news, him and I never see eye to eye. I'm all about love and the art of fucking, but that bastard flies off the handle at the smallest thing.

Let's hope Cain can tame the Sin Demon of Wrath.

ARIA

The streets are busy, unlike anything I've seen before in Hell. Plus, we are now in Hell City, a decrepit place with high-rises and demons running all over the place.

We stick to the alleyways, which stink so bad I can't stop gagging from the putrid smells.

Maverick is leading the way, with Dorian close behind him. Cain is at my side, and Elias is at my rear. We don't exchange any words, just Maverick pointing which direction to take. He's leading us through the intricate web of a city filled with demons in an attempt to avoid us all being identified.

Cain would be the first to be spotted, as he's the most well-known, especially after being expelled from Hell.

I look over to him where he stares straight ahead with a focused gaze. I want to ask him what it feels like to be back home and if there's any nostalgia at seeing a place like this again. Or has it been so long since he'd moved to Earth that nothing feels familiar anymore?

I keep my mouth shut for now though. We'll

have time for that later, if we all survive this crazy mission.

At the end of the alley, we wait in the shadows for slug-like demons to make their way across the road, each dragging black sacks with something that's writhing frantically inside. I don't even want to know what's in there.

I must have winced because Cain slides his hand in mine and squeezes slightly. When I meet his gorgeous blue eyes, his lips pull into a tight smile and he mouths, 'We'll be alright.'

I want to say I believe him, but we're in Hell and wanted by Lucifer.

Maverick waves us on and we sprint across the road and into another alley. We move with speed and I lose count of how many turns and stops we take.

Finally, we emerge from a back street into one empty home and there is an explosion of woods across the road. They're packed in tight too, branches twisted, trunks growing at weird angles, and vines coiled around everything.

"Please don't tell me we're going in there?" I whisper.

Maverick's looking my way, raising an eyebrow

as though he wants to say yes, but restrains himself. "Not quite."

"We're here," Cain states, and takes the lead with Maverick.

Elias and Dorian fall in by my side, while I glance behind us to the dark, stone walls of the buildings with no windows. Wherever we are, it's isolated.

"This place is fucking creepy," I murmur under my breath.

"Torryn is not a fan of people, yet he wants to live close to Hell City. So, he's carved himself a small paradise," Dorian explains.

"This is the farthest thing from paradise."

"Can't agree more," Elias adds, then takes my elbow and has us rushing to catch up with the others.

Maverick and Cain have stopped on a narrow sidewalk, facing the woods, and only then do I notice it…

Realization flashes over my mind. There's a black door within the forest in front of us, and it's attached to a house swallowed by trees and vines sporting huge thorns.

The whole explosion of forest is an actual mansion…a monstrous castle. Except it's concealed so well, entangled by trees, that it's impossible to see at first.

The front door opens and a huge man stands in the doorway.

"What in the name of all things Lucifer is going on here!" The man stares at all of us. He's large, equal in height and width to Elias, and his upper lip must had once been half torn off and never grown back. I can see the top row of his teeth when he closes his mouth. His eyes are similar to Cain's when he's furious. With his short-cropped dark hair, his cargo pants, and black tee, he reminds me of a soldier.

"Torryn." Cain strolls toward his brother. Sin Demon of Wrath. Despite his title, I don't see an angry demon in front of me yet. Someone more annoyed than anything at having visitors.

"Cain!" His shoulders rear back and he seems lost for words, his face shocked.

"Brother," Cain says and slaps his shoulder. "We have lots to talk about but not a lot of time."

"We do." He turns to wave Cain into the house. We go to follow, but he stops in front of us to make the rest of us halt. His pleasant expression quickly morphs into one of hatred. And when his dark gaze hones in on Dorian, it increases ten-fold.

"You step a foot in my home, and I'll break every bone in your body."

"Got it," Dorian responds sharply, and I don't make a move to enter his home either. Maverick marches inside.

When Torryn lifts his chin at Elias for him to join them, he states, "I need the fresh air."

"Suit yourself." His eyes land on me, and he studies me for a long time. "Human…you wear Cain's ring, but I can still sense you. I won't ask. If you are with Cain, then I give him the benefit of the doubt."

I swallow the lump in my throat and watch him go inside, shutting the door behind him. As much as curiosity has me wanting to go into his forest home, it also petrifies me. Part of me pictures the walls adorned in the heads of all the creatures he's butchered. The demon has that savage hunter vibe going for him.

"What the hell was that about?" I spin toward Dorian.

He shrugs nonchalantly. "You steal someone's woman five hundred years ago, and he still holds onto the grudge."

Elias raises an eyebrow at Dorian. "Well, you did use your powers to seduce his wife."

"Oh, that's bad," I mumble.

"I was in a different head space then," he groans, his brow furrowing. "I did a lot of shit that I'm not proud of, but the past is just that...the past. So, what's going on with Maverick then?" Dorian asks, and part of me wonders if this is distracting us from talking about his shady past.

Elias is staring at me just as intently, and I'm not surprised. With so much happening, I haven't had the chance to talk to them as I had with Cain.

"I'm guessing Cain told you about Maverick and me?"

"Bits and pieces," Dorian answers curtly.

I reach over and take each of their hands in mine. "I didn't expect this to happen, but Maverick's wriggled into my heart. Yeah, I know he's also been a jerk to us in the past. He's lied and done some unforgivable shit, but I believe he's changing. He wants to fight against Lucifer, wants to be close to his brother. And we're grown closer, too. Bonded."

They both watch me, almost incredulously, as if they aren't ready to accept this.

"Don't look so shocked. He's actually a surprisingly decent guy. Did you know he paints beautiful portraits? He makes me laugh, and there's just something about him that awakens me, just like you two and Cain do. I don't even know how to explain it, but it feels right in my heart."

"He does not paint," Elias mutters.

"See, you don't even know him properly, yet you hate him."

"When someone behaves like a monster, then they usually are a monster," Dorian says.

"I understand you've all had a bad history with him, but people change. Look at you two and Cain. Maybe Maverick was that way because of how Lucifer and others treated him. And not all monsters do monstrous things." I arch a brow at Dorian.

His lips thin, while Elias just watches me.

"Look, I know this is going to take time. All I ask is give him the benefit of the doubt for me, please? I honestly believe he is a man with a huge heart, and he's let me see enough of it that I am drawn to him."

It doesn't surprise me that neither reply right away. So, I go and sit on a log near the edge of the woods near the doorway, both men soon follow and take a spot next to me.

"I don't know what else you want me to say," I add.

"That you won't fall for any more demons because sharing you is hard enough," Dorian says.

"I know, and I promise that if we can just survive Hell, literally, we can be a huge happy family. And I'll have all the time in the world for us to do more things together."

"I want to also hear that he is shit at sex," Elias says.

I burst out laughing, because my memories of Maverick only spike my arousal. When Elias doesn't smile, I say, "Oh, you were being serious."

He sits back. "I've seen his dick once, and it doesn't compare to mine."

"Or my two," Dorian contributes, both of them staring ahead at the black stone building, seeming content for now to know they are better than Maverick.

Well, who would have thought that my conversation with two powerful demons on jealousy would come down to dick size.

I lay my hands on both of theirs. "All I care about is that I have you all by my side."

They shuffle closer and hold me, and I melt against them. I still couldn't believe that after my foster father sold me to pay his debt, the very demons who owned me now loved me.

I never used to believe in truly happy endings because they don't happen to people like me. But look at me now. I am so close that I might actually believe in such fairy tales. If we survive, that is…

"So, what do you think is going on there?" I ask.

"Three sin demons together…hmm," Elias says. "Definitely lots of chest puffing and ego stroking."

"Or maybe getting into a fight. Nothing would surprise me," Dorian adds.

I don't know how long we wait outside, but I'm sweltering in the heat. When the sound of laughter comes from the open door, we all leap to our feet as the three brothers emerge. Cain and Torryn exchange a few quiet words, then Cain and Maverick stroll in our direction.

"So?" I ask. "Is he joining our cause?"

Cain nods. "He was easy to convince, seeing that just last week Lucifer took away his legion of demons. Torryn is pissed, and he wants revenge against Father." The smile on his face is warm, and I'd go as far as to say that bonding with one of his brothers might be exactly what he needs after being away from Hell for so long.

"Fabulous. Where to next?" I turn to Cain, knowing that while this brother seems easy, I doubt the others will be so cooperative.

"Raziel. But first, we change our clothes. He won't appreciate us turning up like we've walked out of a war zone. As the Sin Demon of Sloth, he is very particular about respect from others, and we need him on our side."

I groan internally. Great. This should be fun.

ARIA

I watch Cain as everyone pours into his castle. The way he looks around makes him almost appear out of place in his own home. As we all enter the grand room, he glances over to the throne and a shadow crosses his expression, like the sight pains him.

I can't begin to imagine how it must feel for him to return to Hell after so long.

Maverick, Dorian, and Elias make their way upstairs, chatting like this is normal for them. They don't seem to be as bothered by their return to Hell like Cain is.

"How are you holding up?" I approach him.

His earlier expression morphs into a more confident one, the kind where he conceals the truth of his feelings. "I'm fine."

"Cain," I say with more force. "Don't lie to me. You can talk to me about anything. You haven't been home in such a long time, so this has to be strange for you. It's understandable."

He takes in the dark room once more, a frown appearing and revealing the truth. He feels lost here. In his old home.

"I'm a stranger in my own castle." His words are pained, and they clench at my heart. "This place used to be own of Hell's crown jewels. It used to give me such pride. But not anymore.

He glances at me, gaging my expression, and when I wait for him to go on, he does. "I've been gone for so long… Yet I thought that once I returned I could pick up from where I left off. Like my banishment never happened. But now that I'm back, I can't help but feel out of place."

A sense of pity spreads through me, hearing the uncertainty in his voice. Of course, I'd never let him know that. He's too proud to ever accept my pity, but it shows me just how much humanity has affected him during his time on Earth.

"Just give it time," I say. "A century away is a long time. You've just gotten used to Earth."

"I didn't care for it until you came into our lives. You've changed everything. Me included."

"That's what I like to hear," I tease and hug him hard.

He lowers his face and his lips graze mine, igniting my arousal like he always does, but he remains tense against me. "Our time here is dangerous. Lucifer won't give up once he discovers we're back," he whispers against my mouth. "And no matter how things turn out, my priority is keeping you safe."

Well, talk about a mood killer. My shoulders sag. I guess this is the part where I am supposed to agree with him, except I can't make such promises. We've come so far. I won't stop fighting by his side.

"But what if you're in danger?" I ask, remembering that terrible vision I saw of him sacrificing himself and Maverick. "I don't want to lose you either. Or any of the guys upstairs."

"I know you don't." Of course he doesn't offer me any promises I want to hear, like nothing will happen to him or no one's going to die. He can't, not when danger is all around us.

He wraps an arm around my waist and guides me to the staircase in the hallway. "I'd give you a grand tour of the place, but you've probably seen it all."

"Nope, not even close, but I got the gist of how monstrous it is on my first visit."

He laughs, throwing his head back, and I adore how he sounds. There's something comforting, reminding me of being home. And that's when it hits me too...that I've grown so close to my men that my home is where they are.

Up on the next floor, I make my way into one of the several bathrooms, leaving the others in a main common room with couches and golden statues.

Washed and dried, I wrap a towel myself and rush on bare feet right into Cain's walk-in wardrobe. I make a beeline for the back corner where I found the leather pants last time. Not sure if I want to deal with demons in a skirt.

If I learn anything from this Hell trip, it's to never let Nix and Maverick pick out outfits for me again.

Racks of clothes surround me in every color, and across the back are shelves of shoes and acces-sories. I reach for the drawer filled with women's underwear, some still brand-new by the look of them. I pluck out a simple, black thong. No bras, but the one I wore from home will do.

I drop the towel and it falls to my feet just as the whoosh of the door shutting sounds. I flinch around, grasping onto my underwear to my chest.

Of course I'm completely naked.

And he's nude too, drying his hair with a towel. But now, he's frozen mid-action, and his cock twitches as it hardens. I won't lie…the sight does have me staring longer than I should, bringing with it a surge of fire deep between my thighs.

His gaze roams over my body as his mouth curls into a devious grin. "Came to check on you," he says in a husky voice as he strolls toward me.

"Is that what you call it?" I exaggerate my stare down his body and back up.

"If you want to touch it, you just have to ask, my little rabbit." He palms his dick a few times, his eyes rolling backward at his touch, then they lower onto me. They're glazed over, and a grin spreads across his face, wider than before.

He stands before me, so tall, so huge, and my libido twists into lustful knots. We're so close now, I feel the edge of his cock against my lower stomach.

"I missed you so much," he says, running a hand down my arm. "I missed your laugh, tasting you, fucking you, the way you scream when I make you come."

I stare at his lips and think about how much I want them on mine. His touch and words set off all kinds of explosions throughout my body.

I reach down and wrap my fingers around his beastly cock. He's so big, so hard. He growls, and I love when he does that.

"Is this what you missed?" I pump my hand up and down his shaft, and a shuddery breath slips past his lips.

"You have no idea." Suddenly, I'm in his arms, and he's groaning against my mouth. He kisses me savagely, and my breath hitches.

Running my hands to the back of his head, I fist his hair, holding on while I curl my legs around his hips like a vice, hooking my ankles just under his ass. I kiss him back just as hard, my lips already feeling bruised.

With one hand on my ass, his other shoves aside clothes hanging from the metal frame, tossing some of them to the ground.

My back hits the cool wall between clothes, and

he's nipping on my lower lip, then sucking on my tongue, keeping me caged by his body.

"You have no idea how hard I resisted fucking you the moment you got back." His hand is on my breast, and he lowers his mouth to a nipple, slipping it into his mouth.

In seconds, his cock is pushing into me. I stiffen and adjust, preparing to take him. He lets go of my breast and kisses me again, hungrily. His hands fall to my hips, and he lowers me down to the hilt.

I arch my back, loving how big he is, but he never stops kissing me. Then he begins his rhythm, quickly picking up speed.

It's a wild ride, and I know he's not holding back. This is my Elias when he's been starved for too long, and I love when he gets this way. It leaves me feeling adored and wanted.

My heart slams inside my chest the faster he takes me. I desperately kiss him harder, taking his tongue into my mouth. A spark of electricity buzzes across my body, my pussy throbbing with each thrust.

I moan, but when he pauses and pulls out of me, the sound coming from my mouth is one of protest.

"What the hell, Elias. I was so close."

"Good," he growls, his amber-colored eyes flashing. "That's what I like to hear." He steps back and lowers me to my feet, then takes me by my hand to the middle of the room where he turns me to face away from him.

"On your back," he commands, his hands pushing down on my shoulders.

When I follow his instructions and glance up at him, his eyes are blazing brightly.

"I dreamt about you while you were gone. I woke up with such a hard on, I was in fucking pain."

"Well then, the more reason you should get back to fucking me."

He chuckles and runs his hands from behind my knees to my ankles, drawing my legs straight into the air. Grabbing my feet, he spreads me wider, and I feel him settling in place.

"Fuck, your pussy is glorious. So wet and swollen." This time, there's no ceremonial preparation, he just slams into me so hard and fast, my entire body convulses. I might be going cross-eyed at how furiously he thrusts into me. He nips at my foot as he holds on.

I'm completely coming apart, chasing my breaths.

"You are so beautiful," he snarls, and this is him really fucking me. A man with a desperate hunger who holds nothing back.

He breathes harshly and I moan louder, sweating, rocking back and forth with his motion. My breasts bounce from each thrust, and he eyes them hungrily.

Labored exhales rush past my lips. He's going to kill me. My head falls back, and I'm moaning his name. "Elias." Every inch of me is taut, and the wave of climax slams into me so fast, I lose myself.

I scream as an orgasm rips through me. My body trembles with the most incredible pleasure.

Elias bellows his own explosion, and I feel him pulsing inside me, flooding me. My head goes slightly hazy with how high I'm floating. He shudders against me, and I peer up at him, loving the way he looks when he's coming.

He notices me watching, and a sexy smirk teases his lips.

"That was exactly what I needed," I say as he lowers my legs onto the floor.

He rubs his closed fist across his chest and

blows over it. "I'll be your de-stressing fuck-man anytime."

I laugh and he groans as I squeeze his cock with my pussy.

"Seriously, if you keep doing that, we're going another two rounds." He slaps the curve of my ass.

"Hey," I gasp breathlessly.

That's when he sits back and pulls out of me. As I sit up, he spreads his legs and draws me closer. His skin is clammy like mine, and when I look up at him, he kisses me tenderly.

I press my breasts against his chest, wanting so much more of this gorgeous demon.

The ache between my thighs is delicious and reminds me of what we'd just done… It always happens after he fucks me.

I'm breathing hard again, and when he breaks our kiss, my lips feel full and sore, while my head still buzzes. I'll never get enough.

Our brows are touching, and my mind is racing with so much going on. "Do you think we'll survive going up against Lucifer?"

"We have to," he answers instantly, without hesitation. "I never thought I'd find love again. At this point, I'm not sure I ever had it in the first place—but then I found you."

I blink at him, and I might be on the verge of tearing up.

I press myself against him and kiss him slowly, wanting nothing more than to show him that he never has to doubt how I feel about him. About us.

MAVERICK

I open the door to Cain's castle and stroll through with Nix not far behind me. The moment he steps inside, his wide-eyed gaze sweeps across the onyx floors and high vaulted ceilings.

"It's been so long since I've been here," he mumbles to himself. "I forgot how dramatic it was."

"You mean melodramatic," I correct.

"No, dear Brother, that's your home."

I snort at that. "No, that's *you.*"

He grins. "Guilty."

I start to walk down the hall, toward the throne room where the others are waiting, but when I glance over my shoulder, I notice Nix has stayed behind.

"Are you coming?" I ask him.

He pauses, still taking in the room, but there's a frown weighing down his expression.

"What is it?" I hiss, my irritation growing. "Why are you just standing around?"

He waits another second before replying. "Why did Cain ask me here again?"

Not understanding where this is going I stare at him, dumbfounded. "Cain needs information on Raziel, and you want dirt on all our brothers."

He says nothing.

"You said you wanted to join the cause, right? Help anyway you can?"

"Yes, I do. But…"

"But what?"

"Do you think he's still pissed at me for leaving him for the sharks the last time?"

What the fuck is he getting at here? "Sharks?"

"Father," he says dryly.

Oh. He's worried about Cain's motives for summoning him here now. Especially after he abandoned the cause last time they'd attempted their coup. He's afraid he wants revenge.

A justified thought, I think. I'd be wondering the same thing if I were in his shoes.

"Is he still pissed?" he whispers. "I let Lorcan get in my head, and my fear outweighed my loyalty. But not this time. I'll stand by his side until the end."

"Good."

Nix and I snap our gazes up to the very top of the staircase landing where Cain stands, dressed in a slim-fitting suit—black on black—his hair slicked back to emphasize the sharp lines of his face. He's looking more like the son of Lucifer now than when we left the living plane.

I guess some old habits die hard.

"Cain." To my surprise, Nix bows his head as Cain leisurely walks down one of the two curved staircases. "Welcome home."

Cain says nothing as he crosses the room. His shoes click loudly against the polished floor, and somehow, he's able to take full command of the space just by being there.

He goes straight up to Nix, and for a tense moment, I wonder if he really is going to punish him for the past.

His narrow blue-eyed gaze roams over him, and a boulder of worry sinks in my gut.

If he does decide to hurt him, there's nothing I can do, is there? My allegiance is with Cain.

But then, Cain does the unthinkable and grabs Nix by the arms in a welcoming embrace. A pleased smile stretches his lips. "It's nice to see you again. *Brother.*"

Nix still hesitates, unsure if he can trust him, but when he realizes Cain's welcome is genuine, he beams. "Glad to see you, too. Back where you belong."

Cain's smile falters a bit at the last comment, but he quickly turns and gestures for us all to follow him into the throne room. Before we even get inside, the voices of Elias, Aria, and Dorian echo to us in the hall. When we enter, everyone goes silent, and Elias's and Dorian's hateful glares pinpoint on Nix.

He glances at me for help, but all I can do is shrug.

"Cain is one thing. Dorian and Elias are another," I mutter. "They might not be as forgiving."

"We have a common goal," Cain begins, overhearing us. "And to achieve it, we need to work together."

"Unlike last time," Elias growls.

"Yeah, when *some* of us were too chickenshit to stick around when it mattered," Dorian tacks on.

Nix holds up his hands as a sign of surrender. "I hear you. And I'm incredibly sorry. Won't happen again."

"So, you've grown balls in the last hundred years?" Elias says.

"Big, big hairy ones," Nix quips, without missing a beat. "Like yours."

He huffs a laugh. "We'll see about that."

Aria steps forward in an attempt to calm some of the rising tension. "Nix is here to help us now. That's what matters."

"Right," I add. "He's been keeping tabs on everyone while you've been away from Hell. And he knows what Raziel's most recent rules are. If we want to have any chance of converting him to our side, we need to know what we're in for."

"Wait, rules?" Aria glances between us in confusion.

"Raziel may be the Sin Demon of Sloth, but he expects everyone else not to be. All visitors must comply to his rules as a form of respect, however ridiculous they may be," Cain explains.

"And they change almost every week. Sometimes every day, if he's particularly bored," Nix says.

"Like, as his entertainment?" Aria asks. "He wants us to be his dancing monkeys?"

Nix thinks about her question then nods. "I'm not sure what that means, but it does sound right."

"And what if we refuse?"

"It's the hole for us," Dorian answers. "He still has it, doesn't he?"

"Absolutely. It's the hole and an eternity of servitude. You'll be forced to be his *dancing monkey* forever," Nix says.

She gasps. "A slave! That's unethical."

"That's Hell, sweetheart." He smiles.

"So, what's his ridiculous requirements for today?" Dorian asks and crosses his arms.

"White," Nix replies.

Dorian balks. "Wearing white? In Hell? Talk about there being slim pickings."

"Oh, that's the easy part," he goes on. "We all have to talk in hypophora."

"Excuse me?"

"That's the spirit."

Dorian clamps his mouth shut and glances around the room. Everyone but Cain looks confused as hell, including me.

"Cut the shit, Nix. What does that mean?" I demand.

"Talking in the form of a question," Cain explains.

"Wait, like in *Jeopardy*?" Aria asks. When no one responds, she goes on, "You know...the game show?"

"Is this another human thing?" Nix whispers my way.

"I think so."

"Ah, yes then. Like that—whatever that is. But always. Anything that comes out of your mouth has to be in the form of a question."

"What the actual fuck?" Elias snaps, his anger growing. "Is he out of his damn mind?"

"You're doing quite well so far," Nix chuckles.

"And if we refuse or mess up, we're done for." Aria's fearful gaze flicks to Cain.

"Then I will do the talking," Cain replies with a stiff nod. His mind has been made up for a while; he was just waiting on when to say it aloud. "We need Raziel on our side, so we must follow his rules, but I will not risk any of you because of it. I will do the interacting."

Nix claps his hands together loudly, the sharp sound bouncing off the glass walls and hitting us from every direction. Elias flinches with his enhanced hearing.

"Now that we got that settled, how much white do you all have in your closets?" Nix asks, to which everyone groans.

None.

White is a rare color down here for…*heavenly* reasons. And that's just what Raz wanted. To make it difficult.

Cain rubs his lips together in thought. "I may have a shirt or two…But definitely not enough for us all. Pants will be harder to find."

"I'll fucking go naked," Elias growls.

"Knowing Raz, he'll make you paint your body too," I respond and roll my eyes. All of us have our *things*, but Raz is just a pain in the ass.

"You're right," Nix adds. "I wouldn't put it past him."

Cain clears his throat. "I'll go. There's no need for us all to speak with him. It's better if Aria goes out as little as possible. She should stay here with protection." He's looking primarily at Elias and Dorian—which doesn't go unnoticed by me —but whatever. I don't want to stay behind anyway.

"I'm coming, too," I say. "Two sin demons is

better than one. Especially when dealing with Raz's attitude."

"Make it three." Nix grins. "That is *if* you have enough white clothing for us."

Cain glances between us, seeming unsure about bringing me and Nix along, but he doesn't refuse it. Instead, he says, "I'll see what I can find."

CAIN

My younger brother's castle sits in the very middle of the Styxx river. He's made himself a little island there, the rapid water current just another way to deter visitors, on top of his ludicrous demands.

Unfortunately for him, I'm not afraid of wearing white. Nor am I afraid of getting a little wet.

As expected, it was hard to find pieces of appropriate clothing for us each to wear. I was lucky to have a white dress shirt and a pair of white shorts among all my darker colors. Don't ask me why I have them because I truly have no idea, but they're splattered with blood, which isn't uncommon for living down here. Hopefully the outfit meets my brother's approval, and the few red spots can be overlooked.

For Maverick, I was only able to find a night-gown, which is too short for him, and fits more like a woman's dress. While Nix is in a ruffled white blouse and a skirt—both things I'm sure were left from one of the many women I used to…court.

Even though Maverick has been scowling since we left my castle because of his new attire, Nix has been enjoying his a little too much, flashing Maverick his ass any chance he gets.

It seems the two have made somewhat of a friendship during my time away.

On the river's edge, Maverick side-eyes me. "We could fly across…" he suggests.

"That'll mean losing the only white clothing we have or stripping," I say. "And one of us will have to carry Nix."

"Swimming it is, then." He claps his hands together. "You can swim, right Nix?"

He waves a hand at him. "Of course I can."

"Then let's get this over with." Maverick is the first to dive in and paddle against the strong current toward Raz's castle. It's smaller than the others and made up of moss-covered stones he'd found at the bottom of the river. But like most things in this god-forsaken place, it's not what it seems.

Nix jumps into the murky water next and just manages to keep his head above the rapids. He's struggling, and ends up needing Maverick to haul him out on the other side.

It doesn't take me long to get across, but unlike the bodies of water on the living plane, the River Styxx's water feels more like slime across my skin. Thick. Sticky.

When I reach the island, I climb out, but the disgusting, mucus feeling remains on my skin.

"I'm going to need a shower after that," Maverick says, rubbing his arms.

We walk up to double doors.

"Remember," Nix starts, "everything you say needs to be made into a question."

I nod and use the giant metal door knocker to signal our presence.

It takes some time but, finally, the door cracks open. An old man dressed head-to-toe in white, with a frilled neck piece and exaggerated hips, stands on the other side.

"What do you want?" he asks. The clown-like getup means he has to be one of the unfortunates who have fallen prey to Raziel's stupid rules. He's been forced into servitude.

My mouth dries. Since I'll be the one carrying the conversations in hypophora, I'll have to think about my sentences carefully before I say them. "Is Raziel available?"

The man's hooded eyes dance over us, suddenly realizing who we are. He drops to a knee and his gray head bows.

"Can you tell my brother we'd like to speak with him? Now?"

When he stands again, he nods frantically. "Will I get him promptly?" Then, he turns and disappears, leaving the door open a fraction.

"This is stupid," Maverick grumbles, his voice low.

"It is, but it has to be done," I whisper back.

"Why is Raziel always such a pain in the ass—" The door opens wider, revealing our brother, looking as I remember him. Shorter in stature than me by a few inches, with gold curls, tan skin, and hazel eyes. There's no doubt women on Earth would fawn over him and his pretty-boy meets surfer looks. He's even wearing only a thin pair of white boxer shorts, as if he's been enjoying himself on a tropical island.

But we know better. The demon underneath is almost the opposite of his human form in every way. Slippery, scaly, and more like a man-eating monster than a person who enjoys the beach.

His unique powers can be quite handy, though. He can make any person fall asleep at the drop of a hat and then wiggle his way into their dreams. Even cause hallucinations if they're awake, making them see and believe whatever he wants with just a touch of his finger.

"What was that, Baby Brother?" Raz asks, glancing over our white outfits. "Was there a *question* you wanted to ask me?"

Maverick grinds his teeth. I can see the insults and curses he's trying to hold back, but he has to remember Raz likes playing these games. He wants to make you mess up; He wants there to be a reason to punish you.

I throw Maverick a glare. I am supposed to be the only one talking here. That was the plan.

Instead, Maverick says, "Yeah, why are you always such a dickhole?"

Raz laughs. "What could you possibly mean?"

"Maverick," I growl, "don't you think that's enough?"

He ignores me. "Making everyone talk as a question? What's up with that?"

"Ah…" A slow calculated smile lifts Raz's lips. "For the fun of it, Baby Brother. To see people like you suffer through it."

"Wait, was that a question?" Nix glances at me and Maverick.

"The rules don't apply to the one who made them, silly. Only to the players."

Maverick steps forward, ready to unleash verbal hell on him, but I whip out my arm to shut him up.

"We came here not to fight, did we not?" I ask and turn to Raz, who is watching me with one brow arched in interest. "And may we ask you a question?"

"Big brother Cain has come back home." He leans lazily against the doorframe and pretends to pick at his nails. "I almost didn't recognize you there. The living world really did make you weaker, didn't it?"

Anger begins to bubble up, but I suppress it, reminding myself not to fall for his traps. I keep my expression as smooth as possible.

"Let me guess…You're back to finish what you

started? Or should I say, what you failed at the first time?"

"How can we have your help?" I asked through clenched teeth. "Don't you agree that it will take all of us—all sin demons—to defeat Lucifer?"

My tongue ties from reforming my statements into questions. What I really want to do is grab him by the shoulders, look him in the eyes, and tell him to put his damn ego aside for once. This is bigger than us. It's bigger than Hell. Grow the fuck up.

Raz seems unimpressed. He shakes his head, his curls dancing across his forehead. "You know, Lorcan warned me you may be stopping by. After you harassed Irno and stole the harp's pieces—"

"You mean the ones he stole from us first?" Maverick bites back.

But Raz waves that one away. "So, I had a feeling you'd be knocking on my door, Cain, begging me to help you try and take Father's throne again."

Begging? Aggravation prickles up my neck. *I wouldn't go that far.*

His gaze flicks to Nix. "You're seriously going along with this?"

He opens his mouth to respond but closes it

quickly to rethink his words. "Is-Isn't Father too unstable? Haven't you said that yourself before?"

Raz shrugs.

"Won't his antics end up killing us all?" Maverick asks next. "Including you and all of Hell?"

Raz peers up for a long moment, pretending to contemplate our words, but it's clear he's already made his decision long ago by his aloof attitude. "Well, I'm sorry to have wasted your time, Brothers, but I just can't join in your suicide mission this time."

Maverick is shaking with fury, his hands balled into tight fists. But I don't blame him. We'd have better luck reasoning with a corpse. At this point, if he goes to hit Raz, I may just let him.

"You know you're never going to get the throne…right?" Maverick adds on that last part to assure it still classifies as a question. "No matter what you and Lorcan have planned?"

Raz's gaze hardens on him, confirming Maverick's suspicions. If Lucifer takes us all out, he and Lorcan have plans to try and swoop in and share the crown. Only Lorcan, out of all of us, would *never* share power. He's the Demon of Envy, after all.

Either Raz is incredibly stupid or he's planned a double-cross of his own.

I shove all that nonsense aside. It's too easy to get caught up in the dirty politics and backstabbing of it all. It's just normal, everyday occurrences in Hell, and frankly, I don't have time for it anymore.

"Nice seeing you again, Cain. And may I say, you all look just show-stopping in your white outfits," Raz drawls as he pushes himself off the frame and starts to shut the door.

"You sonofa—" Maverick lunges, but Nix grabs him by the shoulder to pull him back.

Pausing with the door still open a crack, Raz grins wide. "Na-uh-uh, Mavie. Questions only."

"Yeah, well how about you suck my asshole, Raz? How's that? Question enough for ya?"

Raz slams the door shut, but his laughter booms from the other side.

Nix, Maverick, and I exchange concerned glances. There's no doubt we're all thinking the same thing.

Without Raziel and Lorcan's help, our chances of beating Lucifer are rapidly declining. We need all the sin demons to match his power, and without them…this plan very well could be a suicide mission.

But we do have one weapon now that we didn't have before. Aria.

She's the one who's keeping my hope alive. So, I won't give up just yet.

Fuck Lorcan and Raziel. There is still one more sin demon to recruit. Valdim. Gluttony. With his help, we'll be much better off.

I unleash my demon, my wings ripping through the fabric of my white collared shirt. Maverick follows suit next to me, grabbing Nix under the arms, and together we launch ourselves into the air.

ELIAS

After Cain, Maverick, and Nix came back from Raz's with the bad news, things aren't going in our favor. It's starting to remind me a bit too much of the first time we tried taking Lucifer out, and we definitely don't want a repeat of that failure. Especially since, this time, it'll most definitely end in death, not banishment.

Everything relies on the last sin demon of the seven. Valdim. Or Gluttony. So once they return and change clothes, we regroup to discuss what our plan is.

I, for one, am done fucking around and asking politely. Fuck the pleasantries and then getting the door slammed in our face. I say we start flexing our muscles more. It's the only way to get anything done down here.

Unfortunately, Cain doesn't agree with my methods, at least not yet. He wants to be civil with his brothers. For once.

I personally think it's to distance himself as far as possible from his father. That's my hunch anyway.

Before we can even make plans about how to handle Valdim, there's an ominous knock at Cain's castle door.

Every single one of us freezes in place.

Maverick glances at Nix from across the throne room. "Nix…Who else knows we're here?"

He shrugs. "I didn't tell anyone, if that's what you're assuming. But you heard Raz. Hell's buzzing with rumors about you five. It was only a matter of time."

Aria's face pales. "You think it's Lucifer? He's found us?"

"This would be the first place he'd look," Nix replies, matter-of-factly.

"Shit, Nix." Maverick throws him a glare.

"What? It's true."

Cain holds up a finger to his lips to silence everyone, and the room grows still. Then, he whirls around and hurries down the hall into the foyer.

My ears prick up, listening for any sounds that could tip off an attack. Dorian and Maverick shift closer to Aria, too, waiting for my word. If things get nasty, they know to grab her and run.

But, to my surprise, I hear nothing but Cain's footsteps fading away, a rustle of paper, and then him returning. Stranger still, when he emerges from the darkness, he's holding an envelope in his hand. When he flips it over to the back, there's a purple wax seal that he pops open with a flick of his finger.

"You…got mail?" Aria asks in disbelief. "There are mailmen in Hell?"

"No mailmen," Cain begins, his eyes dancing over the script. His pinched frown has my chest tightening. "It's from Valdim."

"No fucking way." Maverick hurries over and snatches the letter from him to read for himself, and Cain doesn't protest. He reads it over too, and his face mimics Cain's. They both glance at Aria.

"What? What is it?" she asks, voice rising with fear.

"We've…been invited," Maverick starts hesitantly, "to a dinner party."

He's joking, right? He has to be joking.

"I don't understand. Is that bad?" Aria asks and glances around the room for some kind of comfort.

Cain answers, "He's asked for all of us by name. Including you, Aria."

"Me?" she chokes out.

"That means he knows we're all here in this castle. And that means Father knows," Nix says.

The seriousness of the situation slams into me and nausea roils in my gut. It won't be long before Lucifer comes busting through the door like he did in our home on Earth. This time, with his army of marble-made assholes. "We need to get out of here."

"I agree with dogboy." Nix points my way.

Anger mounting, I snarl at him and chomp my teeth. "I'll give you dogboy."

He ignores me and says, "We aren't safe here anymore."

"But where are we going to go?" Aria throws the question out that we're all thinking.

"We're going to Valdim's dinner party."

Everyone looks at Cain in disbelief.

"But, what if it's a trap?"

As always, his expression reads calm, but

there's fire behind his eyes. "Then we kill Lucifer. It either happens now or it happens later. It won't change the outcome."

"But Cain—" Dorian tries to argue, but Cain cuts him off.

"If this isn't Lucifer, and Valdim is trying to reach out, then that means we have a better chance of him joining us. If it's a trap, we'll prepare for it." He glances at each of us. "Get dressed. We're leaving immediately."

That's it. That's Cain's final word on the subject.

He turns and walks out, disappearing down the hall again.

He's right, of course. If we take out Lucifer now or later, not much will change. Valdim's help is needed, but if this invitation is a trap, then we never had a chance for him to be on our side in the first place.

As I glance around the room, I take in the uneasy looks on everyone's faces. Especially Maverick's, who's still holding the invitation in his shaking hand.

I hope to hell what we're about to go to is only a dinner party. And that's one thing in my life I never thought I'd ever say.

MAVERICK

I feel like a jackass.

Here we all are, standing in front of Val's castle, dressed to the nines, waiting for him to open the door like it's a family reunion or a holiday dinner.

Standing around, waiting, like a bunch of jerkoffs.

Does anyone else see how weird this is? Just me? And that's saying something, since I was just dressed in an old lady's nightgown when visiting Raz.

I sigh and peer down at my polished dress shoes. Why is it that I seem to feel like a fool a lot around these four? Now add Nix to the mix, and that's just a cherry on the vanilla frosted jackass-cake.

This is most definitely a trap. Has to be. With the way word travels in Hell, Lucifer has to know we're here and what we've been doing. He must know Valdim and Lorcan are the only ones we haven't visited yet, and by some simple process of elimination, he'll know exactly where to cut us off.

Although, if he really was the one to send the

invite, why not just ax us off at Cain's place? Skip this embarrassing step? That was Cain's other argument when I tried to protest this plan on our way here, but still…Father does enjoy the game. And the torture.

So do I, but that's why I try to stay one step ahead of him. And my gut is saying T-R-A-P.

The door swings open wide, and who else is standing there but our brother, Gluttony himself, Valdim. Average height, slender build, with reddish hair and a wide smile that looks genuinely happy to see us. Which only makes me more suspicious. Val's always been on the more…extroverted side of us seven, along with Nix, but that doesn't mean I trust him any more than the others.

Somehow, Val manages to squeeze past the massive wall that is Elias and get right to Cain to wrap him in a hug, which Cain only awkwardly stands there for. Dorian edges a little closer, just in case he tries anything devious, but Val only steps back and looks Cain over from head to toe.

"You look good," he says and pats him affectionately on the arms. "Must be all that non-sulfuric air up there, hm?" His laughter booms, but no one returns it. We're all so tightly wound, waiting for the bang to come, but instead, Val's giving us friendly nods and hellos.

"You all got so dressed up!" He nods hello to me and Nix. "Brothers." Then, his eyes roam us all over and linger a little longer on Aria, for obvious reasons. She's absolutely stunning in a slinky black dress that's swooped at the neck and held up by thin straps. She didn't put on an ounce of makeup or do much of anything to her hair since we were in a hurry, but does she really have to? She's sexier than sin naturally.

And I should know. I'm a *sin* demon.

Val waves us all inside. "Come in, come in! We don't want the food getting cold."

I want to say I'm not sure how it could, seeing that Val's castle is built into the volcanic rock near the pits, a place where most of Hell's nastiest monsters thrive. So, of course, because of the steam geysers and pools of lava, it's hot as the dickens outside. And inside, it's like walking into an oven on broil.

I may have lived in Hell my entire life, but even demons have limits, and just stepping through Val's foyer has sweat dotting my forehead and upper lip. The air is so thick, it's hard to breathe, yet Val seems unbothered by the temperature.

"Excuse the ash," he goes on as he leads us through the open foyer and into a massive room with an actual wall of moving lava as the focal point. It falls like a waterfall from the ceiling, making it easy to miss the long table in the middle and the servants standing along the opposite wall, all waiting silently. "It's impossible to keep up with it all when living in more or less a volcano."

Aria leans closer to Elias and whispers, "Where's the food? I see eight places but no food?"

Elias glances at the people standing there silently. So, not servants, like I had thought. Souls waiting to be feasted on.

It must've registered with Aria too because she covers her mouth to quiet her gasp.

But something else strikes me—something else she'd said.

Eight place settings at the table...

I count them myself to find she's absolutely right. Eight. But why?

There's six of us, plus Valdim is seven. There's an extra.

Shit.

My heart falters.

Who else was invited to this dinner party?

A man strolls in at that second, wide at the

shoulders with a bald head that's covered in demonic symbol tattoos.

Lorcan.

I knew it. This was a set up. Not with Lucifer, but still.

We all freeze in place. Elias's skin ripples as the power of the shift passes over him, ready to unleash his hellhound at the drop of a hat if necessary. Dorian's steps forward and bounces on his toes, itching for a fight. There's no doubt that if Cain said the word, he'd be on Lorcan faster than a blink.

My own demon surges to the forefront, wanting to tear into him for breaking into the mansion, stealing Azrael's relics, and making everyone believe it was me. Instead, I unsheathe my daggers and spin them in my hands.

Surprise flashes in Lorcan's gaze the moment he sees us all standing there, followed by blazing fury. His head whips toward Val. "What's the meaning of this? Why are they here?"

"Us?" I bark. "Why are *you* here?"

Lorcan glares at me. "I got a fucking invitation, asswipe."

Turning to Cain, I mumble angrily, "Give me one good reason why we aren't detaching his hard-boiled egg of a head from his shoulders right now?"

"Let's hear him out first," Cain replies calmly, and that only enrages me more.

"Hear him out? He. Stole. The. Relics. Or did we all forget? Because of him, you almost couldn't get down here again."

"Maverick…" Aria whispers in warning.

Am I the only one who wants revenge here? Lorcan almost fucked up everything for us. And he's right there. Why aren't we doing anything?

"Enough." Cain's voice is sharp and vibrates with power. He doesn't say much, but it's my cue to step back.

I don't want to listen to him; following orders has never really been my thing, but I've made my choice and pledged my loyalty, so I reluctantly put my daggers away.

Lorcan's head falls back and his laughter booms. "It's true? You've turned into one of Cain's lap dogs too, Mav? Nix?"

I clench my jaw as my rage continues to whip inside me like a violent storm.

"You have quite the circus there, Cain," Lorcan continues to hoot and howl like it's the funniest thing in the world. It only grates on my nerves. "A bunch of clowns."

Aria shouts over his obnoxious laughter. "And you keep sucking Lucifer's limp dick. Now *that's* hilarious, isn't it?"

Lorcan stops abruptly, his hateful gaze landing on Aria. His top lip curls over one of his fangs.

But she doesn't back down, only holds her head high and meets his glare head-on. Her ferocity and protectiveness make my heart pound harder. I love when she's fiery like this.

When Lorcan takes two threatening steps toward her, Valdim's hand shoots out to stop him from getting any closer.

"This isn't why I brought you all here," he says calmly and shoves Lorcan back.

"Yeah? Then why did you?" Dorian calls out.

Valdim's big smile is back, but this time there's a sinister twist to it. "Because, my incubus friend, I'm a glutton for many things. But being used as a pawn in someone else's game isn't one of them."

Lorcan rocks back on his heels, and even Elias and Dorian relax some.

"That's right. I knew you'd be visiting me soon regardless to try and sway me to your side for whatever nonsensical reason. But I decided to beat you to it."

"Nonsensical? This is life and death. The fate of the living and nonliving worlds," I protest. "This is the complete opposite of nonsensical."

Valdim only shakes his head. "I don't want any part in either of your plots to rule the underworld. I figured I'd cut out the middleman, so to speak, and bring you all here to tell you directly."

"But he's working for Lucifer," Aria says, pointing to Lorcan. "And they're going to destroy everything—all of existence—if we don't do anything."

"That's where you're wrong, girl," Lorcan spits. "I only work for myself. Fuck Lucifer."

"Then why take the relics from us if you weren't doing his bidding?" I ask.

Instead of answering, Lorcan crosses his arms. Blatantly ignoring me.

What a massive prick.

"Come on, Lorcan. Fess up," Valdim says, but Lorcan only hisses at him, showing off his vampire-like fangs.

"What is this? A family therapy session?" I throw at Val. "And who the fuck do you think you are? You're just as fucked up as the rest of us."

Also ignoring me, Val turns to Lorcan again. "I'm asking you nicely, Brother. Explain your motives then, if you claim to not be under Father's thumb."

Still, Lorcan doesn't answer.

Val tsks and hold out his hand, palm up. "Alright then. We'll do this the hard way. *Dagger.*"

The prickle of magic caresses my hip, and when I glance down, I find my one sheath empty. There's a spark of light and, suddenly, it reappears in Valdim's waiting hand. He grips the handle and points the tip at Lorcan's neck.

Aria gasps, having never seen Val's power to summon things before, and I guess it could be seen as a nifty parlor trick to a stranger but, like most things, it comes with limitations. Still, it can be useful in a fight...or to tame an unruly brother, like now.

Lorcan sneers at him, craning his neck to keep away from the sharp blade. "Point that thing somewhere else," he warns.

Val responds by nicking his skin. Blood wells up from the small cut and drips down his neck.

Lorcan growls in defeat. "Without the relics, Cain couldn't come back. Without him, Raziel and I would take out Father and then take the throne."

Elias snorts a laugh. "You? You honestly thought you and Raz could kill your father? You're even dumber than you look."

"You underestimate me." He bares his gritted teeth. "You all do."

In one swift move, he throws up his arm, knocking my dagger out of Valdim's grip. It slides across the floor and I rush for it. But in a blur of speed, much faster than any creature alive or dead, Lorcan rushes me and slams all his weight into my chest. I fly backward and crash into the stone wall, so close to the waterfall of lava, that it singes my right arm and shoulder. I land on the ground in a heap, the pain making it hard to breathe.

I glance up to see the air shifting in a zigzag— another sign of Lorcan using his unique power of speed. He's so fast, it makes him hard to track, sometimes even seeming invisible to the naked eye. But there are things that give him away. A flash of darkness, a smear across the air...I've become accustomed to his tricks, and from the looks of it, he's heading straight for Cain.

"Cain! You!" I shout, the words raspy from my bruised ribs.

His demon snaps out of him and he leaps off the ground just before Lorcan's on him. He stumbles, tries to make a right turn, but gives away his location. Elias is there suddenly and manages to throw a punch in perfect timing and catches him right in the jaw. It sends him reeling back.

I hop to my feet, but since we weren't able to feed before our trip to Hell, my body's taking its sweet time to heal.

I may have lost one of my daggers, but I have another to spare. I rip it out of my belt, aim for Lorcan's bald-ass head—right between the eyes—and…

A resounding boom shakes the walls around us, and more ash rains down.

Everyone stops and looks around, confused.

Another earth-shaking boom. Lava spills over the table and red cracks line the floor at our feet.

"What's happening!" Aria asks and clutches Dorian's arm. "Earthquake?"

Hundreds of heavy, clunking footsteps come from outside the castle's doors, and dread seizes me. Not an earthquake. Much, much worse.

"Lucifer!" Val's panicked whisper confirms my fears. From his own horror, it's clear this wasn't on the itinerary for the dinner party. "And he's brought his guards! Hurry! You must leave!" He runs over to the lava and steps on a spot on the floor, triggering a secret escape route. The curtain of magma separates in the middle to reveal another doorway. "This way, Brothers!"

Lorcan and Nix rush for it just as we hear the crash of the castle's front doors being smashed through. Dorian shoves Aria forward, too, knowing that protecting her matters above everything else.

Lucifer's marble soldiers march into the room, weapons drawn.

With Elias transforming into a hellhound and Dorian freeing his own demon, they both dive into the fight without a second's hesitation. Chaos erupts as they clash, and Cain lands in the middle of it all, his massive wings taking out several of them at a time.

Spotting my missing dagger across the room, I sprint for it and snatch it off the ground just as a marble guard swings his broad sword down like a battle-ax. I leap out of the way, narrowly avoiding a wide gap in the floor that has more magma bubbling up and spilling over.

Shit! That was too fucking close.

The truth is, my daggers can't do much damage against an army of stone. The good news is, their heaviness and rigid stone bodies make them slow, so it's easy to I kick the sword right out of the mobile statue's hands.

Picking it up, I twist the handle in my hand.

Bulky, heavy, and clearly a weapon made for brute strength instead of skill.

Eh, it'll do.

With two hands, I swing it through the air and strike the guard right through the middle. When the metal hits the rock, the blow vibrates up my wounded arm, and I'm hit with another wave of pain.

The sword may have not sliced through the guard, but it causes it to teeter over and crash to the ground into a million tiny pieces. Only a small victory, since these bastards can't actually die; they can reform themselves like a giant evil jigsaw puzzle with some time.

I've got to move fast.

Sword in hand, I'm about to join the others in battle when a chilling thought comes to me.

Cain, Dorian, Elias…They're all there, locked in the fight with Father's soldiers. But where's Father?

Better yet…Where's Aria?

Terror ices me over.

I whirl around just in time to see Lucifer

holding Aria captive in his arms on top of the dining table, her head flopped forward like she's unconscious. Or dead.

"No!" I bellow and run for them.

Lucifer smirks as his leather wings shoot out from his back and wrap around the two of them. Ditching the sword, I reach for my daggers, but I'm not fast enough.

They both pop out of existence right before my eyes.

*L*ucifer is in my face, his strong hand grasping my wrists, wrenching my arms over my head, and in seconds, cold shackles snap around them.

"Get off me," I yell, writhing against him.

His other hand grabs my jaw, stilling me, sharp nails digging into my skin.

He sneers, smoke wafting out from the corner of his mouth, and I'm on the verge of screaming because I've ended up as Satan's prisoner. This is what nightmares are made of…except he wants something from me, or I'd be dead already.

My back is plastered to the wall. Fear ripples over my skin as I stare into the eyes of this monster. I woke up in this dark room that smells of sulfur, with only the dim burning torches on the wall. Mud covers the floor, and it's stiflingly hot. I'm sweating profusely.

He's wearing a black suit with a matching dress shirt underneath, and as much as I hate him, the similarities between his face and Cain's are too close for my liking.

"All that hard work, sneaking into Hell behind my back, collecting your relics, and look where it got you," he snarls, his upper lip peeling over a perfect row of white teeth. And I can only guess they'd turn to fangs or something hideous if he wills it. His grip on my jaw tightens, and I wince on the inside, refusing to show him my fear. He's the kind of asshole who'd get off on it.

My teeth grind together, and I barely breathe through the bout of anger and dread consuming me.

"What? You're mad that you couldn't stop Cain from returning home?" I should shut my mouth, but my pulse is racing and I'm so furious, so scared, that my mouth does its own thing.

Fury dances across his face, darkness spreading over his eyes. I expect him to go full demon on me, but he doesn't. He just offers me a terrifying grin that curls on his thinning lips, which is a lot worse. He's holding back.

From the first time I met him, I knew Lucifer was unhinged.

He strokes his short beard, pulling back slightly. An air of regalness surrounds him, as it always has—the kind that belongs to an arrogant serial killer who thinks he's untouchable.

"Your words are empty," he barks. "And I will deal with my son soon enough, but that's not who I'm interested in right now." He reaches over and his nails scrape across to my collarbone, over to my shoulder, pushing the strap of my dress aside.

I swallow hard, trying really hard to not fall apart or cry. Within me, I sense Sayah stirring, sensing my dread. Hell has roused her since we arrived, making her more responsive. What I don't know is how she would stand up against someone like Lucifer...

Lunatics like Lucifer are full of ego and love to brag, and I am all for hearing his plans so I can help Cain overthrow him.

"We're going to play a game," he tells me, then fists my dress and rips it so hard, I lurch forward from the force. It tears down the front, and at the seams under my arms.

I gasp, earning me a deranged smile from him.

Shit, I really hate him. "Look, I get you're pissed at Cain, but your family squabble has nothing to do with me."

He just stands in front of me, not responding, and takes something out from his back pocket. It's a curved blade with a ring holder on one end, which he slides onto his middle finger. The flaming glint of the torches shine across the silvery blade.

Fear zips down my spine and I fight hard not to scream at the sight.

"This has nothing to do with Cain." He spits the words in my face like a venomous viper. "Everything I want is standing in front of me." He grazes the side of his weapon across the top of my breasts, then down between them.

I hold my breath. One wrong move and he'll cut me.

He pauses at my stomach, pressing the sharp tip against my flesh.

I tense, my heart hammering.

"It'd be easy to just gut you. Enjoyable too. Will that make your little shadow come out to play?"

It's a test.

This fucker wants Sayah.

I narrow my eyes at him, determined to give him nothing, and with that, I push down further on Sayah. She can't come out, not for this monster. I don't even want to know what he has planned for her…for me. But it can't be anything good.

"Go fuck yourself."

"I was hoping you'd say that," he says and slowly drags the blade across my stomach, slicing skin. Not deep, but it hurts like shit all the same.

The sting sharpens instantly, and I scream this time, my body convulsing.

"Now, that's the sound I like to hear." He lifts the blood-stained knife to my face, while my stomach is on fire, blood dripping onto my dress.

I jerk my head up, and the room seems to sway. "Y-you're a psychopath."

"Why, thank you." He huffs, pressing his knife to my cheek and slashes downward.

I hiss, clenching my teeth through the pain. "Your sons hate you. Each one of them fears you. There is no love."

He barks a laugh, while I tremble. Sayah's just below the surface, longing to escape, but I push her back. I can't let her. Not when I don't know what he has planned for her.

"Their fear is all I need," he snaps.

"Even if that means they see Cain as their true leader over you? That you destroy everything you touch?"

An ugly expression flares over his face, and he shows me the real beast with red eyes, protruding brow, fangs, and thick horns.

He's the creature of nightmares. Terror clings to my skin while blood drips down my jawline, my wounds scream with pain, but I hold Lucifer's stare. He's pissing me off.

"You'll get nothing from me."

"That makes this all the more fun. So, as I said before, let's play a game. It's simple. I will cut you, and when you want me to stop, release the shadow."

My body trembles on its own. "You're a fucking dumb piece of shit. Wasting your time with me." Distraction is worth a shot.

For a moment he pauses, churning over my words no doubt, but when the corners of his eyes wrinkle with his grin, I know he's beyond the point of insanity.

But if I show Sayah, then what? He'll kill me for her?

I keep thinking about how much easier she flows from me in Hell, how quickly she responds, and that somehow this place just resonates with her. Does that mean Lucifer will gain control over her easily?

If she really wanted to come out, she'd do it already, like she's done in the past.

She knows this bastard is dangerous to her and me.

Then he starts cutting—my arms, my chest, my stomach. The burning pain is like acid on my skin.

My cries fill my head, and I'm convulsing, teeth chattering. I don't stop even when he pauses. Fear crashes through me. I'm thrashing against the restraints on my arms.

Everything hurts so much, and I can't stop the tears drenching my cheeks.

But with all the dread, rage also surges forward, my thoughts filled with memories of Cain, Elias, Dorian, and even Maverick. How much they suffered, how we've bonded together, and it's worth all the agony in the world. I grew up with Murray, but there was no real love. Joseline was more a friend than a sister. My true family, my love, is with my demons. And for them, I will get through this. No matter what. I will survive.

I lift my head, blood dripping down nearly

everywhere, and my stomach turns at the devil staring at me with such pleasure on his face.

"I have so much in store for you, Aria. So do keep resisting me. Your body will be marked with scars that will ensure you will never forget me…if I let you survive, that is. Though, I have been needing a new footstool."

"You don't scare me," I snap back, exhausted. I never want to become the girl who's too scared to fight back.

In a flash, the back of his hand flies to the side of my face. His knuckles crack hard, and my head is flung sideways, my world blurry. I cry from the throbbing ache zigzagging across my face and head.

He snatches my hair and yanks my head back up. "The tough ones are the most fun to break. Let's keep playing, shall we?" He releases me, and my head flops back down, my chin tucked into my chest.

I tense up, expecting more, but instead, the click-clack of heels hitting the stone floor catches my attention.

"What are you doing here?" Lucifer snarls.

"You think I'd miss this? No fucking way." Her

voice has me instantly stiffening, and I raise my head, my gaze clashing with Serena's eyes.

What is she doing here?

She approaches us, flicking her blonde hair off her face. Her skin-tight, black bodysuit leaves nothing to the imagination. How is she not sweating up a storm in that?

I blink the blood and sweat out of my eyes as she pretends to show me pity.

"Oh, you're in a terrible state." She mocks.

I want to rake my nails down her face.

Lucifer raises his blade and I flinch against the wall behind me.

"You really are stupid," she drones on, while I'm shaking and bleeding.

"Just get out of my face," I hiss.

"I bet she doesn't even know how you found her." She chortles like a freaking hyena in Lucifer's direction, then glances at me. "It was me, in case you're too slow to work it out. When you hit me the ring cut me, and I smelled who you really were after that, human, along with it being Cain's ring. And I saw instantly that it was you… the bitch who took Elias from me. You were your own undoing."

I look at her, and one of my eyes is twitching, the eyelid not wanting to completely stay open.

"What the fuck do you want? A pat on the back? And for your information, you destroyed your relationship by betraying him." I'm burning up on the inside over the fact that she ran straight to Lucifer.

I blink at her while grazing my thumb over Cain's ring. It felt amazing to smash my fist into her face, but knowing that was how Lucifer found me, I now regret it.

"Listen here, human filth. If you had half a brain, then you wouldn't be in this mess."

Lucifer cuts her a hard side glare, which she doesn't notice. She is so clueless, having no idea that Lucifer will betray her in an instant. But his look also tells me she has no clue why he really wants me...she thinks it's for her.

Ah, bless her black heart.

Serena laughs again and steps back, watching from the shadows.

I don't even have the energy to come back with a witty response. But when Lucifer presses the edge of his knife to my collarbone, the sharpness biting into skin, I start screaming. Darkness feathers around the edges of my eyes as he cuts me while he smiles.

Rather than fight it, I let myself fall.

y eyes open and I groan with pain. Every inch of me aches, even my ears, which I don't understand.

I must have passed out, because Lucifer is no longer torturing me. Serena isn't around either. Thank fuck.

But when I glance down, I want to scream all over again. I am covered in blood and sweat, so are my clothes, with more blood dried across my skin. How long have I been out? Lucifer must have still cut me when I fell unconscious. Bastard.

My throat burns when I swallow. What I wouldn't give for a cold glass of water right now.

Or better yet, to get the hell out of here. I wrench my gaze across the room this time, just in case Lucifer or someone else remains in here watching me. I keep blinking to clear away the blur.

And now, instinct drives me. *Sayah,* I call to her in my mind. *Get me out of here. Please.*

Desperation is clinging to my thoughts because if Lucifer didn't get what he wanted, how long before he eradicates me?

She slips out of me like a rushing river,

spreading out across the stone floor, then she rises before me like a storm, taking no particular form. She's fraying at the edges, and goosebumps cover my skin. It's not from fear, but from her surge of anger overwhelming me. She's furious that we allowed that prick to do this to me.

Escape. We need to get out before he gets us, I tell her. That's what matters now. Get back to my demons and pray to everything that hasn't been captured as well.

Sayah sweeps over the top of me. I crane my head up as she threads into the locks on my restraints.

In moments, the metal braces snap from my wrists. My arms fall by my side and my legs wobble. They give out and I drop, my knees kissing the floor, my arms too numb to catch myself. I whine quietly from how much it hurts to move. How every cut stings like I'm on fire.

I raise bloody fingers in front of me, and anger billows to the surface. It bears down on me, almost crushing me from the inside.

Next thing I know, Sayah sweeps under my arms and around my middle. She lifts me up and off my feet. It feels like I'm on a rollercoaster. I have no control of my body when we move forward, which makes me queasy.

She opens the door and part of her slips into the dark hallway.

Everything swims around me, and I can't help but think I might pass out again.

Someone grunts up ahead, followed by something heavy hitting the floor. That doesn't sound good.

Sayah carries me around the corner seconds later, and that's when I spot three demonic, hairy goat-like creatures, complete with hooves, strewn on the floor. Their limbs are twisted, and blood pools around them. As Cain kept saying, no one really dies in Hell...well, except me. But these things will come back soon enough.

As if on cue and sensing my concern, Sayah rushes us forward. We move fast now. I don't know where we are, but panic flares at the thought of being found.

Each time the wounds throb, I clench my teeth. My mind races with images of Lucifer in my face, how he was going to keep going until he killed me. My chest tightens again, and adrenaline thumps in my veins.

I never want to be alone with that maniac again.

And in that precise moment, an ear-piercing alarm goes off, blaring through the hallway, deafening me.

I flinch and look back, expecting guards, but there's only darkness. Shit!

"They know I'm gone," I mutter to Sayah. Desperation roars through me, and I'm wriggling to be free, to run faster, anything to escape.

My feet are skimming along the floor in the dark hallways, and I try my best to stand up on my own, but we never stop moving. Sayah takes the lead, but when we come to a dead-end, my stomach drops. My hands push against the wall, just in case there's a trap door…but nothing.

"Crap." My heart slams against the inside of my chest. I twist back around and, with Sayah still curled around my middle partially holding me up, we move again. We swing around another corner when thunderous footsteps sound straight ahead of us, shadows dancing at the end of the long hallway.

Sayah's holds around my middle constricts and she wrenches me backward into a dark passage.

Silence.

I don't dare take a breath while she spreads out in front of me like a shield, concealing me.

An army of soldiers storm past us—marble guards—and I feel the blood draining from my body remembering their attack from earlier and how I ended up kidnapped in the first place.

Once they pass, we wait and I quietly try to catch my breath.

Then Sayah nudges me forward. I swing my attention to the left where the guards went...and we go right, hoping it'll lead us outside.

I stumble on my feet, holding onto the wall for balance. I'm walking faster now, almost running, when a flood of bright light comes from up ahead. Cautiously, I keep going and when we reach the turn, I peer around to find large double doors, sitting open, natural light spilling inside. Outside stands a large courtyard and more buildings nearby.

Nerves dance up my spine since I'll end up walking right into the open to be seen...but what other choices are there?

Sayah, still wrapped around my waist, tugs me in the opposite direction. I twist around to see her pulling open what appears to be a side door heading outside directly across from the courtyard.

You're amazing, Sayah. I frantically lunge after her just as the walls seem to tilt around me. I stumble and crash into one, then shake my head. I have no idea how much blood I've lost, but this is the worst place to pass out. I have to get my shit together.

I push my legs to move before they slip out from under me again. Time isn't on my side, but I can't stay here, so I step through the door with Sayah.

We find ourselves in a dingy passage encased by two granite stone buildings. Behind us is a dead end, but up ahead a street runs adjacent to the building. I look back and quickly shut the door to not give away our position.

A way out. *Yes, please let it be the case.*

I've had so much bad luck that I'm desperate for something to go right.

I wobble awkwardly away from the door, my breath strangling my lungs with the burning hot air. My skin tingles, and a thrumming sensation fills my head. I feel Cain, Dorian, and Elias like they are just out of reach. Our connection flares awake now that I'm outside the building.

I'm drawn forward as though I'm magnetically pulled to them.

Our bond… It'll help me find them.

Sayah is stretching out ahead of me. But I don't need anyone spotting a huge shadow by my side and drawing unwanted attention. *Sayah, come back.*

She obediently complies.

At the end of the alley, I careen away, following the call to my men toward the left. I need to be as far from the prison or whatever the fuck this place is as possible.

But something dark suddenly falls over me.

Panicking, I raise my head just as I slam straight into a solid wall of muscle.

Panic flares over me, and I'm curling my hands, raising them, ready to defend myself.

But he snatches my wrists before I can even push away.

"Aria," he snarls with a deep husky voice I don't recognize and is already dragging me toward the street where a black car waits.

My heart lunges to the back of my throat so hard that I might pass out again.

19

ARIA

"Hush, I'm not here to hurt you. I'm helping," he says as he shoves me roughly into the back seat of a black car that looks like a hearse.

"Help how?" I hit the leather seat sideways just as the door slaps shut behind me.

What the fuck? I scramble back up and frantically pull at the door latch, but it doesn't budge.

Sayah's already edging out of me as the man wearing all black climbs into the driver's seat, and I hold her down so she's just brimming below the surface.

"I'm not going back to Lucifer," I practically yell.

He twists his head around to look at me with a downturned mouth. He's red all over, just like Lorcan's boyfriend. Thick, bushy eyebrows crown dark eyes, a wide forehead, and thick stumps of sawed-off horns at his temples. He has that look on his face like he's constantly pissed off...or maybe he's constipated. Could go either way, really.

"Neither do I. But you want to see Cain again, right? Then we need to go quickly before Lucifer comes after us."

My head spins, and he's already got the engine roaring, sounding more like a dragon than a motor. I don't even want to know what's under the hood.

Except, I don't trust this guy.

"Let me the fuck out! And how do you know who I am, or about Cain?"

"I'm a friend," he says quickly over his shoulder. "Cain came to my home and asked me to help find you. And I drove past just as you rushed out of the building with your shadow. That's when I knew instantly I'd found you."

We're driving now; I'm huddled in the corner by the door and panic curls in my gut. Sayah is begging to come out to hurt this demon. But then what? I navigate through Hell in this car? I wouldn't be opposed to the idea, except with my luck I'd end up driving into a lava pit or something. Especially considering this demon isn't even sticking to the road. He swings abruptly between two houses, tearing up the ground, then we come out on a dirty path. What the fuck?!

I keep staring at this beefy, red man driving like a lunatic, taking turns fast, dodging fucking trees growing in the middle of the road so suddenly that I'm white-knuckling the door handle.

"You haven't answered my question. Who are you? And don't bullshit me with your friend story." Not that Cain wouldn't have friends, but I doubt he'd trust someone he hadn't seen in years to track me down. "Why isn't Cain with you? For all I know, you're one of Lucifer's lackeys."

"He's searching for you, and we split up to cover more ground. Lucifer is a fucking bastard. He killed my wife, so I can promise you that I have nothing but loathing hatred for the demon." He growls as he turns left and takes us farther from the compound. "I tracked you down here because this is one of his homes where he takes pleasure in torturing anyone who crosses him."

"Well, sorry if I don't believe you. Let me out

now!" I shout. "Or would you prefer to personally meet my shadow?"

I'm certain I hear him snarl under his breath, then suddenly the entire car comes to an abrupt stop. The motion throws me forward and I smack face-first into the back of the passenger seat.

I groan and push back. "Goddammit, warn a girl first." I rub my nose, convinced I'm bleeding, but luckily I'm not.

"You want to threaten me, then get out, go!" He hits a button on his dashboard and my door swings open on its own. "Find your way back to Cain on your own. But keep in mind, Lucifer will be sending every guard he has to search for you, and I'm talking flying guards, too. Then, if you manage to somehow outsmart him, the local demons will come after you. There are creatures roaming the streets, desperate for a feed." His eyes glint, and a forked tongue slips out from his mouth, licking his lips like somehow the idea excites him.

Everyone here is so depraved.

I tremble and stare outside, the heat pouring over me like a furnace, burning my nostrils with each breath. There are no homes in this area, only block buildings with black charred trees bare of leaves everywhere, roots having broken out of the ground. It's almost like a scene out of a zombie movie at the end of the world.

Going out there on foot alone has me tense... but it's also suicide. Even I have to admit that, even though I'd like nothing more than to prove this cocky demon wrong.

When I don't move, he says, "My name is Bolgaun, and you must know that a demon giving you their name gives you power over them."

I recall one of the guys telling me that...or maybe I'd seen it in a movie, but regardless, it doesn't instill confidence in me. My suspicions remain because I struggle with coincidences, and him being in the right spot just as I ran from the alarm that went off in the compound is a bit too much. Yet, a part of me wants to believe him, and that Cain does have all his contacts roaming Hell for me.

His dark gaze studies me then settles on Cain's ring on my finger. It leaves me uneasy.

"Cain and I grew up together," he tells me. "Lucifer has always been a prick to everyone, so Cain spent a lot of time hunting in the nearby woods. Sometimes I joined him, just to get away from the reality of my life. This one time Lucifer sent his guards after me for daring to speak ill about him in public, Cain fought the guards and let me hide in his home until Lucifer cooled down. If he hadn't, I'd be sentenced to hundreds of years in the prisons down in the pits. So, I owe him."

I square my shoulders, unsure how much I should believe. So, I state curtly, "Cain wouldn't tell you about my shadow."

The corner of his mouth curls upward, and I half expect him to reveal the truth of who he is, as though I'd caught him out. "He didn't have to. Lucifer put a target on your back to all the hunters and assassins in Hell before he found you, giving details on your shadow. All for a massive reward of souls."

My hopes of keeping low key are completely shattered. It shouldn't surprise me that Lucifer outed me once we escaped his clutches at The Ring. Though, dread fills me when I start to wonder if this red demon has any intention of being the hero for Lucifer.

"So, what are you doing?" he asks.

I study the strong man, whose fingers are tapping his impatience on the steering wheel. We did just escape from Lucifer, so that explains his urgency to get moving. Going through all my options, along with not remembering Lucifer ever mentioning this demon, I decide in the end that I am safer with him…mostly because I have Sayah if crap goes sideways.

So, I reach over to pull my door shut, when I notice half a dozen black creatures with six legs, the size of German Shepherds and sporting fangs watching me from feet away. I startle at the sight since I hadn't even seen these creatures sneak up on me. And here I was with my door gaping open for the attack.

Rapidly, I grab the door and slam it shut, my heart in my throat. Shit! Had Bolgaun seen them but didn't warn me? I look out of the window as they pace nearby, then two of them get into a fight.

Damn hell mutts. Damn demons. I hate everything in this place.

"Assuming Cain's castle is the best place to deliver you?" he asks, drawing my attention to him as we start moving again. He speaks so nonchalantly when I could have just become demon dog chow. "Like I said, he came to my home so I'm not even sure if he'll be there waiting for you."

Bolgaun looks at me through the rearview

mirror, waiting for my confirmation. "I don't know where he is, but I can sense the direction, so keep driving and I'll tell you which direction to turn."

His gaze narrows. "Okay."

The pull in my body sweeps right. "Go right," I say, knowing that's not a great way to travel seeing there are no right hand turns.

But Bolgaun abruptly swings in that direction, tearing down someone's fence as he zooms past their stone house and yard.

I jostle about in the backseat, madly tapping for a seat belt, only to find there are none in this car. We're now on a road again, and the sensation drawing me to my men seems settled in this direction.

"Keep going straight," I confirm.

We fall silent as he drives like a maniac past demons and skeletons in his path, making me feel as though we're in a race car and he's trying his best to hit everything he passes.

After all the stuff I've been through with Lucifer, I honestly did not see this coming. I settle in close to the door, my pulse still shuddering, and I stare outside as we pass through Hell. Part of me always imagined this world burning, with flames and terrifying monsters everywhere, yet right now it looks like a deserted dystopian setting. Dried vegetation, stone structures, dark mountains surrounding us, and a sky that looks like it's on fire. No one is around, either.

Yet, they have roads and demons who live in homes. That's not what I expected at all.

I can't judge how long we've been driving, or if we're going in circles based on my instructions. There are no clocks in the car…the dashboard is completely black with no indication of how fast you're going, gas level, nothing.

When we finally roll down a street with only one massive mansion I recognize right away. It's Valdim's, where we came for dinner before Lucifer and his guards attacked. "That's it." I sit upright, my gaze scouring the front for any sign of my men. Unlike the last time I was here, the huge building now has cracks running down the walls like the structure is about to collapse any moment now.

The front yard is as dead as his burnt lawn, and I pray Cain is here, or at least one of the other men, because everything about Bolgaun makes me uneasy.

Once we come to a complete stop, the bond

between us pulls me to the mansion. A creepy black thing, but if Cain's there I don't care.

Pushing open the door, I turn to Bolgaun. "Thanks for the lift. I'll be sure to let Cain know of your help."

I take quick steps through the open gates when the bang of the car door sounds behind me. Looking back, Bolgaun is coming in my direction, and I pause.

"What are you doing?"

"It'd be rude of me not to deliver you personally," he mutters. "Plus, Cain mentioned something about maybe helping him with another project." The red demon arches an eyebrow, and he towers over me upon approach. He's at least twice my width, and my whole body tenses.

"Maybe I should see if he's even here first, and I'll let him know." Just something about this demon is giving me the wrong vibes, and I'm not the trusting kind when it comes to strangers in Hell.

He shrugs. "You have little faith in someone who just saved your ass."

I narrow my gaze at him. "Let's not pretend you know me or are my friend."

Something flares behind his eyes, but the chance for him to respond is stolen when he glances up at something over my shoulder. That's when I hear the creak of the front door.

"Aria!" Cain gasps.

I twist around, and I start to cry out his name but Bolgaun grabs my arm, his grip squeezing hard. I struggle to break free and turn on him. "Let me go!"

"Bolgaun," Cain growls his name, and it's not friendly in the slightest. These two aren't friends, are they? He lied to me, and I bought it like an idiot!

I stomp my heel into his foot, which is just enough for his grip to loosen, and I wrench myself from his hold.

Throwing myself to Cain's side, his demon bursts forth—wings, dark veins beneath his skin, and black eyes.

"Did he hurt you?" he asks me as I stand pressed to his side.

I shake my head.

Bolgaun's upper lip peels back over fangs, and he puffs out his chest, smirking.

"What the fuck are you doing here?" Cain barks as he pushes me to stand behind him.

"He said he was your friend," I say, feeling guilty that I fell for his lies and brought him here.

"He's Lucifer's personal assassin," Dorian announces, making an appearance out of the castle. He steps up alongside us, as do Elias, Maverick, Torryn, and Nix

Assassin? My blood turns cold, and my stomach does that thing where it hurts really bad because I might have fucked up.

A flash of something crosses Bolgaun's face… It almost looks like hesitation. Did he only expect to find Cain, not his whole crew? His lie is so transparent now and I want to kick myself for not noticing earlier.

So, what did he want? To capture us both, then become the big hero to his boss?

Bastard!

He sneers, his gaze narrows and never looks away from us as he retreats.

"Four against one. Sounds like my kind of odds." Maverick cracks his neck, fists raised. "It's long overdue that Bolgaun got his just desserts." He glances over to me. "Did I say that correctly? Trying to use more human terms." He winks at me, and I just don't have it in me to smile or react with anything but dread right now.

"Why is this scumbag here?" Elias spits.

"Fucking filth!" Dorian booms.

"Dorian," the assassin growls. "You are nothing to me and Lucifer. Dirt under our boots. Just like your parents were, before Lucifer eliminated them."

The news strikes me right in the chest.

"What the fuck!" In a heartbeat, Dorian roars and hurls himself at Bolgaun. *Shit*...Did Dorian not know what Lucifer had done?

Oh shit!

The two of them hit the ground near the enormous metal gates, coming together in a ferocious clash and rolling across the ground.

The rest of us head toward them, though I mostly stumbled there.

Maverick and Elias do not pause, just leap into battle. Cain places his hand on my arm to keep me back. But I'm shaking with anger at being tricked.

The others have kicked up so much dirt it conceals them. The snarls are deafening, and I swallow hard at the viciousness. Movement is all I see, faces here and there filled with hate and unleashing terrifying growls.

Revulsion flares in my belly at what Dorian must be feeling.

I stare at the fight, my legs refusing to work, and I suck in jagged breaths.

"Go inside," Cain commands. "I don't want you to see this." The darkness beneath his words worries me.

"I'm not running away. My life is with you, and that means embracing Hell. I'm no longer the shy girl you first met."

He half grins, turning his attention back to the fight. "I would disagree. You have never been a shy girl."

Bolgaun is suddenly thrown across the ground, skidding and coming to a halt right before Cain's feet. He's slumped on his side, bleeding, clothes torn and bloody. A blade sticks out of his back, too. *Ouch*.

"Beg," Elias howls, emerging from the plume of dust. "And maybe Cain will show you mercy."

"Fuck that. Did he and Lucifer show mercy to my parents?" Dorian points out, heaving and gasping for air. He's shaking, his jawline clenched tight.

My hands clench, fisting them as I watch the agony flare across Dorian's face. I hear the grief in his words. I want to drag him into my arms, to tell him I love him and he'll never be alone again. But I'm also no fool and know that nothing could ever eradicate the heart-wrenching agony of losing his parents.

With the jumble of emotions tearing me, anger also surges, and a nerve dances in my temple with how furious I am at Lucifer and all he's done.

Bolgaun cranks his head up, blood dripping from his chin, and grins, revealing bloody teeth. While part of me wants him to suffer, to take a pound of flesh from him for each death he's caused, it's just not enough. He deserves an eternity of torture. To scream, to suffer, to cry for help just as his victims had. To understand the agony of what Dorian must have gone through…is going through.

"Fuck you." He spits blood at Cain's feet, and I glare at him. "Lucifer is the one true king."

Just then, Dorian hammers a fist to the back of his head so hard, I hear the crack of bone breaking. "Shut the fuck up!"

The asshole drops to the ground, unconscious.

"He needs to die. We need the angel blade, now," Dorian demands. He's shaking violently and wearing a sheen of sweat over his face. Under the harsh, fiery sky of Hell, Dorian has gone pale, all the blood drained from his face.

"They killed my parents," he says, his words

barely audible while tears well in his eyes. "Lucifer butchered my parents and all this time I had no clue." His eyes glint and his shoulders tremble. My eyes prick seeing him this way. So lost, so angry, so heartbroken.

My heart clenches hard, and I can't take another breath.

Cain releases me, and he pulls Dorian into a strong embrace. Elias is there, too, hugging them.

I'm mesmerized. The three of them have gone through so many devastating ordeals together, suffering and being abandoned. Yet, they stuck together through all the shit.

I wipe away the single tear that slides down my cheek. Maverick is at my side and wraps an arm around my waist, both of us watching. There's no smartass comment from him, and I hear him swallow hard, like this pains him as much as the rest of us.

No one speaks for a long pause, all the while I choke back my own tears.

Dorian emerges from his hug, and I can't stop myself. I run to him. He takes me into his arms, and I hug him hard. I finally let my tears fall for him.

After a short moment, he says, "I'll be alright, gorgeous. But thank you."

I wipe my eyes, drawing back from him, and turn to the rest of the guys. My three demons stand across from us, looking as pissed off as me.

Between us lies Lucifer's assassin, the one responsible, and I side-step him.

"We need to kill Lucifer now. No more waiting," I state. For so long, all I've known is to escape and to fight to stay alive. Now, my stomach trembles, my heart hardens as I stand tall. My thoughts flood with the reality that the only way we'll survive is by eradicating the evil darkening our world.

Cain nods, his mouth opening with words that never come.

It's as if someone hit the slow-motion button on my world.

Bolgaun surges up onto his feet like a missile, gripping a blade in his hand despite the one still in his back.

The bastard is flying at me.

Large eyes and a brutal expression are all I see.

The men scream around me, their movements erratic.

Bolgaun's shadow falls over me, the blade glinting in the light, coming straight for my face.

In that heartbeat, I swear my life flashes before my eyes. Each image filled with my demons, with all the times they made me laugh, brought me to orgasm, and showed me how much they loved me. All things I'm not ready to lose…

My body tingles, and in that exact same moment, as the blade arches down toward me, I raise my hands to block him and Sayah zips out of me.

Her black shadow gushes out, engulfing Bolgaun instantly.

One second, the blade is flying at my face, the next, a wall of darkness blots out the light.

Someone grabs me from behind, strong arms around my middle, and wrenches me away. I'm off my feet, Cain whipping me as far from the attack as possible.

But my gaze never leaves Sayah, who snaps around Bolgaun. The last thing I hear are his gurgled cries before she shrinks in on herself until she's a flat shadow on the ground.

Sayah breaks away and withdraws back into me.

My mouth falls open.

Bolgaun is gone. Where he'd been standing seconds earlier, now only two blades lay on the ground.

"Oh, fuck!" I murmur.

"She ate him!" Maverick blurts. "She fucking ate him!"

20

DORIAN

*D*eath doesn't exist in Hell. Not without an angel blade.

Healing is slow for those souls condemned here—it prolongs the suffering, since this is Hell after all. But we all just witnessed Bolgaun die like the rest of the Nightwalkers and the hellhounds and imps. He was swallowed up by Sayah, gone into oblivion.

It was scary as shit when we were on Earth, but when the magnitude of what just happened hits, it's even more terrifying.

Aria's powers are stronger than we imagined. She can *kill* where no one else can. Not even Lucifer by his own hand, and that means she is more powerful than him.

We all stare at her in stunned disbelief, and my mind still whirls with everything that just happened. I can hardly keep up.

Somehow, my gorgeous girl escaped Lucifer by herself. We had even called in Torryn and Nix, and were about to fast-track our plans to storm Lucifer's castle, but she hadn't even needed us to save her. Her and Sayah had gotten out of there on their own. Unfortunately, Bolgaun had tracked her down, but fortunately, he was also a greedy arrogant asshole who thought he could nab both Cain and Aria at the same time for Lucifer, and it was that mistake that ended him.

Sure, me and Elias were a given, but he didn't count on Cain to have recruited Nix, Maverick, and Torryn to his side. Or that the leviathan creature Aria was harboring inside her was capable of...well, *that*.

I'm glad he's dead. Red bastard didn't deserve such a quick death, but at least he's dead. Bolgaun had always been in competition with me and my family, since we were in the same trade. He especially didn't like it when my father sliced off his horns during a fight and mounted them on top of our fireplace, like a trophy. He'd been trying to take us out ever since. So, do I believe him when he said he had delivered my parents personally to Lucifer to be killed because of my allegiance to Cain? Yes. I do. The sick twisted smile he wore when he'd delivered the news said it all.

And why do I care if my family is gone? I'm asking myself that question over and over, but honestly, I don't have the answer to it. When I refused to carry out their wishes and become bounty hunters like them, they disowned me. Hadn't spoken to me in centuries for it, and I had vowed I hated them. I was just fine living my eternal damned life without them.

Yet, here I am, grief and fury lashing through my chest, knowing they're dead—truly dead— because of me.

Sayah definitely delivered him a kindness by finishing him off easy, something he didn't deserve at all.

When the silence and the weight of my parents' deaths are too much for me to stand anymore, I turn, pushing past Torryn, Elias, and Nix, and head back to Val's bunker.

"Dorian…" I hear Elias call out in worry, but I don't hesitate. I need to be alone.

No one follows me as I enter Val's mansion, over the debris, the fissures running across his rooms, many with lava. Blood splatters stain the wall and there are broken marble guards all over the place.

I don't give a fuck about how destroyed his home is, seeing as demons all have multiple mansions and castles in Hell. Plus, he has a bunker.

The curtain of magma remains parted in his house just as when he'd summoned it. I push into its darkness and step forward. Instantly, a swoosh of hot air blows in my face, then the darkness fades, replaced by a faint blinking light from several candles in a chandelier.

It still amazes me that Val's definition of a bunker isn't a small room to hide out in until all is safe to reemerge. Nope, for him, it must mean hiding with all the creature comforts and in luxury. The bunker even has a full bathroom, complete with a golden-claw-footed tub.

The room is extensive, adorned with several leather sofas, a very well stocked bar against the back wall, and even a piano for entertainment. I try not to overthink it because, in truth, I don't care.

I stroll through the room and into one of two hallways, leading me to a bedroom that looks unused. I reach for the door, only to find there isn't one. I huff. Of course not.

I run a hand through my hair and just slump on the edge of the king-sized bed.

My mind is running rampant over Bolgaun's words. The enjoyment in his voice destroyed me. My arms tremble and I lean forward, elbows pressed into my thighs, my head in my hands.

It's been so long since I had anything to do with my parents, and yet the news is like someone had wrenched open the old wounds. Pain that I'd worked on forgetting.

They rejected my decision to not join their bounty hunter business. They rejected me from the family as a result. Disowned me. It was bullshit and I hated them for a long time. Still do...but now, I feel regret and it's shredding my heart.

Fuck!

I don't know how long I stay lying on my back, the lights switched off. Only the glow from the main room glinting in the doorway.

When the soft tap of footsteps approaches, I don't look up. No need to when I know who it is. Demons walk with heavy footfalls, making their presence known. But not her.

"Are you sleeping?" Aria whispers.

"No." I frown, even if she can't see it, and push myself up, throwing my legs over the edge.

"You sound croaky like you *were* sleeping," she teases, with that sing-song voice of hers. I can't help but grin, even if it does feel strained.

"Are you going to join me, or are we having a conversation from across the room?" I ask, tapping the bed, motioning for her to come on over.

She strolls through the dark and flops down beside me, then she takes my hand in hers, and silence stretches between us. Her hair is wet and slicked back, like she's just taken a shower. She's wearing a loose black tee that looks too big for her, and it hangs off one shoulder where her cuts have been bandaged. The one on her cheek is red and slightly puffy.

"I'm fucking furious at myself for not getting to you before Lucifer hurt you. But I'm going to murder him." I tense and hold her hand, hating how fucked up things had become.

"I survived," she answers, putting on a brave smile, which I adore. "But I may get to him first because he's a raging lunatic. And there was nothing you could do. We are on his turf. I was just fortunate that I passed out and he left me alone. Guess monsters like him only enjoy torturing if they can hear their victim's screams," she says, with a lopsided grin.

My heart constricts and I move to embrace her, taking her into my arms. Part of me wants to somehow push her inside of me where I can keep her safe forever. Where no harm can come to her ever again. I admit I'm extremely possessive over her. In a perfect world, she would smile every day.

The quiet between us is a mix of understanding and thoughtfulness, coupled with the kind of tenderness I've become accustomed to from Aria.

She cares for all of us, ready to fight to keep us protected, as much as we look out for her. Her passion radiates from every word and action she takes. And there is no doubt in the way I feel about her.

"How are you with all that stuff about your parents?"

"I'm fine," I finally break the silence, shrugging. "I worry more about you."

"Yeah, I know. You're strong and tough, but I worry about you, too."

I give her a sarcastic stare, and even with only the faint light from the hallway, I see her warming grin.

Running my thumb over the back of her hand

tenderly, I say, "Have you noticed how each one of us has shit going with our parents? Maybe that's why we clicked in the first place. Perhaps when someone's parents royally fuck you up, it makes their kids a certain kind of person. For a long time I thought I was better off without mine, that they made me weak anyway. Now, I'm not so sure. I can't even let go of them after all this time."

"I prefer to think it makes us fighters and we take nothing for granted," she says. "And I don't call it weakness. It lets you appreciate that there is so much more to fight for in life than yourself." Her fingers curl around my hand. "I mean, Sayah just killed a demon. To me, that's what family is."

"Yeah, and even more reason why I shouldn't give a shit that my parents were killed. They booted me out when I needed them the most. But you know what fucks stings now? It's that I feel guilty that they died because of me."

"It's not your fault."

I look down at our fingers interlacing, my chest tightening like someone had stabbed me in the heart and is now twisting it to torture me.

I swallow hard and hate that my eyes sting. "Lucifer killed them to get revenge against me. He punished me for going to Earth with Cain." I shut my eyes, tucking my head low. "So, of course it's because of me."

Aria's hand holds onto mine, making sure I don't pull away. "It's not your fault."

"Yes, it is." I get to my feet, our hands breaking apart. "They died because of me, and I shouldn't give a fuck, yet I feel like crap about it."

Aria's on her feet, coming to me and taking my hand. Her touch is so warm, so comforting. "I hated my parents for a long time, thinking they left me. That I wasn't good enough. Turned out I was half right." Her attempt at a laugh came out strained. "But it doesn't change who I am or what I choose to do with my future."

Her words spin in my mind… I know she's right, but the ache drowning me isn't letting go. Perhaps I just need time to let it all sink in, to accept their fate.

I draw her into my arms, and she wraps me in her embrace. With her tucked against my chest, I kiss the top of her head. Our pasts are just as broken, which makes her so much more special in my eyes.

For so many years, I had assumed that the most I needed out of a partner was sex, and to feed my arousal. After all, my parents showed me that love was a useless emotion. I thought I had it all worked out, except I'd been wrong.

What I have with Aria is the true definition of Heaven, which is so ironic I could laugh.

"We can't control what our families do or what anyone else does either…especially psychopaths like Lucifer. But we choose our decisions and what emotions we decide to take into ourselves."

"That sounds deep," I say, staring at this gorgeous creature who is so much younger than me and is spouting off wisdom I need.

"I read it once somewhere and it stuck with me. It said each of us can choose what emotions we feel by what happens around us. Lucifer made the decision to punish you, and he wears the entire burden. Not you. And your parents pushed you away. That wasn't on you, Dorian. So, don't take his emotions on yourself."

Her words strike a chord and something deep inside me twinges. And maybe she's right. I blink the haunting thoughts as far as they'll go for now, trying my best to focus on something else…something that doesn't feel like I'm drowning.

I gave her a small smile, and she presses up against me, lifting herself up on her tippy toes. Her breasts are crushed between us, and they are all I can focus on at first. Until she fists my shirt and pulls me down to her lips. Our mouths clash, and she kisses me like someone who knows what they want…and what she wants is me.

There's never any doubt in my mind what I want, too. Not when it comes to my gorgeous girl. Arousal awakens within me, it flares, burning through me.

I adore the way she licks my lips. My cock twitches, wanting her.

I grab her by the back of the neck, holding her closer, and kiss her like I mean it, my other hand following a trail to her breast.

She moans against my mouth, and I adore the sounds she makes. But when she winces, I pause and break our kiss.

"Did I hurt you?"

"No. I'm just a bit worse for wear after Lucifer was a dick."

"Come sit down," I say. "I'm being fucking selfish and should be waiting on you hand and foot."

She giggles. "I'll hold you to that once we get out of here. But who said we can't just have a bit of fun now?"

I reach over and push a loose strand of hair back off her face. "You are a temptress."

She laughs, then flashes me a smile that has me caving in.

"I want you naked," I say, reaching for her shirt, my mouth on the curve of her neck.

"How about you go first," she moans as I lick all the way up to her earlobe.

"I'm going to fuck you now, and you're going to scream for me."

She shudders against me, and I make quick work of stripping her from the tee and leggings. Clothes I assumed she found in the bunker.

In moments, she stands naked in front of me and she's the most beautiful thing I've ever seen. Even with bandages across her stomach and over the top of those sexy tits, she still destroys me.

"I promise to be gentle."

"Please don't," she answers quickly, batting her eyes at me while pulling savagely at my shirt.

I drag her to me and kiss her, taking her tongue into my mouth while I rip my clothes off. She tugs at the button and zipper on my pants, and I shuffle out of them, along with my boots.

It's a frantic rush, both of us breathing like

we've just finished racing a marathon. "Tell me to stop anytime I hurt you."

"I'll tell you when you're not hurting me," she teases, then kisses me hungrily. She's beautiful, absolutely spectacular, and everywhere her hands touch, she leaves a streak of fire on my body.

My hands are on her breasts, squeezing them while my thumbs roll over her stiff nipples. Then we're kissing again and I walk her to the wall, our bodies plastered together. She shudders against me like she's been waiting for this, craving it.

My fingers trace the sides of her body and they glide over her ass, then I scoop my girl off her feet. Immediately, her legs curl around me. She's moaning, her nails digging into my shoulders, our kiss all consuming. Her body, her kiss, her taste are all intoxicating, and I can almost feel my soul drawn to her forcefully, and I'd give her my life if she asked for it.

Her gaze fixes on me as I shift and my cock presses to her entrance. She draws in a sharp breath, her body quivering. We kiss and I push all the way into her in a swift motion. Her moans drive me crazy.

"I want every inch of you," I murmur against her mouth. "I will never get enough."

I drive into her, she's jostling on my cock and in my hands. There's pure euphoria over her face, and I feel the heat and wetness over my cock. My world is floating and nothing else matters but us two.

"I love you, Dorian, so much," she breathes the words that wrap around my heart. Words I've wanted to hear for too long.

Pausing, I press my brow to hers, both of us drawing in air rapidly, our chests pumping, her sweet pussy squeezing down on my cock.

"Oh, Aria. I've loved you for a long time. This is everything I've wanted."

She grins at me. "I love hearing you saying it."

I pull and push back into her, coaxing her moans out. "I love the way you grin, I love the way you smell when you're turned on, I love fucking you. I love that you fight back, that your passion for those close to you is vicious, and most of all, I love that you love me."

"Dorian," she whispers. "You're going to make me cry."

Her mouth is soft and she holds the sides of my face, giving me the kind of kiss where I lose myself to her. Even when the world falls apart around us, all I think about is her.

Possessiveness rises through me, as it has always done, and it tears through me, how much I crave to keep her safe.

I fuck her harder now, and she gasps, and gives me those huge heart-in-her-throat gazes. I carry her over to the bed, lay her down, and I follow her body, covering hers.

"Do you want more?" I ask seriously, my hand already moving down between our bodies.

"Please," she begs, those sweet lips and voice ruin me.

I draw out of her and exhale, the tingle at the base of my groin growing. When she raises her head up to take a look, she notices that both my cocks are now alert and so ready.

"Two," I say. "In one hole." I wink at her and rub my finger over her spread pussy. She's drenched and so ready.

"Don't just talk about it," she says, then spreads her legs wider, lifting that gorgeous ass. With my cocks stacked on top of each other, it's easier to grab them together, then push against her opening.

She's gasping for air but doesn't flinch. Fuck me, but it's a tight squeeze...I work my way in slowly, gradually widening her.

Her cries are escalating, her chest heaving for

breath. I look down, absolutely loving the way her pussy is swallowing both my cocks at once. How she greedily sucks on them, seeming to pull me in.

I push all the way in, and her eyes are glazed over, her hands pinching her nipples. "Fuck. I'm going to come so quickly."

A thrill rushes down my back.

"You're mine, gorgeous. All mine. Now scream for me." I rock my hips back and forth into her, hard and fast, giving her everything she desires, reaching deep within her. Spreading her, stretching her. Our bodies rock back and forth.

Her moans escalate while I'm pounding into her.

I growl, my balls tightening, and it's a losing battle. The sensation of her tight pussy is destroying me.

The horny little sounds she makes make me harder and the buildup comes fast.

She suddenly screams, her whole body shuddering. Her pussy clamps down and constricts my cocks. And that sets me off.

I snarl, buried deep inside her, spilling my seed. We're both sweating, gasping for air, our voices thundering through the room.

Losing track of how long we float on ecstasy,

when I finally look down at Aria, she's breathing heavily and staring at me with a delicious grin.

"Damn, this whole time we could have been having sex with both your cocks inside me? Why have you been holding out on me?"

I laugh and draw out of her, the leak of my cum seeping from those plump pussy lips. "Let me clean you up." I head out, cross the hallway and grab a towel from the bathroom. On the way I notice the bright light of the main room at the end of the hallway where I see the back of Elias, and there are others there with him. Waiting for us, no doubt.

Back in the bedroom, Aria is spread and divine. I wipe the mess from her sweet pussy and her thighs, then toss the towel aside. Taking her hands into mine, I draw her to her feet.

"Thank you," she says. "It was everything I needed."

"I wish I could drag you into my arms and have you fall asleep there, but I think the others are waiting for us now."

"I know." She hugs me tight and I embrace her, kissing the top of her brow. "My stomach is so antsy. Is this how it feels before big battles?"

"They say being nervous before a fight gives you an advantage."

"Fuck, I hope so," she answers and breaks away from my arms. There's a bittersweet sensation rolling over me. How, after such a perfect moment, the last thing I want is to dive into battle. Which says a lot for me. I'd never back away from a fight...

The hum of voices dances in from the main room of the bunker.

Aria's looking at her torn shirt. "Give me a sec to grab some clothes from the other room. There's a wardrobe with all kinds of clothes."

She vanishes down the hallway and I get dressed, then run my hands through my hair, needing to get my head in the game.

This is the battle of all battles. And we have to win.

It isn't long before Aria reappears outside the room dressed in all black. "You coming?"

She takes the lead and I'm close on her heels, heading through the dimly lit hallway, soon emerging in the main room of the bunker.

Six sets of eyes are on us instantly... And with the wicked grins on the faces of Val, Nix, and Torryn, I'm going to say they've all been privy to all the sounds from the bedroom.

Aria moves to the bar without a care in the world, grabbing herself water from a pitcher.

"So, what's the plan?" I ask, wanting their attention on me, not on her.

"Well, we're ready to head out," Cain answers in a clipped tone. "We've just been waiting for you two."

"Was thinking," Maverick pipes in. "I'm happy to give you some pointers on how to make it last longer in the bedroom. I'm pretty sure I calculated less than three minutes."

Nix and Torryn burst out laughing.

"Fuck off," I spit, not giving a shit in all honesty.

Elias is howling in laughter, while Cain is up on his feet and strolls over to Aria by the bar, his hand on her back. The issue has nothing to do with what we did, but that each man in this room wishes they'd been in my shoes.

"Well, unless all you limp dicks are gonna sit around and compare notes on how long you last during sex, I'm with Cain. It's time to kick ass," I declare.

Elias stands tall and joins me, while Cain has Aria in his hand, drawing her toward the exit. There's defiance and determination crossing her face when she looks back, and I love how strong she is. Hell, Sayah killed a demon, so maybe we stand a greater chance against Lucifer than any of us realize.

Torryn and Nix stroll out too. I look back to find Val behind his bar, mixing himself a drink.

"Calming last minute nerves?" I ask, drawing Cain's attention as well.

Val shrugs. "I'm sitting this out, taking neutral ground."

Fire rises through me instantly. "You're not taking sides? What the fuck, man?"

His gaze lowers to his drink and he shrugs nonchalantly, which irks me.

"Let's leave," Cain growls, scowling at his brother.

We make our way out, one man down. I had just assumed he'd join the fight, which was my mistake. It shouldn't surprise me that Val chose the gutless way out.

"This day will go down in history when we defeat Lucifer," Maverick states, drawing my attention. "Especially since we have Aria's shadow on our side."

Everyone turns to Aria, who doesn't shy away, but holds her head high. "What Sayah did to Bolgaun has never happened before, and I am definitely feeling the pressure right now to perform."

Maverick chuckles, eyeing me. Bastard.

"This fight isn't just on your shoulders," Cain answers confidently, his arm still wrapped around her waist. "It weighs just as heavily on each one of us. We all have reasons to want Lucifer gone. Just as we all have a lot to lose if we don't win."

Those last words whip through my mind. We are risking our lives, but we've come to the end of the line. Time has run out, and either we let Lucifer come for us, or we take him out first.

We all march out of the bunker because war waits with the lord of Hell.

And today, one way or another, the end will come for someone.

I just pray that the swift call of death doesn't visit us.

21

CAIN

This is it. This is what I've—*we've*—been waiting for.

Everything's come down to this.

Today, my father will fall.

We stand in front of Lucifer's castle gates. As Hell's biggest and center feature, it looms over his mighty kingdom with high peaks and stone walls. Black smoke billows from the underground crematorium, where Father likes to set fire to his victims that can never die. It's running double-time today, the pungent scent of burning flesh and singed hair poisoning the air.

The last time I was here, things went to shit fast. I was sure I'd let everyone down for convincing them to be a part of my plans to overtake my father and then failing. I blamed myself for decades for getting Elias and Dorian banished and stuck with me on the living plane.

And here we are again.

But I've grown a lot since then. I've learned that I didn't need Hell or my father's stupid crown to be someone. Elias, Dorian, and I—we built ourselves up from nothing. Made an empire from the ashes and became kings among the living. And because of Aria, I discovered what love is, how powerful and consuming it can be, and those are things I'd never thought possible for a demon.

I'm not the same sin demon I was when I left here.

I'm stronger. Wiser. Better all around.

I look to my left. There's Aria, dressed for the fight in ripped jeans and a tank top, a sword in her hand. I wish with everything I didn't have to include her in the upcoming danger, but she's proven time and time again to be able to hold her own in a fight. And with Sayah, I know she's protected.

Beside her is Dorian, my oldest friend. Like the rest of us, his demon is out and his gaze is locked ahead of us. Determination crinkles his brow, and the tattooed runes on his chest glow bright as his power heightens.

On my right, there's Elias as his hellhound—a massive black beast with lips curled over fangs and hackles up. My brother, Maverick, spins his daggers expertly in his hands on the other side of him. He glances over at me and gives me a stiff nod. He knows what lies ahead, and this time he's not going to run. He's going to fight at my side.

I turn to see the others who've chosen to join us. In his demon form, Torryn is an impressive sight. He's a ten-foot monster—part man, part bull, with long horns, a stretched snout, and hooved feet. Behind him are his legion of minions. Like with Lucifer and his marble soldiers, Torryn can call on and command hundreds of damned souls and make himself an army. It's one of the unique sin demon gifts he was given and, most importantly, it allows our numbers to rival Father's.

Even though Nix's power to shapeshift is more on the defensive side, he's still one hell of a fighter. Maverick even convinced him to use one of the weapons in his collection. He picked a battle axe.

Of course, I wish my other brothers were here. Lorcan, Raziel, and Valdim. I wish they had seen that we all have a place in this battle, but I know now that their loyalties lie only with themselves.

And when this is over and we win, they're going to have to beg for mercy.

Everyone is waiting for my word. They're looking to me for guidance, and it's time for me to be the leader they need me to be.

It's time to give Lucifer hell.

My wings whip out, spreading wide, and the darkness inside me roars to life. Hellfire blazes in my fists. *"Donec ipsum finem!"*

Until the very end.

And with that, we charge.

Torryn's thunderous bellow shakes the ground. Maverick and I take to the sky, while everyone on the ground rushes toward the castle. With one swing of his arm, Torryn breaks the magical and non-magical locks holding the gate closed and his legion of tortured souls spill into the overgrown courtyard.

Lucifer's castle is surrounded by vine-like thorn bushes, with points as sharp as a surgical scalpel, and they crawl all over the ground, walk-way, and up the sides of the monstrous building. Hovering above, I spot Aria struggling to avoid the branches. A thorn catches her and slices across her arm. She gasps, leaping back, and is about to stumble into another patch when Elias appears and, mid-stride, throws her onto his back. As they head toward the front door, she grips onto his fur and ducks her head down low.

"Cain!" Maverick shouts, and when I look his way, I see he's pointing at the stones on Lucifer's castle. And they're shaking, quivering before our eyes.

What the fu—

Suddenly, the stone-men pop out of the walls—dozens of them—and leap onto the ground below.

"Watch out!" Maverick shouts.

The stone soldiers swing their weapons, taking out many of Torryn's men at one time.

Shit.

Maverick flies at the wall, knives slicing the air, and when I realize another wave of stone guards are about to come to life, I throw a blast of hellfire their way. But it only sends them back instead of stopping them. The second my fire extinguishes, they push themselves off the wall and leap into the battle, now glowing orange-red and blazing hot.

Well, that's not going to work. I've only made them more dangerous.

When the next group of guards start to wiggle

their way out of stone, I throw my body into one, smashing it to rubble.

"Ah, brute force. Sometimes that's the best way," Maverick says, sheathing his daggers, which hadn't been making much progress against solid rock, and follows in my method. We slam ourselves into the wall over and over, and it isn't long before numbing pain shoots up and down my arm.

As if we're on the same mental wavelength, Maverick yells, "We can't keep this up forever. They won't stop coming."

He's right, and I know it. We're just wasting time.

Flying backward, I glance at the castle turret. There's a window at the very top. We can use it to get in and weed Lucifer out from the inside, while Torryn and Nix try to get through those doors. We'll surround him.

"Dorian! Elias!" I shout. Both their heads perk up to find me hovering above them. I point to the window to leave our new plan unspoken but clear. It doesn't need to be said; we've fought alongside each other enough to know how we each fight.

With Aria still on Elias's back, the three of them

round the castle and do all they can to get past the soldiers and the prickly vines.

I turn to Maverick. "We need to help them get up here."

He nods, understanding, and we swoop lower.

Elias shifts rapidly, and Aria drops to her feet. Without much effort, I scoop her into my arms and beat my wings against the air to gain altitude again, while Maverick tries the same for Elias. His takeoff's a bit more wobbly because of Elias's size, and he curses as he struggles to get them higher in the air.

"Shit, man. You need to go on a diet or something," he grumbles. "You're too fucking heavy."

"Shut the fuck up," he growls back. "It's 'cause I eat baby demons like you for breakfast."

Dorian chuckles as he scales the side of the castle like an overgrown primate with the grace and pose of a feline. Holding Aria tight, we swing toward the window. Dorian beats us there and punches through the glass, swiping away the rest of it so that I can help Aria inside without injury. Once she's in, I climb in next only to hear a loud thud and Elias cursing wildly. A second later, Elias is thrown through the window and tumbles across the dusty floor. He lands with his naked ass in the air.

Maverick slides in next, his wings folding into back. "Next time, you get the gorilla and I get the girl."

"You little shit." Elias stands and goes toward Maverick, but Dorian presses a hand to his chest.

"Focus, King Kong. Focus," he teases.

My gaze roams the room. It looks like we've ended up in some forgotten attic space. There are abandoned furniture pieces covered in white cloth, a broken chandelier, and a grand piano from what I can see. When I find Aria, she already has her hand out, the ominous orangey-yellow light sparkling around it. At her feet, Sayah's dark tentacle wiggles across the floor and down the spiral staircase.

How very clever of her. Having Sayah check for danger is the safest way to go on from here.

Outside, the sound of fighting intensifies, and the walls around us quake as more of Lucifer's stone soldiers manifest and join the battle.

The only way to get them to stop is by defeating Lucifer—whatever that entails. Killing him or capturing him and having him renounce his hold on Hell. We are hoping for the later, but knowing the devil, we're expecting the former.

When Sayah zips back into the room and back into Aria, her power's light dims. She glances at all of us. "She says it's safer for us to go down the west wing. And Lucifer is in the throne room."

"Of course, he is," Maverick says with a dramatic roll of his eyes. "He's waiting for us there. Probably has traps set up for us."

"Probably. But what other choice do we have?" Dorian asks.

"Actually…" Maverick starts, an idea forming, "the element of surprise may still be on our side." He makes a beeline for the broken window and unfurls his wings again.

"Where the heck are you going?" Elias barks angrily.

Hopping on the ledge, Maverick looks back at us. "Trust me on this, okay?"

Elias growls, "Trust you? What the fuck is that supposed to—hey!" But Maverick jumps out, cutting him off mid-sentence. His gaze whips to me. "What the fuck? He just bailed on us."

"He did say he has a plan," Aria chimes in.

"It would've been nice for him to let us in on it, don't you think? Our asses are on the line here."

I don't know what my brother's intentions are, but fleeing or not, I agree with Elias. He should've told us of his plans.

I guess Maverick still has some work to do when it comes to being on a team. But I can't worry about him now. I can only hope that whatever he's doing, it doesn't get him or any of us killed.

"We go on without him," I tell everyone else. "Our objective hasn't changed."

Dorian nods. "Take out Lucifer. Don't get killed. Got it."

I turn to Aria. "Can Sayah lead the way?"

As if hearing me, her shadow elongates and spreads across the stairwell.

"I'll take that as a yes, then," I say, and together we follow Sayah's shifting form to the lower levels.

Besides the commotion raging outside, every floor we pass is deadly silent. No marble guards, no screams of torture or ecstasy…all the familiar things I have come to expect when visiting his home. This time, there's no movement, no sounds, nothing.

It's looking more and more like Maverick's mention of a trap awaiting us is right.

Sayah stops suddenly at the very bottom of the steps, making us all halt. We wait for Aria to translate the Leviathan's thoughts to us.

"Lucifer's through there, across the foyer, in the throne room," she whispers so low she barely makes any sound at all. "He's alone."

"Bullshit," Elias replies, only to be shushed by Dorian.

Aria shrugs. "That's what she says."

My first thought is that it's impossible—his guards must be waiting in the walls for his command—but then I realize this must be a test of some kind. A power play to show us that he isn't afraid and that he can squash our coup for a second time without much effort at all.

It's something I would do if I was in his shoes, and what does that say? It's his pride getting in the way of logic.

I should know. I'm made from that part of him.

But unlike him, I've evolved past that baser part of myself. We can use his ego against him.

"I'm going alone," I say, and pull back my shoulders.

"What?" the three of them snap in unison.

I lower my voice even more. "Listen to me. I know Father. His inflated ego is refusing him to show weakness, so he's pretending that this—all of this—doesn't matter to him. It's nothing but a mere nuisance. A pestering fly he intends to catch and squish."

"Wrap it up Shakespeare," Dorian says and whirls his finger in a winding motion.

"He's playing a game. Don't you see it? One he thinks only he can win. And we need to use it against him."

"I still don't understand why that means you have to sacrifice yourself," Aria answers in a panicked rush, and I know what she's thinking. She's remembering the foot relic's little step into the future, or at least, that's what we think it was.

"I'm just going to talk to him. Distract him. He knows we're coming, but if I can keep him busy long enough, maybe you three can get the angel blade. With it, we'll have the power we need to kill on this plane."

"And what about Sayah?" Dorian asks. "Can't she just…swallow him up too?"

"I don't know." And it's the truth. I don't know the extent of Sayah's powers and what will and will not work against the king of the underworld. "Lucifer's an entirely different animal than

Bolgaun. We don't know what will happen if Sayah faces him. Or what it'll do to Aria."

That is my main concern, of course. Will consuming the most evil being in all of existence affect my beloved in a negative way? I don't want to find out if we don't have to.

"We try to dethrone him without Sayah at first, just in case using her hurts Aria. But if it comes to it, then we let her do what she must."

Everyone nods in agreement.

"I am trusting Sayah to keep Aria safe from any harm," I say carefully, knowing the creature in her is listening, too. "Am I right?"

Aria sighs. "She's got the message."

"Good." My gaze passes over all of them one last time, and my chest clenches with fear. They mean so much to me. I love them each in their own way, which is something I once thought I could never feel for another being, let alone three. We've been through a great deal together, and I hope that by the end of the night, I don't have to mourn the loss of any of them.

Then, retracting my demon and trying to rebutton what's left of my shirt, I leave Elias, Dorian, and Aria behind and walk into the throne room alone.

I find him sitting on his high-backed throne, twirling his unholy crown of bones and gems around his two fingers. As suspected, he's not surprised to see me. His dark eyes find me and a tight-lipped smile curls on his face.

"My first born," he purrs. "How nice of you to give your old father a visit while in the neighborhood."

"You know why I'm here," I say, not wanting to play into his games.

"I do." He jumps to his feet. He tosses the crown onto the chair and hops down the steps. "And I have to say, I'm a bit disappointed. Not surprised, just disappointed."

I watch as he walks around the room, circling me like a predator. His eyes flash red, the evil creature within him wanting to come out to play.

"So, what now, son? You try and kill me again? Take my throne? Hell? Become king?"

"I don't want the throne for myself," I reply. "I just want you off it, so either you come with me willingly, renounce your claim to Hell, and live out the rest of eternity in a cell somewhere, or I will remove you forcefully."

His head snaps back and his laughter booms like a gunshot. "And you honestly think you can do that? You?" He glances around the room. "Where are your little friends? The girl? Aria."

Hearing him just say her name has my temper flaring. And he sees it. He knows how I feel about her, and it only makes him smile wider.

"I expected something like this from your brothers. This weakness. Letting your dick guide you into disaster. It'll be your undoing."

"You know nothing about me."

He stops and rocks back on his heels, looking down at me. "You're right. When I ripped you from my own flesh and bone, I expected you to be just like me. Strong. Powerful. Ruthless. You've done nothing but prove me wrong. You're pathetic."

I clench my jaw and tell myself he's trying to get a rise out of me. That's all.

Unsatisfied with my lack of response, he continues to circle me, his hands clasped behind his back. "Apparently banishing you the last time you tried to dethrone me wasn't enough. You learned nothing."

At the corner of my eye, I see movement in the shadows of a doorway. Aria, Elias, and Dorian? Or more of Lucifer's guards?

My heart beats a little faster.

"I'm going to have to go a little darker with my

punishment." He taps his chin in fake thought. "Something involving the girl, perhaps?"

My thoughts jump to the worst possible scenarios, and my stomach lurches in fear. How could they not? I know Lucifer and the way his deranged brain works. He'll torture me by torturing her. Raping her. Making her suffer while I watch.

My demon shoves forward without my say-so, my hellfire surging to my hands and my wings snapping out from my spine. Whatever was left of my shirt falls to the ground, and my vision sharpens as my eyes go black.

But Lucifer only grins, pleased. "Ah, there you are. Now this fight will be more fun."

Closing his eyes, he rolls his shoulder back and tilts his neck side to side. The muscles underneath his skin shift and move. His body stretches upward, gaining height until he's towering over me. Skin graying, his clothes rip at the seams as every inch of him expands and two horns push from his forehead.

Then, when his eyes snap open again, they're a hellish, fiery red.

22

ARIA

*L*ucifer's real demon form is terrifying. A monster with thick gray skin and black veins lining every inch of it, like Cain's. He's grown two more feet, and with his clothes in shreds on the floor, it's clear his body is rippling with solid muscle. Two horns curl back from his forehead and his eyes are a blazing red.

The true King of Hell.

A shudder runs through me, and any confidence I may have had of us winning this dwindles. We're watching from the shadows of a doorway, waiting for our time to spring into action. It'd be nice to have Torryn, Nix, and Torryn's undead army to help right now, but they're still fighting the stone soldiers outside.

Lucifer grins eerily at Cain, showing off a mouthful of fangs. Then he holds out his hands as if introducing himself for the first time.

"Let's get this over with," he says, the beast's voice much deeper and gravelly than his other form. Then he rushes Cain, and they crash into each other into a blur of fists punching, claws slashing, and wings whipping. Snarls erupt, blood splatters, and it's not long before I turn to Elias and Dorian, unable to watch the fight unfolding.

"We need to go in and help," I say. "We can't let Cain do it all alone."

Elias's heavy hand comes down onto my shoulder. "We will. We need to figure out the best time. When Lucifer is distracted enough, and we can do the most damage."

"Does anyone see the angel blade?" I ask, scanning the room.

Dorian peers around the corner more and curses. "There. On the throne. Under the crown."

That's in the middle of the room, up on the dais, in plain view.

So much for sneaking our way to it.

"How are we handling this?" Elias asks Dorian in a rushed whisper. "Cain won't be able to fight him off for too long alone. Not when he's in this form."

"I'm thinking. I'm thinking!" He hits himself in the forehead. "Cain's usually the one to make the plans."

"Well, considering he's getting sucker punched in the stomach right now by a red-eyed, two-horned gorilla, I'd say he's a little busy."

"Can you two stop?" I snap at them. This bickering definitely isn't what we need right now.

I rub my lips together and try to think of what we can do without getting ourselves or Cain killed.

Sayah wiggles inside me, giving me my answer.

Shit, why hadn't I thought of her before?

"Sayah," I called to her, and she pulls out of me instantly. "Can you grab that blade for us?"

Her ghostly forms spreads across the floor, giving me my answer.

"Quick. Try not to be seen."

She zooms outward toward the throne. As she lifts off the ground, her form begins to solidify, and I can feel the familiar tug of her using my energy to become real. Now that I can control her, it's not as draining as it used to be, but I do grow more tired. Especially when the orange sparks dance along our tether as more power transfers from me to her.

Elias grips my arm to help keep me upright, which I am thankful for. But the moment Sayah pulls out the dagger, Lucifer spins around, finding her there.

I gasp. *Shit!*

His eyes widen at the sight of Sayah, a life-sized shadow with a shifting form holding the angel blade.

"What the—" He follows the dark string linking us, and when his gaze lands on me, Dorian, and Elias hiding in the shadows, his nostrils flare.

Double shit!

Cain tries to use the distraction to his advantage and punches him hard across the face then round-house kicks him. Lucifer stumbles back a few steps and blood leaks from his mouth, but it doesn't do much damage and the next time Cain comes at him, he grabs his fist mid-swing, wrenches it back until bones snap, and then uppercuts him so hard, he flies backward, skidding across the smooth marble floor.

"No!" I shout automatically. My panic causes Sayah to drop the blade and yo-yo back into me so fast, I jerk back into Elias's chest.

Lucifer's eyes are still pinned on us, disbelief and excitement flashes in them. "No way. A Leviathan? She's a Leviathan?" He laughs happily, the terrifying sound grating against my eardrums. "Things are getting interesting now!"

When he trudges our way, Dorian grabs me and pushes me back. "Well, looks like hide and go seek's over. Let's go, Elias!" He and Elias run out and tackle Lucifer at the same time. Cain stands again, shaking off his healing wounds, and joins the tussle. But despite all three of them taking on Lucifer, he's still able to fight them off easily.

Without the angel blade, there's no way to really hurt him.

I withdraw my sword, wondering if I should just burst out of here and make a run for it. Or should I risk Sayah again?

Fuck. Fuck. Fuck.

I can't just stand here and watch the demons fight for their lives.

Boom.

The ground shakes under our feet and the thunder of footsteps pour into the foyer. Seconds later, Torryn's bull-like demon shoves his way into the throne room, taking most of the doorway with him. His zombie soul minions spill in from behind him, followed by Nix.

Lucifer roars, somehow managing to throw Cain, Dorian, and Elias off him. "Spoiled, ungrateful children!" He stomps his foot, and the marble splinters and cracks in every direction under him. The ground shakes again, and the tingle of dark magic caresses my skin.

Suddenly, spots in the walls around us move. Pieces chip away and crack off, forming more of those terrifying marble guards we've fought before.

"Teach my sons a lesson," Lucifer barks, and the guards surge for the demons. They clash, and fighting erupts once again.

Where the fuck is Maverick through all this? I really hope Elias isn't right and he bailed on us. But I can't really worry about him right now. I need to get that blade.

"Alright, Sayah." She slides from me again, taking over my real shadow. "Are you ready for this?"

Her head nods.

"Okay, let's do this." Gripping my sword tighter, I dart out into the chaos.

A marble man's spear swings at me, and I spin, narrowly avoiding it. With a mighty howl, Torryn stampedes across the room, crushing many of them and almost me too. I leap out of the way just in time.

I feel Sayah's warning zip up our connection, and I turn to see two more guards charging at us. Sayah lifts off the ground and overtakes them before their weapons can reach us, swallowing them whole until nothing's left.

"Thanks," I pant. Of course, she doesn't answer, but I know she understands. Another guard appears to my right, and I swing my sword. It hits its shoulder, but the strike does nothing but reverberate up my arm.

Man, these things are hard to break.

I swing again, crossing my sword with its spear, but it overpowers me easily and shoves me back. Falling on my ass, my sword skitters out of my hand and across the floor.

I curse as pain skirts up my back from the hard landing. I don't even have time to see where my weapon went because the spear's tip is pointed at my throat.

I freeze.

Lightning fast, Sayah zips around me and

wraps the guard in her darkness, engulfing it, too. It's there one second, and the next it's not.

As she stands in front of me, waiting for me to get up, I hold up my hand. "Let's call our friends and reduce some of Lucifer's numbers, don't you think?"

I can feel her giddiness through our link, and I waste no time reaching down into myself and awakening our power. Light flares in my palms, the magic tickling me, and soon, the shadows around the room begin to shift and come to life.

Closing my fists, I give them all the silent command to feed. Consume. Destroy.

Like Sayah, they attach themselves to me, using me as their power source, and then dart around the room like mini phantoms. One by one, they pick off the marble guards, moving so fast, they appear as nothing more than a blur.

Perfect. This'll give us a better chance.

A cold hand grabs my arm then and tugs me closer to the wall. It severs my links to the shadows, and, disjointed, they're forced to zap back into their normal places, losing their sentience completely.

Dread seizing me, I'm about to lash out with a

fist when I see it isn't another guard holding me. It's Valdim, Cain's brother.

But what is he doing here?

"I apologize for startling you, but there is only way to end this, and it is with the angel blade," he murmurs.

I nod. *Tell me something I don't know.*

"I thought you wanted to stay out of this fight. Stay neutral," I whisper in a rush.

"Can't a demon change his mind?" He opens his palm. "*Angel blade.*"

There's the familiar tickle of magic washes over me and there's a flash of light. When it diminishes, believe it or not, the angel blade is in Valdim's open hand.

Wow, I almost forgot he could do that. Talk about a handy power. No pun intended there.

He grips the handle. "Transporting something powerful like this, my gift will need to recharge, so we have to—"

From the corner of my eye, there's a flash of silver and he pushes me out of the weapon's path at the last second. I roll roughly across the floor, and when I come up, I see Valdim fighting off a marble guard, the blade no longer in his hand.

Fuck! Where did it go!

I spin and collide with something solid. Peering up, I lock eyes with Lucifer himself, and my breath locks in my chest.

"Hello again, Aria," he says with a fangy smile.

I feel Sayah rushing to leave me again, to protect me, but then there's only pain. It's so sharp and sudden, I don't even register what's happened right away until I glance down and see Lucifer holding the heavenly dagger's handle, its blade embedded in my stomach.

When he yanks it out, I shift backward, clutching my middle and instantly feeling warm blood covering my hands.

The pain is all I can think about. It's fiery, burning, searing, and it steals everything from me. My knees give out, and I fall at Lucifer's feet.

"Such a pity," he says smugly. "I had big plans for us, Aria. Big plans."

Sayah… I call to her internally, but I can't feel her essence within me anywhere. Panic seeps in. *Sayah! Where are you?*

Still, she doesn't respond.

Besides the pain, all I feel is emptiness. Even when she was hiding from me, I knew she was still there, but now, I can't feel her at all.

It's like…she's gone.

Exhaustion weighs heavy on me, and I know I'm losing too much blood. Unable to move, all I can do is glare up at Lucifer, hatred burning in my gaze.

"What-What did you do?" I shout at him. Saying anything is a huge effort, and my head whirls.

"Simple. I rid you of your demon," he says. "And soon, you'll be rid of your life too."

My body begins to shake without my doing, and I know it's from the blood loss and pain. I fight to keep my eyes open. Even when Lucifer raises the angel blade again, like he's about to use it to chop off my head.

Sayah… I search for her again but find nothing. Not a damn thing.

Roaring, Lucifer's arm swings down, and suddenly Cain's there and rams into him with all his strength. The blade clatters to the floor somewhere out of sight as the two wrestle on the floor, tearing into each other and spilling more of the other's blood.

There's a blast of heat to my left and when I look, black flames erupt from the massive fireplace. I keep myself blinking through the pain, knowing that if I let my eyes close for even a second, they will never open again.

Through my blurry vision, I see the outline of a man in the middle of the flames. With so much carnage and chaos happening all around me, no one sees the stranger emerging from the hearth, but when I spot the silvery white hair and boyishly handsome face of Maverick, my heart skips with relief.

So, this had been his plan all along... Use the magical passage he and Lucifer shared.

With daggers in both hands, he bursts from the fireplace, feathered wings out, and sails high above the action. Then he dives straight for Lucifer and Cain who are locked in a fierce battle of their own.

Before Lucifer can turn around, Maverick plunges his knives into shoulders, sending him reeling back and roaring like the monstrous beast he is. Unable to hold on, he's bucked off and lands hard on the marble floor.

Cain uses his chance to spear Lucifer through the chest with his wing's talons, and as he pushes them in deep, Lucifer's eyes widen in shock and pain. Black blood from his own internal wounds stains his teeth and drips down his chin as he screams with all the hatred and rage burning inside him.

For a second, it looks like Lucifer is too weak to stay standing. He sways on his feet and his eyelids droop. But suddenly, he grits his teeth, clutches Cain's wings, and yanks the sharp talons out of him with an annoyed grunt.

The look of terror on Cain's face ices me to the core. A normal man wouldn't have that strength, especially with his injuries. Hell, a normal demon wouldn't either. But Lucifer isn't either of those, is he?

No. He's evil incarnate.

With eyes as black as Cain's, his hand clamps down on his arm and the other grips his wing. Then, while looking him dead in the eye, he twists the leathery appendage hard and tears it right off Cain's back.

My stomach roils as vomit threatens to come up. The sound... The disgusting, fleshy and wretched sound. I'll never forget it. Then comes Cain's screams of agony, of absolute horror as Lucifer carelessly tosses the wing away like it's nothing but an oversized piece of trash.

Unable to bear it, Cain collapses onto his knees,

his demon forced to return and his blood turning crimson as it continues to spill from his wounds.

Lucifer reaches up and pulls out Maverick's daggers from his shoulders without so much as a wince. Chucking them to the side, he whirls on his youngest son next, his gaze shining with vengeance.

"You're fools. All of you!" he spits, stepping closer to Maverick. He scrambles to get away, crawling backward across the floor, but Lucifer keeps coming.

"I brought you into this Hellish world, and I can take you out of it just as fast."

Sayah, I plead with her again in desperation. *Sayah, please. Our demons are in danger. They need our help. Please!*

But I can't feel her at all anymore. There's not even a flicker of her dark presence inside me.

Sayah!

Tears spring to my eyes as the realization finally sinks in.

She's gone. I've lost her. And now I am going to lose my demons too.

Maverick's pain-filled cry has me panicking. Lucifer has stomped on his leg, crushing the bones in his knee. But still determined to get away from his father's wrath, he hauls himself up the steps of the dais.

A tingle of familiarity wiggles through me at the scene.

I can't think too long about it because there's a flash of dark fur and Elias's massive hellhound leaps onto Lucifer's back, clamping his jaws into his neck. Cursing, Lucifer spins, grabs Elias by the scruff, and wrenches him off. Elias's jaws take away a large chunk of his neck, but it doesn't seem to matter. Despite the blood gushing down his back, Lucifer's still able to hurl Elias into a column so hard, it crumbles all around him. As does a part of the ceiling, which rains down chunks of marble.

Dust erupts, cloaking the room in a dense cloud.

"Damn mutts," Lucifer growls.

A scream tears from my throat. I can't see Elias, but I can hear his hound's soft whines from under all the rubble.

For what feels like the millionth time, I try to push myself up, but my body feels too heavy and I am too weak. It was ungodly painful when Lucifer stabbed me through the stomach with the angel blade, but its magic is relentless. Blazing like fire, like it's burning me from the inside out.

Blue light cuts through the dust cloud, and when I see the ghostly glow of Dorian's rune tattoos, I hold my breath. He rushes at Lucifer at full speed, claw-like fingernails aimed for his face, but Lucifer somehow snatches him by the neck.

He lifts him off the ground with one meaty hand, and even though Dorian slashes at his arms desperately, he doesn't let go. Instead, he squeezes his throat hard.

Dorian gasps for air, his eyes bulging from their sockets, and all I can do is scream and cry. Helpless. Completely helpless.

It takes only seconds, but Dorian's body goes limp and Lucifer drops him. He lands in a heap, unmoving. Lifeless.

"No!" The pain in my chest is paralyzing. My world comes crumbling down all around me. Cain, Dorian, Elias, Maverick… And Sayah. I'm going to lose them all.

As if remembering me, Lucifer's head whips my way. His red eyes brighten, and a malicious smile twists his mouth. My heart drops.

He stomps towards me.

Frantically, I search around for a weapon—

something to help protect me from this raging monster coming right at me—but find nothing other than some pieces of broken rock from his fallen marble guards.

To my surprise, Lucifer stops mid-step, nostrils flaring, his face pinching in anger. He spins on his heel.

"No!" he bellows.

That's when I see what he's staring at. Cain's there on the dais, blood painting every inch of him. His one wing is out, the missing one nothing but a gaping hole in his back. Maverick's near the throne, laying on his back, and looking up at his brother, eyes wide in terror.

Oh my god... Recognition slams into me, making my head whirl. I've seen this scene play out before. Not exactly like this but close enough. When we were on top of mount Kirkjufell and we had touched the foot relic of Azrael's harp.

Acid burns its way up my throat as I remember how that ended. With Cain and Maverick dead.

As a last-ditch effort to win this war, Cain's going to kill himself and his brother to weaken Lucifer.

But he can't... He can't!

"No! Cain!" I yell as panic surges forward. "No!"

Cain lifts his hand and something metal glints in his hand.

A dagger. The angel blade.

"I'm sorry, brother…" he whispers, pain lacing his voice.

Knowing what's coming next, I rip my gaze away. I hear the blade cutting through the air, and then the final thud, my heart seizing. I choke, more screams trapped in my throat, and when I glance up, Cain is wrenching the dagger out of Maverick's chest.

Oh my god…

Lucifer stumbles, as if struck by an invisible sledgehammer. "You fool! You'll kill us all!" he shouts, furious.

We were right. He's getting weaker.

"I plan on it." With hands covered in blood, Cain turns the blade on himself. Lucifer snarls and charges him.

My heart twists. Time seems to slow in that moment, and Cain's black eyes flash my way and automatically change to their beautiful crystal blues. I expect the same sadness I saw in the vision, but to my surprise, I see nothing but fierce determination.

Those eyes flick right, then back at me, and

that's when I realize he's trying to tell me something.

I follow his gaze and see the hint of something silver under the fallen rubble.

What the...

Is that...?

But if that's the angel blade, then what is Cain about to stab himself with?

My brain scrambles to catch up with everything, but I don't have time to sort it all out now. Cain thrusts the dagger into his chest and I'm up and crawling madly across the floor. Clutching my stomach, the pain is unimaginable; every part of me screams to stop, but I can't. Too much depends on this.

Lucifer wobbles on his two feet, and his monster starts to recede. His horns retract and his massive form shrinks right before my eyes.

As I reach the spot, I grit my teeth against the pain and force myself to shift through the rocks. Underneath the mess is the modestly engraved handle and curved blade of heaven's *real* weapon.

Cain faked him out. If he hadn't used the angel blade to stab him and Maverick, they would heal. And that means Lucifer's weakness is temporary. I'll have to be quick.

"Aria…" The deranged sing-song way Lucifer says my name makes me wince. Breathing frantically, I glance over my shoulder to see him still stuck in mid-transformation, his skin gray and scaly, his brow protruding and twisted horns shrinking further into his head, his body the size and shape of a normal man. He rolls his neck and bones crack. "Finally. You're mine now."

Then, he comes for me with arms outstretched.

I wrap my hand around the angel blade's hilt and wait, licking my lips. He's tried to take everything from me. Made my life and my demons' lives a living hell for far too long.

Not anymore.

No more running.

This is it. With no help from the demons or Sayah, it's only me.

And I'm going to kill the devil.

"Come get me," I growl at him, my anger giving me the courage and strength I need.

Right then, Lucifer lunges for me, and I yank the angel blade from its hiding place and thrust it upward, right into the evil bastard's blackened heart.

His eyes widen in shock and confusion, and I drink it in. All of it.

"No…" he croaks, his face paling. "How did you… The Leviathan…"

"No Leviathan here. Just little ol' me. An Ordinary." I push the blade deeper, loving the way he grunts as pain consumes his expression.

The brightness to his red eyes dims as it scans my face in disbelief.

"Bitch…" he whispers on his last breath.

I pull out the angel blade as his body slumps and crumples to the ground.

Dead.

Around me, the marble guards crumble and disintegrate to dust. Torryn, Nix, Val, and the others stop fighting and all look at me kneeling over Lucifer's unmoving body.

Torryn's back in his human form and staring at me with wide eyes. "You… You killed him."

I stand there for a while, my heart thundering in my chest, letting the victory sink in. Then, I lift the angel blade to see Lucifer's and my blood coating the blade.

"She did!" Nix shouts and runs over to me. He grabs me by the shoulders and kisses both of my cheeks. "She did!"

"Well done, girl," Val says with a smile.

I want to smile back—it tickles across my lips—

but remembering Cain, Maverick, Dorian, and Elias, I whip around instead and limp for the dais.

Cain and Maverick are already squirming, eyes fluttering open. Their gazes find me at the same time.

"Ar-Aria…" Cain groans with a smile. "You did it."

Relief washes over me, and now the smile comes naturally. For a moment, I'd thought I'd lost them all, but especially him and Maverick.

"That was a pretty clever thing you did," I whisper, stroking his blood-matted hair away from his face. He presses into my touch.

"Clever and extremely painful," Maverick grumbles and rubs his chest where the wound has already knitted together. "Would've been nice if you told me what your plans were before this."

"It wouldn't have been believable if I had," Cain explains.

I chuckle and watch his skin knit back together before my eyes until only smooth skin and muscle remains.

"I don't know. I think you may have enjoyed killing me a little too much." Maverick sits up and winces, obviously still in pain.

"Maybe."

The sound of rocks shifting has me looking across the room. Elias climbs his way out of the rubble, dust covering him from head to toe. He shakes his head like a dog, long hair whipping across his face. "Where's Dorian?"

"Here." Dorian rolls onto his back and folds his hands over his chest, mimicking being dead. "But I'm going to need a kiss from a princess to wake me up."

He puckers his lips, and I laugh.

I'm about to walk over to him when the pain in my stomach spikes again and sends me onto my knees. The angel blade clatters to the floor next to me.

Cain and Maverick are next to me in the next second, Elias and Dorian striding across the room to us.

"She was stabbed with the angel blade," Cain reminds everyone. "She won't heal here."

"Sorry..." I breathe and pull away my hand to show them that it's covered in blood. "Rain check?"

Dorian frowns. "You bet, gorgeous... Let's get you fixed up first."

Gingerly, Cain scoops me up and cradles me against his chest. "Cain..." I whisper, my voice as weak as I feel.

"Yes, my love." He begins to walk me out of the throne room, all the other demons following behind us.

"Sayah… I think she's gone." Tears sting my eyes, and I'm not even sure why. The moment Lucifer stabbed me, it felt like I'd lost a part of me. Like I wasn't myself anymore.

His tone is gentle, his gaze full of worry as he searches my face. "Why do you say that?"

"I can't feel her anymore. I think the blade…"

He hushes me softly. "Let's get you feeling better first, and we'll figure out Sayah after. Okay?"

I dip my chin in a nod. Being this close to him, I can see the real damage to his severed wing, and I wonder if something like that will grow back. It's a missing limb, nothing like a stab wound. I'll have to remember to ask him about it later.

For now, I lose myself in the warmth of his skin, the rhythmic sound of his heartbeat against my ear, and let my eyes drift closed. Despite everything we've been through, the pain, and all the unknowns still to come, we are finally rid of Lucifer. Hell is free and so are we.

We won.

23

ARIA

"Fuck yeah, Lucifer is dead!" Torryn roars, breaking into hysterical laughter, like he can't believe it.

His brothers cheer, and it should be strange to see them celebrating the death of their father. But we are talking about Lucifer here…a psychopath who deserves everything he got.

The leather chair I sit carefully on groans like no one has sat in it for centuries. Which might very well be the case, considering we're back in Cain's castle, and Elias brought it in from one of the unused rooms for me. Now it sits in the throne room, where I lounge listening to the five sin demon brothers, Elias, and Dorian discuss who will be the new leader of Hell.

I'm just happy to be able to sit down after laying in a bed for a week straight. It's the best feeling in the world.

Despite being patched up and magically worked on by every spellcasting soul the demons could get ahold of down here, every inch of me still aches. The magic in the angel blade is resistant to other magic apparently, and although we were able to stop the bleeding and sew me up, healing properly will take a while. I'm just lucky Lucifer hadn't hit any major organs when he'd run me through. Otherwise, I'd be dead.

It's still a bit unbelievable that we beat him. That *I* defeated him. Especially with no other supernatural help. I'm just glad we finally have the asshole off our backs.

Cain appears at my side, his face a permanent image of concern. "How are you feeling?"

"You just asked me that five minutes ago," I tease him.

"I know. But I want to make sure things haven't changed."

"I'm fine," I assure him for the millionth time. "Sore. Achy. But I'm alive so I'm *fine.*"

He still doesn't seem completely satisfied with

that answer, so I offer him a small smile to really sell it.

"Come on," I say. "This is a big day for you. You should be happy."

His brows pinch. "Big day? What do you mean?"

I lower my voice and glance around the room to see everyone else tied up in their own conversations. "You know...coronation day. You're the oldest sin demon. You lead us all. Because of you, Hell is free. There's no doubt they'll pick you to wear the crown."

He stands a little straighter and his expression smooths over. Not exactly the reaction I expected from him, but it's clear something is bothering him. Something he's not ready to talk about yet.

He walks to the front of the room, in front of his own throne where Lucifer's crown sits, and clears his throat. Everyone quiets down and they all turn their attention to him.

He clears his throat and speaks loudly, demanding everyone's attention with just his voice, like a true king would. "I know we've all already agreed that Raziel and Lorcan will be apprehended and punished for treason, but we still need to discuss who will rule in Lucifer's place now that he's gone."

"It should be Cain," Dorian shouts. "He's the one who first had the guts to stand up to his father and gather us all."

Cheers erupt from the rest of the brothers agreeing, and I clap from my seat.

But Cain holds up a hand to stop them. Then he turns, picks up the crown of bones, and holds it up for everyone to see.

"Come on, Brother! Put it on!" Torryn shouts and raises his fist in triumph.

I can't help myself. I'm smiling from ear to ear. I'm so proud of Cain. He deserves this—all of it. Hell, the throne… He even lost a wing to the cause, something I found out he'll never get back. Even though he said it was worth it, I could see the pain in his eyes, knowing he'd never fly again, and that's just another reason why he deserves to be king. He's sacrificed so much for this. Plus, he's a real leader, one who will care for his people instead of ruling by ruthlessness and fear.

Nix joins in. "Put it on! Put it on!" he chants, and soon, Val's wrapping his arm around him and adding his voice to the chorus too.

Despite their praise and encouragement, Cain's

eyes fall onto me. He closes the distance between us, and the room falls silent again.

Then he does the unthinkable and places the crown on my head.

When he steps back, a smile lifts his lips. "I cannot accept the crown because it does not truly belong to me," he says. "Aria killed the devil when none of us could. And she did it without magic or special powers of any kind. She is stronger and braver than any of us, and she is the ruler Hell deserves."

"Wha-What?" I can't believe what he's saying. Me? Queen of Hell? "No. No way."

Murmurs come from the other brothers, and uneasiness stirs inside me. I can't be queen. I'm not even a demon. It doesn't seem right.

"I don't even have Sayah anymore," I go on, and reach to take off the crown. "The Leviathan's gone. I'm basically human now."

"And that's all the more reason you should lead us," Cain says. "You have the compassion and the insight demons lack. For so long, I thought I was only capable of destruction. You changed me for the better."

"And me," Dorian chimes in and steps forward.

Elias follows suit. "Me too, little rabbit."

"And me," Maverick says from the corner of the room, where he's leaning against a pillar, observing all this from afar. "Which is quite a feat in itself, I'd say."

"And if we want things to change here, too, then it's time we start thinking differently." Cain stops me from taking off the crown and instead adjusts it on my head. Then he holds out a hand to help me up. Elias and Dorian come over, and all together, they help me walk up to the throne.

I still can't believe this is happening. I want to reject it, to argue that Cain is a much better fit for this role than me, but with the three of them beaming at me with such pride and devotion, it's hard to deny them.

When I sit on the large throne and look out at Torryn, Nix, and Val, I see them smiling up at me with the same certain looks on their faces.

Maybe I *can* do this. They all seem to think so. And, if they believe in me, then goddammit, I should too.

Sayah would think so, too, if she were here.

My stomach twists, her absence a heaviness I've been carrying with me since the battle. She hasn't come back; I still can't feel her, and that's only confirmed my fears that the angel blade stole her from me.

After having her with me for so long, it's weird not to anymore. The only way I can describe it is as if my best friend died. But, she took part of me with her. I don't know if I'll ever feel whole again without her, but after everything, I am thankful she did choose me to attach to.

"I think this calls for a celebration! A feast!" Valdim shouts, which snaps me from my grief-ridden thoughts. All the other brothers groan.

"You and your parties," Torryn chuckles and slaps his brother playfully on the back.

"It is sort of my thing," he replies.

With everyone's merriment, I remind myself that I'm not alone in this…even without Sayah. I have my four lovers, my demons, my soulmates. And that's all I really need.

The day goes on and Val gets his party. There's food and music and laughter. Reminiscing about the fight, or about the sin demon brothers' past memories, and I marvel at how these men went from fighting each other to being thicker than thieves in next to no time.

Dorian and Elias are chatting loudly, laughing at something I probably don't even want to know about. Cain's chatting with Torryn, and from the looks of their hand gestures, it's about fighting techniques. Go figure.

My gaze swings around the room again, and this time, I catch Maverick's eye. He's leaning against the same pillar as before, staring at me with a wicked smirk.

Since moving is still difficult for me, Maverick walks over and hops onto the throne's armrest.

Stretching his legs out, he points to my crown and says, "I like it. It suits you."

My face heats up, and I'm not really sure why. "Thanks."

He's definitely managed to crawl into my heart. I just can't believe how quickly it happened.

"It's still a bit surreal," I confess.

"What is?"

"You know. Being queen and all."

He waves a hand at that. "Nah, you were made for this."

I snort a laugh. "This is *me* we're talking about here. *Me.*"

"Yeah, I know. And I still won't change my answer." His hand is in mine suddenly, and he squeezes it lightly. This gorgeous man with golden flecks in his deep, chocolate eyes studies me. We'd been through so much, discovered each other's darkness, and despite being enemies at first, I have found four men who adore me unconditionally. That is the true gift I gained.

He began, "I would never have guessed things would turn out the way they have." He raises the back of my hand to his mouth and kisses it, before leaning in closer. "And I should have told you this earlier, Aria, before things got…crazy, but I'm going to say it now before I lose my nerve."

"Yeah, what's that?"

"I'm falling in love with you."

My breath catches in my throat.

He really said that? Really?

"This is new for me," he explains and rubs the back of his neck shyly. "All of it… Feeling this way. But Cain's right. We are capable of being more than our sin, more than what our father created us for. It just took me a bit longer to see it."

My chest warms, and I don't know what else to say besides the obvious. "I love you so much," I murmur back, and my eyes are close to tearing up.

"All the fear and death is over now," he says. "It's just about the future. About all of us."

Tilting my head up, he closes the distance for a kiss. I love his words and the inclusion of my other men, too. And, for the first time, I think this can actually work, with all of us being happy together.

Someone clears their throat, and we break apart. Everyone is staring at us now.

"Uh..." Who knows how long they were watching.

"So, what is the plan now?" Maverick asks quickly to save us from the awkwardness settling in. "Are we all moving into Cain's castle to rule Hell?"

Oh shit. I hadn't even thought about that. That's going to be a pretty big problem.

I straighten in the chair, facing Cain. "I don't think I can leave Earth behind for good. What about Cassiel? I can't leave him. And Charlotte? What about your clubs? And rebuilding Purgatory." It's all rushing out of my mouth now. Word vomit. "I am still human after all, and without this ring..." I show his crimson ring, still on my finger, "I wouldn't even be able to be here. How is any of this going to work?"

He answers by pulling out something from his pants pocket. When he unfurls his fingers, another ring is sitting in his palm, not too different from his. The band is made of crisscrossing tiny bones and it's crowned with an onyx gem.

I've seen it before…

"Is…is that Lucifer's?" I ask.

He nods. "And now, it belongs to you. It will keep you protected in Hell, body and soul."

I blink at the ring, unsure if I should take it.

Taking my hand in his, he pushes the ring onto my middle finger. The bones shrink to match my size, cradling around my skin with a perfect fit.

He then removes the one that belongs to him and slips it back onto his finger.

As I continue to study Lucifer's old ring, I shift my hand side to side, and find that when I do that and the dark stone catches the light, a hue of different colors shine back at me. Like a rainbow has been trapped inside.

"You have been given a great responsibility," Cain adds, looking at me.

"I understand."

"Which means you cannot dismiss your role," Torryn says. "Everyone will expect you to stay here."

"They will," Nix agrees with a firm dip of his head. "Without a ruler, Hell will erupt into utter chaos."

More than it naturally is? I couldn't even wrap my head around what that would look like.

Swallowing hard, I glance over to Cain again. He's staring at me intently, thinking. Then my gaze sweeps over my other men.

I shouldn't be surprised. Of course, I'd have to stay here in Hell to be queen.

But to leave the living world… My friends? Work? The life we'd built in Glenside?

My stomach knots just thinking about it.

I remind myself that this is what my demons wanted. Ever since I met them, their goal was to return home. To Hell. I can't take that from them, either, and I certainly can't live without them.

Cain must see me struggling because he whispers sympathetically, "It's whatever you decide. We support your decision either way. "

"I've grown rather fond of living on Earth," Elias mentions, which surprises me. "Don't even mind the cold of Vermont anymore. And our house is in the middle of a wild animal's paradise. The woods, the lake…"

"I agree with you there, except Nix is right. Shit will go sideways here, and fast, if we leave," Dorian pipes in.

"Someone else will jump at the chance to steal the throne," Nix replies. "War will break out, a division among all the ranks."

Cain's silent, lost in his head, but his frown deepens. He wants to make me happy, but Hell is just as much his home as Earth is mine. And leaving Hell without a ruler could cause another tyrant to rise in Lucifer's place. I can see the two sides of his thoughts warring with each other through his expression.

My own anxiety climbs. What can I do to give everyone what they want and need?

Then an idea strikes. A crazy one, but it's the only thing I can see that might work.

"I have an idea," I suggest, raising my voice over the growing murmurs in the room. "What if we stayed six months in Hell, and six months on Earth? We have two homes, and get to enjoy the best of both worlds?"

I'm not sure how much the word *enjoy* applies to Hell, but with me in charge, I intend to bring about some changes. Maybe a cafe built in town, or a library. And there's no way I'm staying in Lucifer's castle. That's coming down.

Oh, and air conditioning.

Yeah, I'm definitely installing central air wherever we live.

"And what about the six months you're not in Hell?" Torryn presses, distracting me from my thoughts. "That doesn't solve you being absent for a significant amount of time. What stops total anarchy from reigning?"

Fuck, true.

"Well then…" I pause for a moment, wracking my brain for a solution. Then I glance from one man to another. From Torryn, to Nix, then Val. They'd done so much to help us, had bravely fought by our sides despite the risks… They deserved something, too. "Then, during the six months we are on Earth, Torryn, Val, and Nix will keep things in check. We'll make this more like a democracy than a monarchy. You three will help while I'm away, but keep me in the loop of every-thing, of course." I look over to Cain. "How does that sound?"

At first, no one responds, and in their silence, my worry peaks.

But then Cain lifts his chin and a slow smile spreads his lips. "A shared responsibility. We keep us all accountable."

I can't help myself. There's just something about when the sin demon smiles… It makes my heart flutter. "Yes. Exactly. I was thinking since we work so well when we cooperate. As a team, maybe we can extend that into Hell and prevent another dictator."

"Spoken like a true leader." Cain's eyes spark with pride, and my chest warms. Looking over at his brothers, he nods once. "Would you three be willing?"

"Work with these two idiots?" Nix grumbles and tosses his long hair over his shoulder. That wins him a slap in the back of the head from Torryn.

"We can do it, of course," he says. "Especially since we cut off the dead weight."

He means Raziel and Lorcan.

"There will be a trial period," Cain goes on, "to work out any issues and to make sure the people of Hell are respecting the changes."

The three brothers nod in unison.

His face suddenly turning very serious, Cain's eyes narrow in warning. "And if any of you disobey or try to take too much power…"

"Don't worry about that, Brother. We love Hell and its people. And we don't want another Lucifer," Val says.

"Not to mention we all saw what Aria can do with the angel blade," Nix chuckles. "I like my eternal life, thank you very much."

Laughter bubbles up inside me, too. And it's not long before Elias and Dorian join in.

"Good then, so we have a plan." Maverick dusts his hands like all's well and done. He, Elias, and Dorian walk over to the others and begin to talk about new living arrangements, but when I try to listen in, Cain draws my hand to his chest, capturing my attention fully.

"Thank you," he says, the softness in his gaze making me melt. "I know this isn't truly your home, so thank you for the compromise."

"It's not my home *yet*," I say and smirk. "Maybe with a few little changes here and there."

He raises an eyebrow. "I want to hear all about it."

Cain laughs, and I don't think I will ever grow tired of hearing that sexy sound.

We decide that before we take over the reign of Hell officially, we have to return to Earth to pack a few things, work out what we are bringing with us, plus tie up some loose ends, like Cain's club.

We are barely in the foyer of our home when

power dances up my arms, the kind we all recognize at once.

Elias growls just as the air in the room dances with heat waves, and with a snap of energy that cracks at the back of my nape, archangel Gabriel materializes in the middle of the room. He's wearing a white tunic that falls to his knees, a golden rope tied loosely around his waist, and his wings tucked into his sides. Unlike his previous visits, there is a sense of relief on his face.

"I guess you've heard the good news," Cain announces, squaring his shoulders, standing by my side, a hand across my stomach, protecting me.

"Everyone in Heaven felt Lucifer's death the moment it happened," he says with a grin that makes him look creepier than normal. "My condolences for your loss." And yet, the way he says that with a smile, it does not have the effect he thinks it does.

"I'm picturing all the angles up there, dancing merrily," Maverick says, his eyebrows raised.

Gabriel gives him a deadpan look, and I might have laughed if I wasn't frozen on my feet, knowing exactly why he's paid us a visit.

"Don't taint such a special occasion with your mockery, foul beast."

Elias rolls his eyes, while Dorian adds, "Yeah, let Gabe have his little merriment. This may be the only time he finally gets to jerk off in peace." He stares at Gabriel, grinning. "If angels do enjoy the pleasure of the flesh, that is."

"Filthy hell-vermin. You dare talk to me in such an irreverent manner," Gabriel roars. "I could rip your soul out for such impious words and smite you where you stand."

"I take that as a no," Elias mumbles under his breath. Maverick sniggers.

With a sneer, Gabriel turns his attention to Cain and me. "My time is being wasted. I must deal with the Leviathan."

I loathe the way he refers to me by that name… Sure that might be what Sayah was, but it's not me or my choice that I ended up cursed.

"You're too late," Maverick interrupts.

"What does the demon refer to?" Gabriel asks, not even bothering to look Maverick's way.

"It's gone," I reiterate. "During the battle with Lucifer, I was stabbed with an angle blade and it must have been vanquished because she's no longer inside me. I don't feel her." She's been with me my whole life, so to have her gone leaves me feeling empty.

Gabriel's face twists into a scowl. "Her? Next you'll tell me you named it. Such a weak human trait."

"Hey," I say, louder than I intended, but I'm tired of his arrogance. "Just remember, I didn't create her, but was cursed, and I learned to make peace with her. Maybe you should show respect that I, a mere mortal, survived with a beast created by God living inside me."

His lips thin and eyes narrow, showing no sign of showing remorse. "I will lay my hand on you to check for myself that what you say is true."

I flinch back, and Cain steps in front of me. "Her word is enough," he growls, a direct threat against an archangel. "We defeated Lucifer, and did your work for you in protecting Heaven. That is proof enough."

"I don't trust demons. And don't ever challenge me, sin demon," Gabriel bellows, his wings snapping out so wide, the tips touch the walls on either side of us.

I don't know who would win, but I don't want to find out after what we've just been through. I step around Cain.

"We have nothing to hide, so I give you permission," I state, lifting my chin, even if I am slightly trembling.

I sense my men all watching me, Cain shifting closer to me, and I know they don't agree. "Gabriel is not our enemy," I say. "He helped us protect our home from Lucifer's attack."

Besides, we just got Satan off our tails, and I don't want to worry that a gang of angels will be lingering around, watching me in case I lied.

Gabriel steps toward me, towering over me like a mountain. The archangel is broad too, bulging with muscles, his jawline clenched tight.

Without warning, he places his large hand on the top of my head.

Instantly, a zap of energy snaps through me, where my whole body feels like jelly, and my mind flashes with images as if on fast forward. They speed past my mind's eye, but I see them regardless, running through every memory in my mind, everything I've experienced. From being left at the hospital as a baby, to the foster home with Murray taking me in and promising to keep me fed and warm, to meeting Joseline and how quickly we clicked, to learning to steal to survive.

Even stealing Sir Surchion's orb—little did I

know that night would set in motion so many events.

Days and months zip by so fast, and seeing them again rattles me. My heart pounds in my chest, tears pooling in my eyes at seeing my life flash before me. Murray sold me to the demons, all the fear, excitement, and adventures we underwent, down to how I fell in love with each of my four men. It all rushes through my thoughts all the way to the final battle with Lucifer.

Then, in a crack of power that pricks over my skin, and Gabriel releases me.

My knees give way under me, and I drop to the floor, tears flooding my cheeks, my chest close to breaking from seeing everyone in my life. All the emotions, the heartache, the grief. I was rejected by my family and, despite all that, I found love as though someone always looked out for me.

Unbelievable warmth spreads through my body, flooding me with the kind of intense sensation that promises me, wholeheartedly, passion and love.

I cry in my hands, unable to remember the last time I cried from sheer happiness. From how the single thought of my men reminds me instantly of home…where I know that I feel more at home in their arms than I ever anywhere else in my life.

Cain's at my side, crouching low, wrapping his arms around me. "Are you okay?" I sink against him, letting him hold me, and despite my tears, I'm smiling.

"What did you do to her?" Dorian barks.

"Four against one archangel sounds like good odds to me," Maverick snarls.

"What I said I'd do," Gabriel says calmly. "She speaks the truth and is clean. With Lucifer gone, our business here is done."

"Then leave," Elias warns.

"Aria," Gabriel states, and I lift my head in response, tears streaming down my face. "What is meant to be, will always find a way to happen. Even love with the unloved. Even taming the most dangerous creature God created. Everything happens for a reason. Remember that."

Then, in a flash, the air sparks from his energy, and Gabriel pops out of the room.

Goosebumps race down my arms, and I wipe my eyes. My four men are kneeling in front of me in a semicircle, each of them reaching out and touching me. I lean into their touches, loving how everything they give me reminds me that I've found the answer to happiness.

"What did he do to you?" Cain asks.

I sniffle and lift my gaze to each of my men, drowning in the devotion in their eyes. How did I get so lucky to find them? And, with that thought, Gabriel's words swirl in my mind.

Everything happens for a reason.

What if a great power had a hand in my fate?

"Gabriel's touch showed me my whole life in a flash. It was incredible and heartbreaking." My breath hitches, and Dorian wipes the loose tear running down my cheek. "It made me realize that despite my family giving me up, I deserve love too." I half laugh. "These damn tears won't stop. I think Gabriel did something to make me just cry."

"Right, I'm ready to take down that jerk." Maverick rolls up his sleeves, and it only makes me laugh louder.

"I loved you from the first time I laid eyes on you," Cain confesses. "I just didn't realize it at the time. Of course, you deserve all our love."

"You will always have us," Dorian says.

"We are fated mates, after all." Elias squeezes my hand.

"And I may be late to the party, but I never

thought I'd find love. Not until you came into my life." Maverick gives me one of his gorgeously wicked grins.

"That's why I'm the luckiest girl in the world, because I love each one of you. And, after everything we've been through, how about we draw a line in the sand and start our lives properly from here? No more end-of-the-world adventures?"

Elias howls with laughter. "I'm down for this."

The other three agree, and I lean forward to hug them all. I take a deep breath and smile easily, knowing that, for once, my life might just be normal. Well, as normal as ruling the realm of Hell will permit. But it doesn't scare me. Not when I know I'll never be alone again.

The click of nails scraping the wooden floorboards has us all looking over to the doorway.

Cassiel charges in just then and leaps at us, tongue out, and I swear he's smiling. When he crashes into Elias first and knocks him over, I burst out laughing while the others are all over Cassiel for a hug.

This…this is exactly what life should be. Laughing, chasing a lynx cat through the house for hugs, and wondering if there is a bathtub big enough for five people I can order online.

"Aria, hurry up, we're going to be late," Dorian calls out from downstairs. "We're all waiting on you."

I roll my eyes before yelling back, "Give me a sec."

Exhaling loudly, I glance back at myself in the mirror, and apply the scarlet red lipstick, trying not to smudge it. I don't normally wear a lot of make-up, so I'm a lot slower at getting ready. Give me a demon to fight anyday over keeping a steady hand while using an eyeliner pen.

Making kissy lips, I pull back and look at myself. It's hard to believe I look so hot in all honesty. I still recall the red dress Cain gifted me to wear to Purgatory when I first arrived at the mansion. I looked stunning but a complete virgin in it. And when it came to the heels, I'd been a complete klutz.

Now, this black dress, covered in tiny swarovski diamonds, hugged every curve from the straps on my shoulders, over my bust and the curve of my hips. I seriously had an hourglass figure and it never occurred to me until now. My hair is pulled up and off my face with only a few loose strands around my face, making the whole appearance more dramatic.

It isn't everyday you are invited to a friend's wedding. So, only the best would do.

Besides, I am the Queen of Hell now, aren't I? I need to look the part.

I smile and spritz myself with perfume, then hurry to the men before they hollar after me again.

With all the fabric sashaying around my legs, I take my time coming down the steps. When I glance up, I meet the eyes of my four men, each of them visually devouring me.

My demons are all dressed in fitted suits, each with different colored shirts. My heartbeat speeds up automatically at the captivating sight of them all. I've always thought they resembled gods, but dressed up, it's like they're gods who've just stepped off the catwalk.

"Absolutely stunning," Cain mutters, his crystal blue eyes glinting as they roam across my body. "We may need to go out more often just to see you dressed up like this."

"If you keep buying me dresses like this, you have a deal," I reply, feeling incredibly beautiful.

Once I reach his side, all four of them surround me like predators and study every inch of me.

"I-I thought we were in a hurry," I stammer, the heat from their closeness making my pulse thunder.

"I'm suddenly thinking it can wait," Dorian says, his hand sliding to my ass. He whistles approvingly. "Wait, gorgeous, are you not wearing underwear?"

"Fuck me, Aria." Elias sweeps his hands on my waist, pressing the bulge in his pants against my side.

My head whirls at how amazing he feels, and I'm starting to wonder if there's any way we really can show up late to the wedding. Just a little.

No, stay focused.

"How can you be so cruel?" Maverick leans in, his warm breath feathering across my neck and making me woozy with desire. When I see him grabbing himself through his trousers, I have a hard time swallowing. My throat's suddenly too tight.

"Or," Elias chimes in, "we can bend you over now and get this out of our systems before you give us all blue balls."

I laugh, though I'm well aware he'd been completely serious.

Cain's watching me with an arched eyebrow, while that primal hunger I know all too well flares in his gaze. Is he actually considering Elias's proposal?

"You too?" I ask him.

His lips quirk up at the corner. "You have no idea how fucking delicious you look and smell."

As tempting as this sounds, Charlotte would *kill* me if I missed the wedding.

I push past all of them and head to the front closet.

What amI looking for? My thoughts are a jumbled, sex-crazed mess.

Oh yeah, my coat. That's right. Coat.

"Maybe after the party," I say, trying to hide the trembling in my voice. "But first--"

"Oh, in one of the new VIP rooms?" There's a

mischievous smirk on Dorian's face when he glances at Cain.

"There's an idea," he replies, and a growl of approval rumbles in his chest. "I did want to try out those new beds we just had customized and installed. With the racks and ties."

Oh boy. I'm in trouble.

The ravenous desires on all their faces has me struggling to not give in to the pleasures they promise. Arousal is already thumping in my veins. It's hard to ignore.

An abrupt knocking at the front door douses me with imaginative cold water and shakes me from my dark thoughts.

Is that Ramos? How late are we?

Cain marches past us and opens the door.

To our complete surprise, the Seer, Miranda, stands on the front steps, wearing that lecherous grin. She's dressed in a black coat with faux fur around the collar, and her hair is tucked in a matching hat, like she's just flown in on Krampus' sleigh. The cold instantly rushes inside, chilling me to the bone.

"What are you doing here?" Cain growls.

She slinks into our home without an invitation, looking too comfortable for my liking, and dusts off the snow clinging to her shoulders. "We had a deal, remember?"

Anger instantly stirs in me. That *deal* she's talking about involves being Cain's bride after he dethroned his father and took over Hell. Against all out pleas, Cain had agreed to it, and now Miranda is hoping to collect on her prize.

There's no way in Hell I'm going to let that happen.

I step forward, but Elias's big hands are on my shoulders, pulling me back against his chest. He's radiating heat, but I'm already burning up with fury, and sweat slicks down my back.

When her gaze sweeps over us, she sneers. "Got a big night out planned?"

Bitch.

Elias holds me tighter.

When she turns back to Cain, she fakes a smile. "It's a shame you're going to have to miss it," she says.

Jealousy flares in my chest, and I shrug Elias's grip off of me. As I step up to Cain's side, his hand slides across my back.

"I suggest you leave," he tells her firmly, chin lifted high.

"I've come to secure my contract."

"You heard him. Leave," I push through a stiff jaw.

Anger flashes in her gaze.

"My business is not with you," she snaps at me, then reaches toward Cain's chest. But he blocks her by pushing her hand away.

"We had a deal. Signs in blood," she snaps. "Or did you forget?"

I go over what I know of the deal again in my head. She was to rule Hell beside Cain when he got the crown. But he didn't get the crown, did he?

I did.

So, that would mean the contract holds no power anymore. It's null and void.

It's the loophole we've been hoping for.

Grinning, I link Cain and my hands together, trying hard to make a show of it. I want her to see the onyx Hell ring on my finger and know that Cain's chosen me as his eternal bride.

Once her gaze focuses on it, her eyes widen in shock. "Wait… is that Lucifer's ring?"

"That's right, baby doll," I reply with fake sweetness. "I killed the king of Hell. Me."

Her mouth tugs down into a tight frown. "That's-That's impossible. That would mean…"

"She's queen," Cain finishes for her. Lifting our

joined hands, he places a kiss on the back of mine. "My queen and Hell's."

An excited shiver runs down my back. I do like the way he says that.

"Impossible." She shakes her head like she can't believe it. "I translated Lucifer's diary. I did my part, now you need to hold up your end."

"It's over, Miranda." Cain is as calm as ever, and it only seems to annoy Miranda even more. "Your terms were to be held on the condition of me being king. Which I am not. Therefore, the contract holds no power."

Elise wastes no time to move toward the doorway, as does Maverick and Dorian, flanking Miranda.

She notices but doesn't retreat.

"In layman's terms that means you can fuck off," Maverick says.

"You heard him," Elias snarls and shows fangs. "Out."

Her face blanches, and dread slides over her expression.

Just then, Holmes pulls up in the limousine. When Ramos steps out of the passenger seat wearing a tuxedo, I can't help but think that the albino dhampir cleans up pretty well, too.

Cain instantly waves for Ramos to come over. "Help the Seer off our property, will you? I think she's a little lost."

Ramos moves fast and grabs Miranda by the arm, wrenching her back into the freezing night. She struggles against him at first, spitting curses at me, but once she's out of sight, her shouts silence abruptly.

Good riddance.

"Well, that was a bit of fun," Maverick says and readjusts his suit jacket. "I can't wait to see what a vampire wedding brings."

"Hopefully a happily forever after," I reply.

He chuckles, and with that, Cain, Maverick, Elias, Dorian and I head for the limo.

"I've never been to a wedding before," I whisper quietly to Cain as we enter the newly built club. Seven is the name Cain settled on, to honor his brothers.

It was better than Dorian's suggestion, which was unapologetically, "Lucifer's Limp Dick." That one got Elias's approval... but no one else's. For obvious reasons.

Seven is much bigger and badder than Purgatory was with a more modern, sleek, and sexier feel. It's two stories--well, technically three--with all the offices in the basement, the club and bar on the main floor, and the new VIP rooms upstairs. Antonio and Sting have full range of the bar, which stretches across the entire back wall and also doubles as a second stage for dancers. The dance floor is massive and has smoke effects and under-lighting to really enhance the experience.

For today, the club's gotten even more of an overhaul with the dancefloor being transformed into a wedding ceremony space. With the lights dimmed, hundreds of flickering candles add to the romantic ambience, and a carpet of rose petals line the aisle between the rows of chairs for guests.

My demons and I have picked spots by the front, and excitement makes my knees bounce.

"This will be my first human wedding too," Cain answers.

"It was really nice of you to let them use the club."

"Charlotte and Viktor are good friends. It's an honor, really."

Antonio and Sting sit in the row right behind us, sporting matching white suits and bowties.

Antonio already has misty eyes, but he's trying his best to pretend like he's tired by yawning and being dramatic about it. Sting only pats his arm affectionately.

My cheeks hurt, and I realize it's because I haven't stopped smiling since we got here. Cain was able to hire all the old workers from Purgatory and I see so many familiar faces… it truly feels like I have a family here.

It makes me think of Joseline, and how much I miss her. Without Maverick's soul contract anymore, I wonder how she's doing. How she's been living her life in a new city, hopefully away from dark magic. I promise myself I'll send another messenger bird tomorrow and see if we can meet up.

Elias reaches over and places a warm hand on my bouncing leg. It stops instantly, and when I peer up at him, he gives me a warm smile.

More guests pour into the club, making it a full house.

As music begins to whaff from the speakers, Dorian leans forward in his seat behind us, next to Maverick. "Time to start the show," he says.

On cue, Viktor emerges from a hallway, and everyone falls silent. His smile has me grinning, and just seeing how elated he is has my own eyes prickling with tears. In true Viktor fashion, he wears a traditional Dracula ensemble, with black tails, ruffled shirt, cape, and all.

I mean, the man knows what he likes. And not to mention, he can rock a cape pretty damn well. Not many people can say that.

After making his way up the aisle, he turns to the crowd and says in a strong voice, "Thank you my friends and family for attending. Today is a dream come true for me, and it means everything to Charlotte and I that you could join us." Despite his confident words, he's fiddling with his hands and glancing around.

He's nervous. How adorable.

I clap, as do a few others, and he takes his place beneath an arch made of vines and red roses. Behind him stands Ramos, who was given the task of marrying them.

I know Cain, Elias, Dorian, and I performed the binding ritual, or Hell's equivalent to marriage, but all this love and ceremony has me wondering if I will ever be walking down the aisle too. I've already met the men of my dreams. If they asked, I wouldn't hesitate to say yes, but demons have different ideas about marriage. Cain and I may have talked briefly about it before, but who knows something like this is even on the table for me.

As if sensing my thoughts, Cain runs his hand over mine and begins to twist the Hell ring of my finger. He's watching me intently, and behind his gaze, I can see the same questions hovering there.

He offers me a warm smile, and butterflies dance in my stomach. Forever is a long time, but there's no one else I'd rather spend it with than the four of them.

Just then, the lights dim and the music changes to a soft piano tune. I twist in my seat, anticipation skittering through me to finally see my good friend and the bride.

A spotlight flashes at the back of the room and Charlotte steps out of the dark, making her appearance.

My mouth falls open.

Blonde curls cascade over her shoulders, framing the most beautiful face. Her lips are painted red and match her form-fitting and nearly sheer bridal gown. With all the crystals on the bodice and long train, her dress glints like stars in the sky.

She is spectacular.

She glides past us to her lover, unable to look

anywhere else but his face, and my chest tightens with happiness. As Charlotte and Viktor hand each other's hands, their faces are aglow with joy and love.

Cain's hand squeezes mine, and I realize that I'm captivated by the love in their eyes because I feel it too, times four. I went from having no one to love me to have four of the most incredible demons in my life.

Who would've thought I'd find my heaven in the darkest pits of Hell?

Despite all the shit we've been through, things really have turned out perfect.

Well, besides losing Sayah. If I had the power to change anything, it would be getting her back. Her absence is like a hole in my heart.

I exhale deeply, my body relaxing into the seat as I watch the ceremony go on.

"I wish you could see this, Sayah. I wish you could share in this happiness, too." I shake my head, realizing I'm talking to someone who's no longer there. But she was with me for so long, it's been a harder habit to break than I thought it would be.

Leviathan or not, she was my best friend.

A strange sensation wriggles up my spine. A familiar one and I stiffen.

No… it can't be. It can't.

Impossible.

It happens again, this time stronger. A swirling of ancient magic deep, deep inside me.

Unable to believe it, I gasp under my breath.

Leaning in close to not interrupt the vow exchange happening up front, Cain whispers, "Everything okay?"

I nod, unable to make what I'm feeling into words.

No way.

No. Way.

But, when I reach into myself again, I find the same pulse of living darkness, the one I'd lived with my entire life.

It's her. My shadow…

She's back.

"Sayah?"

Thank you for reading the Sin Demons series.

These books have been an amazing whirlwind of brainstorming, laughter, and mad writing marathons between us two authors who have been friends for a long time.

So to be able to enjoy this roller coast ride with a close friend is a magical experience.

Plus, Aria, Cain, Dorian, Elias, and Maverick have lived in our heads for more than a year, and we doubt they'll be letting us forget them anytime soon.

Lots of love and hugs for sticking with us and enjoying the crazy stories we've adored writing.

And by the way... we've got a brand new series coming out very soon...

If you loved Sin Demons, you'll go wild over Kings of Eden. Turn the page and find out more…

Lots of love and thank you for all your support

Mila and Harper

ABOUT MILA YOUNG

Best-selling author, Mila Young tackles everything with the zeal and bravado of the fairytale heroes she grew up reading about. She slays monsters, real and imaginary, like there's no tomorrow. By day she rocks a keyboard as a marketing extraordinaire. At night she battles with her mighty pen-sword, creating fairytale retellings, and sexy ever after tales. In her spare time, she loves pretending she's a mighty warrior, walks on the beach with her dogs, cuddling up with her cats, and devouring every fantasy tale she can get her pinkies on.

Ready to read more and more from Mila Young? www.subscribepage.com/milayoung

www.milayoungbooks.com

For more information... milayoungauthor@gmail.com

facebook.com/milayoungauthor
twitter.com/MilaYoungAuthor
instagram.com/mila_young_wicked

Join Harper's reader group for exclusive content, sneak-peeks, giveaways, and more! www.facebook. com/groups/harpershalflings

* 9 7 8 1 9 2 2 6 8 9 1 6 0 *